NO
ANGEL

ALSO BY HELEN KEEBLE

Fang Girl

NO ANGEL

HELEN KEEBLE

HARPER TEEN
An Imprint of HarperCollinsPublishers

HarperTeen is an imprint of HarperCollins Publishers.

No Angel
Copyright © 2013 by Helen Keeble
www.epicreads.com

Library of Congress Cataloging-in-Publication Data
Keeble, Helen.
No angel / Helen Keeble. — First edition.
    pages cm
    Summary: "Rafael Angelos thought being the only guy at an all-girls school
would be a dream come true—but he didn't realize that developing angelic
powers and battling demons would be part of the package"— Provided by
publisher.
    ISBN 978-0-06-208227-5 (pbk. bdg.)
    [1. Angels—Fiction. 2. Demonology—Fiction. 3. Boarding schools—
Fiction. 4. Schools—Fiction.] I. Title.
PZ7.K22549No 2013   2012040092
[Fic]—dc23   CIP
                                                                   AC

Typography Alison Klapthor
13 14 15 16 17   CG/RRDH   10 9 8 7 6 5 4 3 2 1

First Edition

For my mother June, who is not at all like the Headmistress.

Mostly.

NO
ANGEL

Chapter 1

The shiny new sign above the towering wrought-iron gates said ST. MARY'S BOARDING SCHOOL FOR GIRLS AND BOYS, which, as it turned out, was wrong by one letter.

"Wait," I said, staring at the Headmistress with a slow-rising sensation of dread. "You mean I'm just the first guy to arrive, right?"

"If you fail to understand the meaning of the word *only*, Mr. Angelos, I will have to schedule you for remedial English lessons," replied the short, severe woman. "But to make it crystal clear, you are indeed the first, sole, singular member of the male gender here." It was obvious that she considered this at least one boy too many. "I trust you will be a worthy representative of your species. Welcome to Saint Mary's."

Declarations of outright war had been uttered in

friendlier tones. I grabbed my dad's arm as he came back from the car, carrying the last of my suitcases. "I've changed my mind," I said, turning us away from the waiting Headmistress. "Don't leave me here!"

"You were the one who begged to come to your mother's old school when you found they were accepting boys this year. 'A way of honoring her memory,' you said." He dropped my bags in front of the school gates and raised an eyebrow. "Not to mention 'a heaven of honeys in very short skirts,' as I recall you saying to your friends."

I flushed. I hadn't realized he'd overheard that conversation. "But I thought there would be at least a *few* other guys around. Who am I supposed to talk to?"

"Girls?" Dad suggested mildly.

"Ha-ha. Seriously, Dad!"

"You want serious?" Dad folded his arms, looking up at me. "It's cost me a serious amount of money to enroll you here, so I expect you to actually make an effort for once, Raffi. Saint Mary's has always been one of the most exclusive schools in England, and we're incredibly fortunate that they're opening up to boys at last. And even more fortunate that they're allowing you in for just the final year." His finger jabbed me in the center of my chest. "You *will* work hard."

Behind him, the Headmistress's expression suggested that she personally thought boys were best put to work down dangerous mine shafts.

I scowled at my feet, stuffing my hands into the pockets of my new suit. "If it's so fabulous here, then why didn't any other guys apply?" I muttered under my breath.

"Our entrance requirements are extremely strict," the Headmistress said as if I'd spoken normally. "There was no shortage of male applicants, I assure you. Were it not for your late mother, I would have rejected you along with all the rest. But she was a personal friend of mine, as well as an outstanding member of this institution." She fixed me with a piercing stare. "I trust you will live up to her legacy."

"You hear that?" My dad poked me again. "This is your last chance, Raffi. You're lucky to get into *any* school, after what happened at your last one. You should be grateful for this opportunity." In my head, I started reciting the inevitable speech along with him. I'd heard it enough times to have it memorized. "You can't keep wandering around in a dream, absentmindedly strewing chaos in your wake."

Honestly, incinerate *one* lousy building by accident *once*, and your dad will never, ever let you forget it. "That fire wasn't my fault!"

"Perfectly ordinary toasters do not spontaneously spout four-foot pillars of flame!"

The Headmistress took a phone out of her pocket and murmured into it, "Memo to self: Mr. Angelos is banned from Home Economics."

My dad was still on a roll. "Your problem, Raffi, is that you're too unworldly for your own good. You have got to quit goofing off and start paying attention to what's going on around you—"

His voice droned on, but I didn't hear another word. I was too busy falling in love.

She was tall, only a few inches shorter than myself, but so light and slender she seemed to float on the breeze. Her feet barely made any sound on the gravel as she slipped around the gate and headed for us, her waist-length blonde hair rippling behind her like a cloak. Even though all the girls must have been warned that boys were joining them this year, she still did a very gratifying double take at the sight of me, her summer-sky eyes widening. For my part, it was all I could do not to gawp at her like a total idiot. The instant I saw her, I knew her. She was The One.

For a moment we stared at each other. Then the girl shook herself, her hair shimmering with the movement. A delicate rose tinted her high cheekbones, but—my stomach dropped into my socks—she didn't look pleased. A small frown marred her perfect face as she turned decisively away from me. "M— I mean, Headmistress?" Even her voice was perfect, so soft and sweet I half expected her to break into a duet about kittens and rainbows with a passing bluebird. "Everyone's ready and waiting."

"Thank you, Faith," the Headmistress replied. She lifted a hand, cutting off my dad's lecture. "Major Angelos, while I am certain your son's head has not yet been filled with your sound advice, time grows short. I must ask you to make your final farewells."

"Of course." Dad put his hands on my shoulders, looking me squarely in the eye. "Now promise me you'll apply yourself, Raffi."

"Oh," I said, staring past him at Faith. "You bet I will."

"That's my boy." To my utter mortification, Dad ruffled my hair, then pulled me in for a hug. "You'll do fine."

"Mr. Angelos, you may leave your bags here for now," the Headmistress said as I disentangled myself as fast as possible. "Faith will escort you to the hall. A last word with you, please, Major Angelos?"

"This way," Faith said, holding the gate open for me. She avoided my eyes, her own gaze lingering on my dad and the Headmistress as they headed back toward his car.

"Your dad seems nice." There was an odd, wistful note to her musical voice. "You're lucky."

"I certainly am." Falling into step with her, I tried out the charming, enigmatic smile that I'd spent the summer practicing in front of the mirror. "Though not because of my dad."

"Yes, of course, we're all lucky to get to go to a school like this," Faith said a little too quickly. She indicated the carefully tended flower beds lining the path, and the landscaped woods beyond. I had to admit, it was all very pretty. Also, unspeakably girly. I could already feel my testosterone draining away. "It's so beautiful here, don't you think?"

I edged a little closer, trying to keep up my smile while also throwing in a hint of smolder. My face was starting to ache. "Yes, I do."

"Some of the buildings we use for classrooms are hundreds of years old," Faith said in the bright, brittle tones of someone determinedly paddling against a conversational undertow. She lengthened her stride, like a tour guide on a tight schedule. "Look, there's the main school building. It has many unique architectural features." I had a horrible feeling that Faith was about to start listing them all. Given that the monstrosity rising in front

6

of us sported everything from Gothic gargoyles to a sort of bonsai skyscraper, she could probably keep going for hours. "It started as a chapel, though of course it's been extended a lot since then. Saint Mary's used to be a convent, you know."

I was beginning to feel like it still was one. Faith wasn't looking at me at all. Time to deploy the big guns. "I know a lot of things, Faith Jones. Especially about you."

That got her attention. She stopped dead, swiveling to face me. "What do you mean?"

Going for broke, I reached for her hand, gazing deep into her astonished blue eyes as I lifted it to my lips. "I mean that you're the reason I'm here."

This was absolutely true. School brochure, page three, full-page picture: "AFTER A HARD DAY'S WORK, NOTHING BEATS A SWIM IN OUR BEAUTIFUL OUTDOOR POOL!"—FAITH JONES. The photographer had captured her rising from the water with her head thrown back and water streaming from her hair, looking like some sort of classic sea goddess. In a red bikini.

The instant I'd seen that picture, I'd known this was the school for me. And now all my research in the romance section of the library was about to pay off big-time. All the wariness had vanished from Faith's face, chased away by incredulous, breathless hope. Her fingers tightened on mine as my lips brushed the back of her hand—

"Ah, Mr. Angelos," the Headmistress said from right behind me. "I see you've introduced yourself to my daughter."

. . . Daughter?

Abort! Abort! "Great to meet you!" I nearly punched myself in the nose in my haste to turn my romantic gesture into a hearty handshake. "Totally looking forward to being your classmate!" I dropped her hand as if it were a live spider, backing away. "I mean, in class. Outside of class, I guess we won't see each other that much, because, uh, I like to study on my own. Really into studying. Doesn't leave a lot of time for anything else. You know. In case you were hoping."

Faith, understandably, looked as if I'd just slapped her across the face. "I wasn't." She started walking away, fast. "And I can tell you're going to fit in just fine around here."

"And I," the Headmistress said, ice freezing around every syllable as Faith disappeared from view through an archway, "can already tell you are going to cause me many headaches, Mr. Angelos."

Too late, I realized that insulting the Headmistress's

daughter right in front of her probably wasn't the best start to my career here. Great. Mentally kicking myself, I trailed behind the Headmistress as she followed Faith into a large courtyard, dominated by an ancient chapel that formed the far side. How the hell was I going to get on the Headmistress's good side now?

Possibly more easily than I'd thought, as Faith's shriek echoed from the walls. The sound yanked me into a sprint, every other thought swept aside by an overwhelming need to respond. In an instant, I was at her side, catching her as she stumbled back from a small group of teachers. "Are you okay? What happened?" I looked past the teachers to try to see what had startled her—and took a step back myself.

An intricate design of white-chalked lines sprawled across the chapel's closed door. It had to be some sort of optical illusion, but the graffiti seemed to swirl sickeningly. I swallowed hard, forced to look away before I hurled. From the uniformly pissed-off expressions the teachers were sporting, they didn't like the weird symbol any more than I did. "What the hell *is* that?"

"A pentagram." Faith's own face was faintly green. Nonetheless, she shook me off, straightening her spine. "It's nothing," she said, though I noticed she was careful not to look at the door again. "Nothing that concerns you anyway."

"It does, however, entirely concern me." The Headmistress had caught up with us. Her mouth thinned as she inspected the symbol. "This is becoming quite tedious." She flicked her fingers, gesturing for the teachers to disperse. "We shall take an alternate route, Mr. Angelos. Faith, deal with it."

If my dad had ordered me to clean up my *own* mess in that tone of voice, let alone someone else's, the resulting row would have been heard in the next county, but Faith just nodded as if she was used to being treated like a slave. No wonder she'd said I was lucky to have my dad. I cast a backward glance at her, alone and fragile in front of the pentagram, as the Headmistress led me into the building through a side door. "I could help her out," I offered halfheartedly.

"I did not admit you to this school merely to scrub graffiti, Mr. Angelos," the Headmistress said, to my secret relief. It was dumb, but just the thought of getting closer to that symbol made my stomach pitch. "There are more pressing matters for you to attend to."

Right. Girls. Given that the one I'd originally picked had turned out to be majorly unsuitable, I was anxious to start evaluating the rest of the candidates. Which made me realize that so far, I hadn't seen any of them. The dark, narrow corridors the Headmistress was leading me down were all deserted. "When are the other students arriving, Headmistress?"

"Approximately two hours ago. You are late, Mr. Angelos. Do it again and you risk becoming *the late* Mr. Angelos." Her heels clicked on the flagstones. "That was a joke, Mr. Angelos."

I really hadn't been able to tell. "So when do I get to meet them?"

"That," the Headmistress said, opening a small iron-banded door and standing aside, "would be now."

Multicolored light streamed through the doorway, dazzling after the dark corridor. I hesitated on the threshold, squinting. I couldn't see anything past the brightness, but I could hear a soft murmur of voices whispering to one another.

This must be my home class. Twenty or so girls my age, doubtless all panting for my arrival. I swallowed hard. *Okay, Raf. Remember, you're the only game around. You just have to not be a total idiot.* I drew myself up to my full height and arranged what I hoped was a suave expression on my face. Smooth. Casual. Cool—

I felt a firm shove against my shoulder blades, and stumbled forward, my feet thumping onto a hollow wooden floor. I shielded my eyes against the bright light, blinking until my vision cleared.

Three hundred pairs of female eyes stared back at me.

I was in a chapel. On a stage. In front of the entire school.

I was dead.

Chapter 2

Weekly Peer Assessment feedback sessions will now take place on Thursday evenings in your common rooms, mediated by staff." The Headmistress swept the assembly hall with a stern glare. "Final-year girls, your Peer Assessment will be of particular concern to you this half term as it will determine whether or not you will be fortunate enough to have an escort to our traditional Masked Ball in October. As usual, pupils from Winchester Boys' School have generously volunteered their services as your dance partners, but as there are only two dozen young men available, many of you must inevitably be disappointed. Selection of escorts will thus be done strictly by Peer Assessment results two days prior to the Ball itself. See your form head, Ms. Wormwood, for further details." Glancing down at her lectern, the Headmistress flipped to the next index card. "The school play this year will be Shakespeare's *Othello*, and auditions will take place—"

She might as well have been announcing the latest football scores, for all the attention the girls were paying her. I could feel the heat of their stares washing over me like a flamethrower. I stood behind the Headmistress with my arms folded and feet braced, my own eyes fixed on the massive stained-glass window at the far end of the chapel.

If my pose seemed cool, it wasn't on purpose. It was just that every one of my muscles had locked, rigid with terror.

"And I remind you once more that the crypts below the old chapel are out-of-bounds for all girls." The Headmistress paused as muffled giggles scurried around the cavernous room. "And boys. Boy. Which leads me to the next topic."

Another, louder mass giggle rippled through the hall. I didn't dare glance down. I was going to be able to draw that sodding stained-glass angel on my deathbed.

The Headmistress carried on, ignoring the interruption. "As some of you may be aware, recent changes to legislation about diversity and equal opportunity in education mean that single-sex schools are no longer eligible for a number of government grants. Happily, we have managed to find a way to avoid painful cuts to our school budget." She gestured in my direction like a conjurer forced to produce a rather disappointing rabbit out of a hat. "I hope you will all welcome Mr. Rafael Angelos—"

My total embarrassment was unexpectedly cut short, as someone at the back of the hall very thoughtfully picked that exact moment to fall off her chair with an earsplitting shriek.

"Although not, perhaps"—the Headmistress raised her voice over the eruption of laughter—"quite as *enthusiastically* as Miss Moon."

The girl scrambled for her overturned chair, her face bright red behind a swinging curtain of poker-straight brown hair. She wasn't much to look at, but at that moment I could quite happily have kissed her. At least now most of the school was staring at someone other than me.

The Headmistress tapped her notes against the lectern like a judge banging a gavel, and the room quieted again, heads turning back to face the front. "And with that excitement out of the way, we move on to more important matters. Renovations to the plumbing in the central lavatories will be commencing—"

With the tension broken, I was finally able to relax my shoulders a little. I risked dropping my gaze to the crowd.

For the first time, I was able to get a proper look at my new schoolmates.

They sat in age order, the front rows occupied by first-year eleven-year-olds, awkwardly sitting cross-legged on the floor in their pleated skirts. I skipped over them, and the first three-quarters of the room. Things got more interesting at the point where the chairs started.

The fifth- and sixth-year girls.

No one was going to be sitting on the floor in *those* skirts. With a heroic effort, I forced myself to focus on faces rather than legs. They knew I was looking at them; a ripple of movement ran across the hall, each girl dropping her head coyly or hiding behind her hair or clapping her hands to her mouth and bursting into giggles the instant my gaze fell on her.

Then my eye snagged on the girl sitting at the very end of the last row.

Mind. Officially. Blown.

She was hands-down the hottest girl in the school. She was the hottest girl I'd ever *seen*, and that was including on the internet. Her deeply tanned skin glowed like burnished gold. Her mass of black hair was pulled back from her perfect face in a loose ponytail, while her long, elegant hands rested casually on her crossed knees. She met my stare head-on, assessing me with cool, dark eyes.

She was, without a doubt, utterly out of my league, and I instinctively started to turn away, in case her inevitable boyfriend caught me looking. Then my brain kicked in. What boyfriend? Even if she had one . . . he wasn't here. And I was. And she was still staring at me with that strange intensity, as if there was nobody else in the room apart from the two of us. . . .

A scraping of chairs and rustle of movement jolted me back into reality. The girls were standing up, starting to file out, while the Headmistress was glaring at me as if waiting for something. I hastily tried to replay her last few words in my head and drew a complete blank. I pasted a general expression of helpful attentiveness onto my face instead.

"I *said*, Mr. Angelos," the Headmistress repeated with an icy bite that wilted my smile instantly, "that lessons will commence after lunch, and that you should use this morning to familiarize yourself with the school grounds." Her lips compressed for a moment. "On further thought, I believe I shall provide you with an escort." Her gaze swept over the back of the hall, where a tall, redheaded woman in jeans and a bright pink shirt was rounding up the sixth-year girls. My dark-eyed angel was lingering at the back of the group, looking over her shoulder at the stage. *Oh please, pick her, pick her—*

"Miss Moon!" the Headmistress called out. The girl who'd fallen off her chair tripped over her own feet, crashing into a group of blonde girls who jumped back as if she might give them leprosy.

The Headmistress clearly hated me.

"Miss Moon will show you around," the Headmistress said to me, turning away. She paused to give me one last, cold stare. "I shall be keeping my eye on you. Behave yourself, Mr. Angelos."

"No worries," I muttered, eyeing the girl as she sidled through the crowd, head swiveling as if she was expecting to be tripped up at any moment. Up close, she definitely wasn't in the top three hottest girls, or even the top ten. I guessed she was half Chinese, but she was hardly about to star on the cover of *Hot Asian Babes*. As she reached the stage, she gave me a weird, conspiratorial look, as if the two of us shared some deep secret. She pulled a palm-sized pendant out from under her shirt, flashing it in my direction. The symbol engraved on the metal winked at me.

A pentagram.

It was definitely the same sort of star-in-circle design

as the graffiti drawn across the chapel doors. This one didn't make my stomach churn, but there was something weirdly compelling about it. My palms itched as if it was the latest and greatest mobile phone handset, begging to be held and fondled, rather than a dorky piece of cheap goth jewelry.

I blinked, aware that I'd been staring with my mouth open. So much for not acting like a total idiot. Stepping off the stage—a six-foot drop, but heights had never bothered me—I landed solidly on my feet next to the girl, irritated with both her and myself. "Put that away," I snapped. My hands clenched as I fought down a sudden desire to grab the medallion from her. What *was* it with these pentagram things? "Now."

The girl's grin widened, but she tucked the engraved metal disc back under her shirt. Her pink-rimmed, heavily made-up eyes gave her an uncanny resemblance to a mascaraed rabbit on an anti-animal-testing poster. She was either the world's least intimidating goth or one of those dippy pagan chicks who ate vegan crap and babbled about some moon goddess. "So you're finally here." She made an abortive motion with her hand, as if she'd started to offer it to me to shake, then thought better of it. "I'm Krystal."

Riiight. Dippy pagan chick it was, then.

Krystal took a step closer, pushing her hair back behind her ears as she scrutinized me. "And I know who *you* are." Her tone made it sound like some sort of secret knowledge, rather than something that had just been announced from a podium. "Rafael Angelos." She giggled suddenly, which I felt was a bit rich coming from a girl named Krystal-effing-Moon. "I thought you'd use a different name."

"Call me Raf," I said, probably futilely. I *really* hated the nickname "Raffi," which made me feel like I was still five, but I'd pretty much given up trying to shake it off. Maybe I just didn't look like a Raf.

Judging from the way Krystal was eyeing me, apparently what I *did* look like was the answer to her prayers. But not in a love—or even lust—at first sight sort of way. Her expression was a weird mixture of relief and expectation, mingled with a hint of impatience, as if I was a plumber who'd finally arrived to fix the leaky taps. Her watery brown eyes stayed fixed on mine, without giving the rest of me even a cursory once-over. "You're here for Faith, right?"

I knew gossip traveled fast, but not *that* fast. I hesitated. If I said no, I might get a bad reputation as a player, but if I said yes, I'd be linked to Faith, which could be incon-venient. "It's true," I said at last, deciding on a strategy. I leaned in close, giving her my best intent, serious stare. "But you mustn't tell anyone."

Krystal's eyes widened. Then she beamed at me, the smile lighting up her face and making her almost pretty for a moment. "I won't." Her face fell a little. "It's not like anyone would listen to me." She fiddled with the chain around her neck. "So . . . I guess I should show you around?"

"Please," I said, seizing on the only thing she'd said that had actually made sense. "I need to know where everything important is."

"Right." Krystal turned away—then hesitated. Before I could fend her off, she whirled around and planted a quick, clumsy kiss on my jaw. "Thank you," she whis-pered. She jumped away again, her hair swinging forward to hide her red face. "Uh-um, come on then," she stam-mered. She hurried off without a backward glance.

Girls were so weird.

Chapter 3

Krystal, as it turned out, had an odd sense of priorities. Her tour of the school neglected to show me any classrooms, but did feature a demonstration of how to break into the crypts beneath the chapel, followed by a tour of a half-ruined building tucked deep in the woods, which, she assured me, had once been a shrine. "I found it myself, on a map of the original convent," she said, gazing at the ivy-covered structure with apparent satisfaction. "I think only me and Faith know about it. Anyway, no one else ever comes here."

"Uh, great." I edged away, wishing we weren't *quite* so far from the rest of the school. "Why are you showing it to me?"

"I just thought you might find it useful." Krystal shrugged. "As far as I can tell from the library archives, it's still sacred ground, like the crypts. The actual chapel was deconsecrated ages ago. So, is there anything else you need to see?"

My stomach growled. "The dining hall?"

Krystal blinked. "Oh. You need to eat?"

"It *has* been a long time since breakfast." *And some crazy goth girl has been dragging me miles back and forth across the school grounds,* I didn't say. I didn't want Krystal to abandon me out here. I kept having an uncomfortable feeling that something was watching me from the thorny undergrowth.

"No, I meant—well, I guess you do. Come on." To my relief, Krystal led the way back without further digressions.

Other students were converging on the cafeteria as well. I wistfully eyed a passing group of leggy blondes, who eyed me right back with equal interest. Unfortunately, Krystal showed no signs of ungluing herself from my side. "Don't let me keep you from your friends," I hinted as we both joined the queue for food.

"Don't worry," Krystal said with a slight note of bitterness. "You aren't." Picking up a plastic tray from a rack, she jerked her head in the direction of the serving counter. "There's only Faith, and she works every lunchtime."

I peered over the line of heads in front of us. Faith stood behind a large vat of mashed potatoes, wearing a white apron and a determinedly cheerful expression. "The Headmistress's daughter serves lunch?"

"The Headmistress's daughter thinks that volunteering to do other girls' chores will make them like her again," Krystal said sourly, as Faith beamed at a group of girls who stared back at her as if she was ladling out maggots. "Can't say it's working."

"No kidding." As I watched, the girl Faith was serving jerked her plate back at the last moment. The ladleful of mashed potato hit the floor with a *splat*. "Watch it, you spaz!" the girl said, vicious glee showing in her face despite her angry tone. "You got glop all over my feet!"

"I'm sorry!" Faith was already on her knees, reaching out with a cloth. "Here, let me—"

The girl screeched. "Get that greasy rag away! You're making it worse! Ms. Oleander!" She waved her hand in the air, attracting the attention of the supervising teacher. "Faith's ruined my shoes!"

"Problem, my sweets?" the teacher asked, waddling over. She clucked her tongue at the sight of the splatter of mashed potatoes. "I do hate to see good food wasted. Who's responsible for this?"

"I am, Ms. Oleander." Apparently, Faith wasn't even going to *try* to defend herself. And it looked like no one else would either. The girls watching had the air of hyenas gathered around a wounded gazelle, bright-eyed and attentive for any chance to snatch their own mouthful of fun.

"Don't." Krystal grabbed my arm as if she thought I was about to charge to the rescue like a knight in shining school uniform. That sort of thing really wasn't my usual style, but to my surprise, I found that I'd already taken a step forward. There was just something about Faith, so alone and pathetic on her knees under all those unfriendly eyes. . . .

Krystal dragged me back into line. "Don't draw attention to yourself," she hissed. "We can't risk you getting into trouble."

Faith was still trying to apologize, without much success. "If the stain doesn't come out, I'll buy you replacements," she offered. "Exactly the same."

"Jimmy Choo's limited edition fall collection," the girl said promptly. She smiled, smug and cruel, as Faith went white. "Don't worry. We'll work out a payment plan."

I hadn't thought it was possible for anyone to know less about shoes than I did, but apparently, Ms. Oleander managed to fall into that category. "Very good, that's all settled then," she said cheerfully. "Come on, my sweets, let's get this line moving again. We're holding up hungry mouths!"

The girl and her friends swaggered away to find seats at a nearby table, stifling giggles. I stared, wondering how they managed to get away with being such obvious bitches—and then I forgot all about them. And every other girl in the room. Because there, seated at the head of the table, sat my dark-eyed angel.

She turned to favor the newcomers with a regal, approving nod, treating me to a view of her profile. Forget a thousand ships, that face could launch a damn Mars mission. "Her," I said to Krystal urgently, unable to tear my eyes away. "That girl there. Who is she?"

Krystal followed my gaze. "Oh," she said, the single, flat syllable conveying volumes of past history. "Michaela Dante." Her voice sharpened. "Why? Is she important?"

"You have no idea," I breathed. "Know anything about her?"

Krystal shrugged. "More than most, actually. Faith's kind of obsessed with Michaela. She's told me all about her." She sighed. "At length."

I grabbed her elbow, nodding toward a deserted table in a shadowy corner. "Let's sit over there."

--- ✗ ---

By the end of lunch, I was ready to worship to the Headmistress for bestowing Krystal on me. The girl might have truly terrible taste in jewelry, but she also turned out to have a piece of information about Michaela that was pure, solid gold. It was so unbelievably good I had to get her to repeat it three times.

"For God's sake, you're worse than Faith," Krystal finally said in exasperation. "Why's it so interesting that Michaela's from an orphanage? Don't tell me you're overcome with the romance of the story too."

"Of course not. It's the specific orphanage. You're *sure* it was the Circle of Trust?"

"Positive." Krystal cocked her head to one side. "Why? You know the place?"

I nodded and changed the subject before she could dig any deeper. I wasn't about to explain that my mother had died there when I was just a kid.

She'd been working undercover at the orphanage, investigating rumors of people-trafficking, when the whole place had gone up in smoke. Officially, it was an accident, but my dad and I had always been convinced it was arson, an attempt to destroy the evidence before my mum could uncover it.

Eyewitness accounts said my mum had run back into the burning building several times to rescue trapped children. The last time, she hadn't come out.

I didn't believe in fate, but it was one hell of a coincidence that Michaela might be one of the children my mother had died to save. Talk about your conversational icebreaker. What girl could resist a connection like *that*?

According to Krystal, Michaela was in my first class after lunch, English Literature. Even better, Krystal wasn't. Having pumped her for all the information she could supply, I finally managed to peel her from my side with the excuse that I knew where to find my class and didn't want her to be late for her own. With a parting thumbs-up sign, she departed for Unicorn History or Rainbow Weaving or whatever the hell it was dippy pagan chicks studied, while I set off confidently for my own date with destiny.

Which was why the bell for the start of first lesson found me wandering a maze of twisty little passages, all alike, in search of a classroom I was beginning to suspect only existed in warp space. Being late to my very first class wasn't a great start to my career here, but as the alternative was to ask a passing girl for directions, I didn't have much choice. I didn't speak Giggle.

"Rafael Angelos?" called a syrup-sweet voice. The red-haired teacher I'd seen earlier with the sixth-year girls was now hurrying down the corridor toward me. "I think you're looking for my class, pet. I'm Ms. Wormwood, the English teacher."

"Yes, miss," I said, heart rising. Ms. Wormwood's too-bright red hair and trendy jewelry clearly stated that she thought she was still young and cool. That sort of teacher—one who desperately wanted to be liked by her students—was my favorite type. You could get away with sheer *murder*. "Sorry I'm late." I offered her a cheeky, we're-all-friends-here grin as I fell into step with her. "You know how it is."

"Of course, pet." Ms. Wormwood patted my arm. "Don't worry, you'll get the hang of this place. I hope I'll be able to help you soon feel right at home—I'm your form tutor as well. I deal with any problems in the sixth-year group. My door is always open to my students, pet." Her fingers lingered on my bicep. "Day *and* night."

"Uh," I said, rather unnerved. Ms. Wormwood had to be in her forties. And there was only so far I was willing to go for a good grade. "Right."

To my relief, Ms. Wormwood led the way into a classroom rather than a secluded storeroom cupboard. She clapped her hands as she entered, in what was probably meant to be a commanding fashion but which came across more as if she was about to encourage everyone to join in a rousing sing-along. "Good morning, girls! Suzanne, what are you doing, pet?"

A blonde girl was standing on a desk, the rest of the class gathered around her feet. Now she jumped down, plastering an innocent expression over her evil grin. "I found a phone, miss," she said, waving the evidence. "And I was just trying to work out whose it was."

"It's mine." Faith's soft voice trembled with either fury or suppressed tears. "I *told* you it was mine."

"But I have to make sure," Suzanne said to her. She turned her wide-eyed expression of totally fake sincerity on the teacher. "Loads of girls have this model, and they're hard to tell apart. So I thought of a way Faith could prove it's hers. All she has to do is tell me the most recent message on it. Go on, Faith."

Faith flushed bright red. Hiding her face behind her hair, she took a deep breath. "Our souls will merge into one when I clasp you in my arms at—"

The rest of her sentence was lost in a roar of laughter. "All right, settle down!" Ms. Wormwood said over the noise. Taking the phone from Suzanne, she passed it to Faith. "No need to be ashamed of such a sweet message, Faith." She patted her on the shoulder. "Whoever sent it must love you very much."

"Definitely," a girl stage-whispered to her friend. "Since she sent it to herself. Honestly, no *real* boys send texts like that."

"Of course they do," Ms. Wormwood said as Faith fled to the back of the room. "A young man can be sensitive and literate." She beckoned me in from where I was still lurking in the doorway. "Can't he, Raffi?" Faith was instantly forgotten as the class caught sight of me. "You'll show us what a real man is like. Oh, you'll need somewhere to sit. Is there anyone who doesn't already have a desk partner . . . ?"

Furniture screeched as every girl scrambled to be sitting alone at a table. Given that there were twenty students and eleven desks, the overall effect was of a really *vicious* game of musical chairs. I was pretty sure one brunette actually stabbed a blonde with her fountain pen.

"There you are, pet, you can sit with Suzanne," Ms. Wormwood said as the dust cleared. The only other empty chair in the room was next to Faith, whose unpopularity must indeed be epic to keep her sitting alone even under these circumstances. Maybe that was why Ms. Wormwood hadn't pointed her out to me—joining Faith would be social suicide for any new student.

So . . . why was I already heading her way?

The possessive smirk slid right off Suzanne's face as I went past. Faith's head snapped up, eyes wide with astonishment. Oh, this was a *terrible* idea. But I was powerless to stop myself. It was as if her body was a magnet, irresistibly sucking me toward her even as my brain screamed that I did *not* want to get involved with this jellyfish of a girl, no matter how beautiful she was—

The door creaked open.

"Late again, Michaela," Ms. Wormwood said, her jolly voice for once betraying distinct dislike. "Hurry up and take your seat."

Michaela ignored the teacher completely. Her black eyes met mine—just for an instant, but I felt the jolt of it go clear through me as if I'd been hit by lightning. Then her gaze flicked sideways, from Faith to Suzanne and back again. Face set in a sour expression, Suzanne immediately got up and went to join Faith, who eyed her unhappily but didn't protest. Michaela sashayed to the now-empty desk and sat down, crossing her long legs before her. Without so much as another glance at me, she opened her book.

Ms. Wormwood glared at Michaela's demurely bowed head, a frown making her look much older for a moment. "Very well. With Michaela then please, Raffi pet." Her voice smoothed back into bright, professional tones. "Now girls—that is, class—let's talk about the summer reading."

My feet feeling about three sizes too big, I stumbled through the ranks of desks to the back row, sliding in next to Michaela. I occupied myself for a second getting my stuff out of my bag, my mouth dry. All my plans had completely flown out of my head. I took a deep breath, surreptitiously rubbing my sweaty palms on my trouser legs. She'd wanted me to sit next to her, I reminded myself. "Hi," I managed at last. "I'm Raffi. I mean Raf. Rafael. Rafael Angelos."

I nearly jammed my pencil case into my mouth to shut myself up. Michaela treated me to the very briefest of glances before turning back to her book.

"And you're Michaela," I continued, grasping wildly for something, *anything*, to say. Michaela shifted position, flashing me a glimpse of bronzed skin past the undone top button of her blouse. My brain lost all connection with my mouth. "Michaela Dante. Romanian, from Rome. I mean, not that being from Rome makes you Romanian, but you are. Romanian, I mean, but you live in Rome." *Someone, please,* please *shoot me now.* "Which is in Italy, not Romania. Where you're from. Originally. Um."

Michaela finally looked at me, a spark of something— possibly interest, but more probably concern that whatever I had might be contagious—kindling in her eyes. They were so dark that the pupil and iris merged together. "You seem to know a lot about me." Her exotic accent was pure, liquid sex. "For someone who just arrived."

Trying to look cool was probably a lost cause at this point, but I deployed my charming smile anyway. "I know more about you than anyone else in this school does."

One perfect eyebrow raised. "Oh?"

"Yes." I leaned in closer, holding her challenging gaze. "For a start, I know the truth about the Circle of Trust."

The response was better than I could have dreamed. Michaela stared at me as if seeing into my very soul. She was so close now that I could feel the heat of her skin, could see her pulse leaping in the hollow of her throat—

"So let's hear from the male perspective. If you would tell us your thoughts, Raffi?"

What few coherent thoughts I had at that moment were

mainly about the view down Michaela's top, but I didn't think that was the sort of male perspective Ms. Wormwood meant. Dragging myself back into the everyday world, I tried to remember what the teacher had been wittering on about. Something about the summer reading assignment? What *was* the summer reading assignment? I hadn't even read the back cover when I'd thrown it in my bag this morning. I glanced down now in search of inspiration and discovered I'd taken out my biology textbook. No help there.

Ms. Wormwood's look of friendly expectation was starting to slide into the wary expression of a teacher who senses imminent bullshit. "Well," I said, stalling for time. "I thought it was very interesting." I snuck a peek at the cover of Michaela's book, catching a glimpse of a winged and gratuitously shirtless angel tumbling in flames out of a dark sky. No doubt it was some sort of girly romance, all forbidden love and sparkly boyfriends.

"I found it very inspirational," I said, deciding that I might as well go for broke. Michaela, still searching my face intently, drew in a sharp breath; encouraged, I plowed on. "I really identified with, uh, him." I gestured at the angel guy.

Ms. Wormwood did not look like she was buying this. "Could you be more specific?"

Not really. "Well, his struggle totally resonated with me," I improvised wildly. "And the way that he decided to go for what he wanted, despite everything trying to stop him."

Ms. Wormwood's eyebrows shot up. "Interesting. So you would call him the hero of the piece?"

"Absolutely," I said, hoping I sounded confident. "That sort of tenacity is definitely heroic."

Ms. Wormwood beamed at me, as a little murmur ran around the classroom. "Very good, Raffi. I do like a student who rejects dogma and draws her—his—own conclusions. Why don't you read us the famous quote summing up his argument? Lines two fifty-eight to two sixty-three."

I cast Michaela a sideways glance, to see if she was rapt with admiration at my sensitive nature yet—and was met with a narrow-eyed glare that suggested that if I asked to share her book I was likely to get walloped over the head with it. Recoiling, I hastily fumbled my own copy out of my bag, trying to work out what I'd done wrong. Had I come across as too nerdy? Too pretentious? What?

Finding the right page, I squinted at the text. Oh, great. Poetry.

"Here at last
We shall be free;
the Almighty hath not built
Here for his envy, will not drive us hence:
Here we may reign secure, and in my choice
To reign is worth ambition though in Hell:
Better to reign in Hell, than serve in Heaven."

. . . Huh?

"Excellent, pet," Ms. Wormwood said as I blinked at the page. "Now, who can tell me what Satan means by his speech to the fallen angels here?"

Satan? What the hell kind of romance was this? I checked the back cover as half a dozen hands shot into the air. *Paradise Lost,* it said. *By John Milton.* Apparently, it was all about the war between God and the Devil.

Who I'd just held up as a paragon of manly virtue.

Whoops.

No wonder Michaela had glared at me. She'd now let her hair swing down like a curtain between us, hiding her face. I stifled the urge to groan and thump my head on the desk. This day just kept getting worse and worse.

Busy kicking myself, I barely noticed Michaela whisper

something Italian-sounding under her breath. Then her fingers brushed my thigh.

Ms. Wormwood broke off midsentence. "Is there something wrong, Raffi?"

From flat on the floor, I managed to make a strangled sort of noise, shaking my head. Aware of all the eyes staring at me, I quickly picked up my overturned chair and reseated myself. Burying my face in my book, I waited until all the girls had turned back to Ms. Wormwood. Then I cautiously peered over the pages at Michaela.

Her face was still hidden, but somehow she knew I was looking. "And now," she murmured in a low, throaty voice that made every syllable sound like an invitation to a dirty weekend, "*I* know everything about *you*." Her knees bumped mine under the desk as she turned toward me. "Do you know what I'm going to do?"

I maintained my smoldering, mysterious silence, mainly because my brain had utterly fused.

Michaela pushed back her hair. Her bloodred lips curved upward, slowly.

"I'm going," she whispered, her black eyes burning with passion, "to kill you."

Chapter 4

That evening found me lying on my bed, flipping through stacks of old school yearbooks I'd borrowed from the library, searching for my mum. She'd always been secretive about her life before meeting my dad—"I was a different person back then" was all she'd ever said—but I knew her maiden name and the approximate dates she had to have been here. So far, though, the only mention of a "Foxglove" I'd found was an English teacher who'd apparently been at the school then. Given that the article was about her retiring due to completing twenty years' service, that couldn't possibly be my mum, although I did wonder if she was a relative. My mum had been completely estranged from her family, but she'd let slip once—while trying to persuade me of the importance of doing my homework—that I had generations of teachers in my unknown maternal background. "The family business," she'd called it and then changed the subject quickly.

With a sigh, I gave up on my research and tossed the yearbook aside. I stretched out on my rock-hard mattress, staring up at the beamed ceiling. "Michaela," I said aloud, rolling the syllables over my tongue. Michaela Dante.

I knew that girls pretended to be disinterested when they actually were panting for you, but when it came to playing hard to get, "I'm going to kill you" was Olympic level. On the other hand, Michaela *had* made a point of sitting next to me in every lesson that afternoon. That had to mean she was interested, right?

A soft, hesitant knock on the door derailed my train of thought. I swung my legs off the bed and reached for the doorknob, a relieved grin spreading across my face. With Michaela's glowering presence at my back all day, every other girl had treated me as if I was surrounded by an invisible force field. I'd spent all afternoon grimly trying to ignore the whispers and stares, feeling an awful lot like a zoo exhibit. At least *someone* was willing to come and say hello.

By the time I realized that my late-night visitor was almost certainly Krystal, it was too late to hide. My expression frozen somewhere between welcome and horror, I peered cautiously around the half-open door.

"Hi!" said the apparently empty corridor.

I looked down. A blonde girl who couldn't be older than twelve beamed up at me over the top of a fistful of large, vibrant flowers.

"Uh . . . hi?" I said.

"HiRaffimynameisClairewelcometoSaintMary'sweloveyoubye!" the girl said all in one breath and thrust her bouquet into my hand. A second later, she was gone.

"Okay," I said, blinking. Random. Closing the door again, I jammed the flowers into my water glass and set them on the windowsill, where they added a cheerful splash of color to the otherwise grim decor. You'd think that as the only guy here, I would have been given one of the best rooms in the place, but as it was I'd been housed in a pigsty. Literally. The plaque on the front of the building said BOYS' DORMITORY (OLD PIGGERY). Thanks, Headmistress.

Still, even if my room was small, at least I had it to myself. In fact, I had the entire building to myself, though the other half dozen rooms were locked. I gazed out the window at the distant lights of the main school complex, just visible through the tangled woods. Nice and private. Far away from all the teachers. That could come in handy.

Another tap at the door interrupted my thoughts. Wondering if HiRaffimynameisClaire had mustered the courage for another hit-and-run sentence, I opened it again.

Same bouquet. Same expression. Different girl.

"HelloRaffimynameisLouisewelcometotheschool-you'rereallyfitbye!"

I was left with yet more flowers and a deepening expression of bemusement. With a shrug, I added the latest tribute to my impromptu vase. I had to admit, the way the girls had decided to greet me was pretty cute.

By the tenth knock on my door in thirty minutes, it was getting a lot less cute.

"Look," I snapped, wrenching the door open yet again and glaring down at the latest admirer, "this is all very flattering, but you guys are starting to pi—"

I stopped. I was yelling at a very short, chubby, plain-faced girl clutching a wilting dandelion and looking utterly petrified.

Way to go, Raf.

From down the corridor, I heard a small, muffled snigger. Glancing up, I caught a glimpse of a couple of young girls quickly ducking out of sight around the corner.

Uh-huh.

I stared hard in the direction of the unseen onlookers for a second, then returned my attention to the girl, who was edging away as if preparing to bolt. "No, wait." She froze like a deer in headlights. "What's your name?"

"L-lydie," the girl whispered at the floor. Her knuckles were white on her tattered dandelion.

"Hi, Lydie. Is that for me?"

Lydie looked at her pathetic flower, then hid it behind her back, her face going red. "I'm sorry." Her barely audible words overflowed like the tears brimming in her big blue eyes. "I picked nicer ones, like the others told me to, but then they didn't let me keep any of the good ones. They said I still had to come, and this was all I could find."

"Thanks," I said warmly, plucking the flower from her fist. Lydie stared up at me, mouth and eyes round, as I tucked it into my buttonhole. I crooked a smile at her. "Yellow's my favorite color, you know."

I got the tiniest, shyest, briefest of smiles in return, before her nerve broke and she was off like a rabbit down the corridor. Well, at least now she hopefully wouldn't grow up thinking that all guys were total bastards.

The warm glow of a good deed well done was cut short by yet another knock at the door. Bloody hell.

"Your future boyfriends can thank me for not giving you all complexes," I muttered under my breath, shoehorning a smile back onto my face. I swung open the door—and discovered I was doing my best Prince Charming impression at the Headmistress.

"Chrysanthemums, Mr. Angelos." For one horrific moment, I thought that she too was about to offer me a love token, but her hands were empty. Despite the late hour, she still wore her neat black skirt suit, but she'd now accessorized it with a long raincoat and a peeved expression. "What do you know about them?"

When my dad had said that they'd make me work here, I hadn't thought that meant late-night pop botany quizzes. "Uh . . . they're a flower?"

"Yes, Mr. Angelos." The steel-capped toe of her shoe tapped dangerously. "A flower that provides delightful late autumn color in the garden. *My* garden."

Oh.

And also: *Uh-oh.*

"Except," the Headmistress continued, as my stomach sank in anticipation, "that my prize specimens now appear to instead be providing autumn color to *your* window. Since I find it difficult to believe that you have taken up flower arranging, I suggest you tell me who gave them to you."

"Um." Lydie's tiny, terrified face floated up in my mind. *Damn.* "Actually, I did pick them. I didn't know they were yours. Sorry."

"Really." The Headmistress's eyes narrowed as she studied me. "Why are you wearing a dandelion?"

"I . . ." My brain stalled. ". . . decided to do a bit of weeding? While I was there? Like, uh, I thought maybe students helped out with the gardening. You know, school pride."

The Headmistress was silent for a long moment, while I sweated my entire body weight. "How very civic of you," she said at last, totally deadpan. "I commend your enthusiasm, Mr. Angelos. Perhaps a bit overzealous, but I shall overlook it on this occasion." She turned away, and I started breathing again.

"On one condition," the Headmistress added, just as I'd nearly shut the door. "I look forward to seeing your map of my flower beds, with the locations of all chrysanthemums clearly marked, on my desk first thing tomorrow morning, Mr. Angelos. Should this fail to materialize, I shall instead expect *you* to materialize in my office for a

45

detention." She fixed me with a look that said she knew I was serving up bullshit, and she wasn't digging in. "I trust it will not come to that."

"You bet," I promised fervently. I retreated into my room, closing the door and collapsing against it with a long sigh. Great. Now I had to sneak out and draw the Headmistress's garden, wherever the hell that was, or get a detention. Was there anything *else* that could go wrong on my first day?

A scatter of gravel hit my window.

I groaned, hiding my head in my arms in the hopes it might all go away. Gravel pattered against the glass again, followed by the louder *clink* of a thrown pebble. Before my would-be visitor escalated to half bricks, I jerked the window open. *"What?"*

"It's me!" Krystal whispered from the bushes. "I wanted to ask how things were going. Can I come in?"

I thumped my forehead against the window frame. "Krystal, I am having a *really* bad night."

"Yeah, I imagine it must be pretty tough for you down here. I mean, it's tough enough for *me*, and I've had a whole lifetime to get used to it." Krystal's flashlight lit her face from below, half-illuminating her sympathetic expression. "Is there anything I can do to help?"

I started to shake my head, and then stopped as a thought struck me. "Actually, yeah. Do you know where the Headmistress's house is?"

"Of course." Krystal jumped back as I slithered out the window. "What, you want to go there now?"

"It's a long story." I disentangled myself from an over-amorous bush and stepped free of the shrubbery. "Let's just say I have a mission, and it's a matter of life and death that I complete it before the morning."

Krystal nodded, as if this was a perfectly reasonable explanation for wanting to spend the night lurking around teachers' houses. Then again, given that this was the girl who wore a pentagram charm the size of a discus around her neck, I could probably just have told her that the fairies wanted me to do it.

She led the way through the woods to an isolated house that looked like something straight out of a horror movie. "This is it," Krystal whispered, pointing at the glowering, ivy-covered structure. I had to admit, it did match my impression of the Headmistress. All it needed was to be surrounded by gravestones. As it was, the immaculately tended flower beds seemed kind of out of keeping. "Now what?"

"Now we search for chrysanthemums."

Krystal shot me a narrow-eyed look. "Is this one of those 'moving in mysterious ways' things that you can't explain?"

"Uh, yeah. You poke around the front, and I'll cover the back." Not giving her a chance to argue, I headed around the house.

A flash of white snagged my peripheral vision, and I had a momentary conviction that a giant albino spider was about to eat my face before I realized it was another pentagram symbol chalked on the stone wall. This one was smaller than the one on the chapel door, but still eye-wateringly weird. The white lines seemed to glow in the moonlight.

What *was* it with this school and pentagrams? I dragged my sleeve across the chalk lines, smearing them, and immediately felt a little better. I took a deep breath, commanding my racing heart to calm down. I was a rational person. So it was dark. So the house was creepy. I was perfectly safe. Nothing was going to leap out at me.

"Get thee behind me, Satan!"

I very nearly died, and not just from shock. Only some primal reflex made me leap aside, so that the shining silver blade skewered the air rather than my heart. My dad's much-hated self-defense lessons—which he'd viewed as essential preparation for an all-boys' boarding school life—kicked in. I grabbed my attacker's wrist, digging my thumb in until she dropped the sword, then twisted her arm behind her back to immobilize her.

Wait a second. Her?

Long, blonde hair tangled across my face as my captive struggled. *"Faith?"*

"Raffi?" To my relief, she stopped trying to stomp my toes into mush. "What are you doing here?"

"Not expecting to get assaulted, that's what!" I was suddenly very aware of her lithe body pressed against mine. I let her go in a hurry. "What are *you* doing?"

"Raf?" Krystal's voice sounded faintly from the other side of the house. "Was that you? Are you okay?"

"Fine!" I called back. "Small misunderstanding. Keep looking, okay?" I turned back to Faith. "Seriously, what the hell?"

"I'm sorry, I didn't know it was you!" Faith brushed her hair back behind her ears, still breathing hard. She pointed at the smudged pentagram. "I was looking for whoever did that."

"With a sword?"

Faith's gaze slid away from mine evasively. "It's for . . . protection. Anyway, you need to go." She looked nervously around the garden, as if expecting the bushes to erupt with zombies at any moment. "It's not safe."

"No kidding." Death threats and attempted stabbings, all in my first day. I hadn't realized an all-girls' school would be *this* crazy. "I don't want to be here. Your mother kind of made me." I briefly explained my predicament, grateful when she didn't laugh. "I don't suppose you've got a map of her garden, do you?"

"Actually, yes. She keeps the designs on her computer. She takes her gardening seriously." Faith's eyes were still skipping from shadow to shadow. "You really need to go now."

"I can't, not without those plans. Look, can you go print me out a copy?" Faith looked dubious, so I added, "You *did* try to stab me through the heart, you know."

"All right," Faith said reluctantly. She took a step toward the house, then hesitated. "It'll take me a while though. Maybe you should come in."

"Are you *nuts*?" The mere thought of the Headmistress catching me with her daughter, alone, in her house, at night . . . I resisted the urge to cup my hands protectively over my groin. "I'll wait here." Scooping up the sword, I handed it back to her. "Hurry, okay?"

Faith bit her lip. Then, to my surprise, she thrust the

hilt into my hand. "To keep you safe," she called over her shoulder as she hurried away.

I hefted the weapon dubiously. It was a thin, whippy thing, dull on the edges like a fencing saber, but narrowing to a sharp, wicked point that would definitely *not* be legal in any sporting venue. "Safe from what?"

Silence answered me. Silence . . . and the growing sense of a watching presence. Try as I might to tell myself it was just my imagination, that there was nothing out there, sweat ran down my spine. I squeezed my eyes shut, determined not to give in to the irrational, rising sense of dread. There was nothing there. Nothing creeping up on me. Nothing—

A twig snapped right behind me.

With a yell, I spun around, lashed out with the sword in pure reflex. I caught the briefest glimpse of the Headmistress's startled face as the weapon hit her solidly in the ribs.

And the blade blazed with white fire.

Chapter 5

The white flames writhing around the sword died as I flung it aside. I dropped to my knees beside the felled teacher, shaking her shoulder. "Headmistress? I'm sorry, I didn't mean it!"

She didn't move.

I was so very, very expelled. And I hadn't even finished unpacking yet.

"Raffi?" Faith's voice drifted down from an upper-floor window. "What's going on?"

"Nothing!" I yelped, huddling over the Headmistress in an attempt to hide the evidence. Thankfully, Faith didn't inquire further. I could only hope that she took a *really* long time to print out those maps.

"I saw a streak of fire!" Krystal's low, excited voice sounded shockingly close. The beam of her flashlight swept over me, searching. "Was that you? What did—"

Krystal fell abruptly silent as the light hit the Headmistress's slack face. The teacher's eyes were rolled right up, showing only the whites.

She didn't seem to be breathing.

"You killed the Headmistress!" Most students would have said that with at least some pleasure, however guilty, but Krystal sounded entirely horrified. Her voice shot up an octave. "You *killed* the Headmistress!"

"I didn't mean to!" Okay, so some things—expensive electronics, kitchen utensils, dormitories—did have a habit of unexpectedly going up in smoke around me, but a sword? "It was an accident!"

Krystal took a deep breath. "Well, there's only one thing to do," she said firmly, sounding like a Girl with a Plan. I looked at her hopefully. "You'll have to bring her back."

Aaand so much for that. "Do what? How?"

"How should I know? However you normally bring people back from the dead!" Krystal flung up her hands in exasperation, glaring at me. "You're the angel!"

I stared at her, mouth hanging open. "And you," I said at last, "are insane."

Krystal froze. "Oh my God," she whispered. "You have

53

no idea what you are, do you?" Letting go of my sleeve, she fumbled for her pentagram charm. "Raf, I know this is going to seem bizarre, but you have to believe me. See, I made this to summon a guardian angel—*Rafael Angelos*—because we needed help fighting the demons, and—"

"And I am *leaving*."

"No! As your summoner, I forbid you!" Now it was Krystal's turn to hang on to me. She was surprisingly strong for her height. "You at least have to heal the Headmistress!"

"What do you expect me to do? Lay hands on her," I said, wiggling my fingers over the Headmistress in demonstration, "and yell 'Arise!'—"

The Headmistress coughed and sat up.

I fell over backward.

"Mr. Angelos," the Headmistress said, blinking at me and sounding vaguely puzzled. "What are you doing down there?" She glanced around, her frown deepening. "What am *I* doing down here?"

"Headmistress?" Krystal shot me a triumphant I-told-you-so look. Then she did a strange double take, alarm flashing across her face. She pointed her flashlight directly at my head while offering her other hand to the

54

Headmistress. "Are you feeling okay?"

"Certainly, Miss Moon," the Headmistress snapped, ignoring the assistance as she got to her feet. She brushed irritably at the dirt on her clothes. "I simply encountered a small obstacle on my way back to my house." She glared at me as if I was personally responsible for this. Admittedly, I was, but *she* didn't know that. "What are you two doing out of your dormitories after curfew?"

"Uh . . ." My mind had gone blank. "We were, um . . ."

Behind the Headmistress's back, Krystal was making urgent throat-cutting motions. I fell silent, but she kept doing the cut-it-out gesture, for no apparent reason. I could really have done without the way she was spotlighting me with the flashlight.

The Headmistress waited for a moment as if expecting further excuses, but as I was already in the hole up to my neck, it seemed like a good idea to stop digging. She let out her breath in exasperation. "Miss Moon, I expected better judgment from you. Mr. Angelos, detention."

"What?" I exclaimed indignantly. Krystal shook her head, but I ignored her. "That's not fair!"

The Headmistress gave me a hard look. "*Two* detentions, Mr. Angelos."

55

"But—"

"If you speak again, Mr. Angelos, I shall have you rusticated."

I had no idea what that was, but it sounded painful. I shut up.

"Miss Moon, return to your dormitory at once. Your *own* dormitory," the Headmistress added as Krystal showed no inclination to leave.

"Uh—can I take Rafael to the nurse, please?" Krystal sounded oddly desperate. "I think maybe he hit his head when he fell over."

The Headmistress treated me to a cursory inspection. "Nonsense, he's practically glowing with health," she said. "I believe he will survive without your company."

Krystal bit her lip, then dashed around the Headmistress to shove the flashlight into my hand. "Keep it pointed at your face," she hissed into my ear. "And come find me tomorrow. I'll explain everything." She disappeared between the trees.

I was left alone with the Headmistress. The Headmistress I'd just hit with a flaming sword.

"Mr. Angelos." The Headmistress's voice was as level as always, but the skin between my shoulder blades crawled. I suddenly wondered just how amnesiac she really was. "I am neither a fool nor your enemy. Do not make the mistake of treating me as either." I followed Krystal's advice about the flashlight, to better display my deeply penitent expression. To my relief, the Headmistress started to walk away, her heels impaling dead leaves with every step. "And, Mr. Angelos," she said over her shoulder, "Miss Moon is not a suitable partner for you. I do not expect to catch you in a compromising position with her again."

"Don't worry," I muttered when I was certain she was gone. Picking myself up, I brushed dirt off my trousers. "You won't."

Soft, silver-gold moonlight made Krystal's flashlight entirely unnecessary as I stomped my way back to my own dormitory. I was too tired to do anything other than kick off my shoes and collapse backward onto the bed. Craving darkness and sleep, I stuck out one arm to flick the light switch off.

The light stayed on.

"Aargh," I groaned, not even having the energy to muster a proper obscenity. I forced my eyelids back open—and found myself staring at the overhead light fixture.

Which was off.

As was the bedside lamp. And the curtains were drawn, not allowing even a sliver of moonlight to penetrate.

I could see all this quite clearly, thanks to the golden, shifting light rippling on the ceiling like sunbeams glittering from the surface of the sea.

Blinking, I pushed myself up on my elbows. The light moved as I did, sending dark shadows scurrying in the corners of the room. The mirror on the far wall lit up with reflected brilliance; I squinted, automatically raising a hand to shield my eyes.

My reflection copied me. It had to be my reflection, given that it was moving like I did and looked just like me.

Except for the halo.

Chapter 6

I finally managed to fall asleep facedown with my head stuffed under my pillow. I awoke restored and refreshed, firmly convinced that I'd hallucinated the whole thing.

And still glowing.

"Oh, come on," I groaned at my resolutely haloed reflection. It wasn't a flaming, floating circlet, at least, but a distinct glow outlined my entire head. I looked like I was being rather badly backlit by incompetent stagehands.

Maybe Krystal had been right, and I *had* cracked my skull on the ground last night. I leaned forward to inspect my eyes in the mirror as I brushed my teeth. My halo helpfully illuminated the fact that my pupils were the same size. As my medical knowledge of concussion began and ended there, further diagnosis was impossible. Vague worried thoughts about internal bleeding circling in my possibly traumatized mind, I finished getting dressed, then headed out in search of the school nurse. Which was where the Headmistress should have sent me in the first place. If I suffered from weird hallucinations for the rest of my life, it would be all her fault.

I cheered up. Maybe I could sue. At the very least, brain damage had to be worth half an hour of extra time in exams.

"Raffi?" called a timid voice. I turned to see a little girl sidling toward me with an apprehensive expression, as if approaching a large dog of uncertain temper.

I squinted at her, checking for any odd visual effects, but she seemed normal. Though for some reason her chubby, anxious face made me think of . . . dandelions? "Oh, right!" I smiled at her, remembering. "Hi, Lydie."

Lydie stopped just out of arm's reach, apparently in order to inspect her suddenly fascinating shoes. "You— you weren't at breakfast," she said to the gravel.

I checked my watch. "Damn. I overslept." Shading my eyes against the bright morning sunlight, I started down the path toward the main school. "Sorry, Lydie, I've got to run."

"Wait!" Lydie hurried after me. Still keeping her gaze averted, she stuck out a hand containing a napkin-wrapped package. "There's never anything good to eat at the canteen, but Ms. Oleander likes me. She showed me the key code to get into the kitchens once. I snuck in and stole you an egg-and-bacon roll from the teachers' stash."

"Hey, thanks!" I took the lukewarm and slightly soggy snack from her and started unwrapping it. "That's really sweet of you."

Lydie went red from throat to forehead. She tagged along after me like a hopeful puppy, though she still didn't quite dare to actually look in my direction. "Thanks for not telling on me," she mumbled to the bushes lining the path. "To the Headmistress."

"About the flowers?" I said with my mouth full. "No worries. Though," I swallowed thickly, "you shouldn't let the other girls push you into stuff like that. Maybe you should tell—er, not the Headmistress. Tell a nice teacher like Ms. Wormwood about it. The bullying, I mean."

From Lydie's horrified expression, you'd have thought I'd suggested that she solve her problem by calling in a SWAT team. "I couldn't do that. I'd get a bad grade."

I snorted. "What in, popularity?"

"Yes," Lydie said woefully. "Claire and her friends are the prettiest and most popular girls in second year." She hung her head even lower. "If I don't do whatever they want, they'll make sure everyone gives me a bad Peer Assessment score. My end-of-year results would be terrible."

I stared at her. "Are you telling me that part of your marks are determined by *other students?*"

"Of course," Lydie said, surprised. "How else could we get evaluated on our 'leadership and teamwork skills'?" She sounded like she was quoting from a school handbook. She finally looked at me, her own expression quizzical. "Didn't they have Peer Assessment at your old sch—" She stopped midword, staring up at my face. "Um," she said after a second. "How are you making your hair do that?"

"It looks like that naturally," I lied. Actually, it took three products and ten minutes every morning to stop me from looking like a blond sheep, but to admit that would be incredibly sissy.

Lydie appeared hypnotized by my hair. I wished it had the same effect on girls past puberty. "What," she said, sounding bewildered, "on fire?"

"It's not—*you can see it too?*"

"Um, yes?" Lydie flinched, looking uncertain. "Sorry? Is it meant to be subtle?"

I grabbed her shoulders, making her yelp, and dropped down to one knee so our faces were level. "Lydie," I said as calmly as I could. Judging from her terrified expression, this was not very calm. "This is really important. What exactly do you see?"

"It's all glowy." Lydie's hands described a circle around my head. "Like, like, a huge candle. It's really pretty," she added quickly as if this might be my main concern. "Just . . . um, I don't think the Headmistress will like it."

"*I* don't like it!"

"Then why did you do it?" Lydie frowned. "*How* did you do it?"

"I have no idea!" I savagely ruffled my hair, and shot Lydie an inquisitive glance. She shook her head, which I took to mean I was still radiating. I pressed both palms to my forehead. "Right. Okay. There's a perfectly rational explanation for this."

Lydie looked at me expectantly.

"While I think of it," I said, getting up again, "I need you to help me with something."

--- ✗ ---

"Nice hat, Raffi," yet another of my classmates—Delilah or Deborah or something, I couldn't possibly be expected to remember all these names—said with a wide grin. "Suits you."

"Thanks," I muttered. I really hoped she was being sarcastic. "I think." I dodged past her into the rapidly filling classroom. History of Art hadn't been that popular a subject at my old school, but it seemed everyone was keen on it here. Apart, evidently, from the one girl I needed to find.

Faith was sitting by herself at the very back of the room, shoulders hunched and face buried in a celebrity gossip magazine as if she could make herself invisible if she concentrated hard enough on the pages. I made a beeline for her. "Hey." She jumped, flinching back as I slid in next to her. "You're friends with Krystal, right? Does she take this class?"

"Krystal?" Faith clutched her magazine to her chest as if she thought I might try to tear it away. "No, she'll be in Advanced Statistics." Her expression of puzzlement deepened. "Why are you wearing a bright pink hat?"

"I'm very secure in my masculinity. When are you seeing Krystal next?"

"In Latin, this afternoon, I guess." Faith was still distracted by my headgear. "Um, Raffi? Did you know that your hat is inside out?"

"It's, uh, got a flaw on the other side." Said flaw was a large appliquéd picture of Twilight Sparkle from *My Little*

Pony. I wasn't *that* secure in my masculinity. "Look, when you see her, can you tell her I really need to talk to her? It's urgent."

Faith bit her lip. "Raffi," she said, turning to face me, her blue eyes wide and earnest. "Krystal means well, but she's a bit . . . Well, she has some strange ideas about you. You aren't taking her seriously, are you?"

"Um." I tugged my too-tight hat a little more firmly down over my halo. "No. Of course not. No way."

Faith gave me a relieved smile. "Good. I think it would be best if you left her alone."

"I think it would be better if *you* left *him* alone," Suzanne said, coming up to our table. "Sit with us instead, Raffi."

"It's Raf, actually," I said coldly. "And no thanks. I'm fine here with Faith."

"Oh my God." Suzanne glanced around with exaggerated caution. She couldn't have been more obvious about wanting an audience if she'd waved a sign saying PLEASE EAVESDROP. "So the rumors are true?"

My fingers twitched as I stopped myself from checking my hat again. "Rumors?" I said, attempting a casual tone. "What rumors?"

"About the real reason you're at this school," Suzanne said. Half the class was listening in now. "I mean, it's beyond weird that only *one* boy would get in. No way that could just be a coincidence. And everyone can see you're not an ordinary guy."

I adjusted my hat again. "Um. I can explain."

Suzanne gave me a sweet, sympathetic smile that failed to reach her eyes. "It's okay, Raffi." She raised her voice a little. "No one blames *you* for being a male model hired by the Headmistress to date Faith."

My mouth hung open as whispers started to scurry around the room. Faith shot to her feet. "That's not true!" she cried.

"Oh, come on, Faith, it's obvious," Suzanne said scornfully. "The only reason a guy would be interested in a nut like you is if he was *paid* to be. Your mother's so scared you're going to end up like your crazy, dead dad, she's handpicked a guy to try to make you forget your imaginary boyfriend." She leaned in close. "Personally, I'd just sit back and wait until you offed yourself like he did. Be less trouble for everyone."

"For God's sake, can't you give it a rest for once, Suzanne?" snapped Something-Beginning-With-D, turning around from the row ahead. I was grateful to her, as I was still speechless. "Michaela's not even here yet. Stop showing off."

Whatever retort Suzanne might have made was forestalled by the arrival of the teacher. At least, I assumed it was the teacher, because stick insects didn't get that big. The gaunt figure glared at the class. "Sit."

I sank back to my seat along with everyone else. Faith had retreated to another table, whose occupants were pointedly ignoring her. Suzanne cast a speculative look at the now-empty chair next to me. I flipped her off from under the desk, and she turned away with a see-if-I-care toss of her head.

"Ms. Vervaine. History of Art. You will learn it." Apparently deciding that this was all the introduction necessary, Ms. Vervaine stalked to her desk, her long limbs moving in jerky stop-start arcs like a broken clockwork toy. "Today we will—what is that?"

It took all my willpower not to cower away from the pointed fingernail stabbing straight at me. "Er, I'm Raf? Rafael Angelos? The new student?"

"Not you." Ms. Vervaine's finger jabbed the air again. *That.*

With a sinking feeling, I realized where she was pointing. "It's a hat, Ms. Vervaine. I, uh, get cold. Please, may I leave it on?" I gave her my best piteous puppy eyes.

Ms. Vervaine looked like she wanted to swat me across

the nose with a rolled-up newspaper. "Remove it." A class-wide snigger died a quick death as her glare swept the room. "Now."

There was nothing for it. Bracing myself for the worst, I pulled my hat off.

"Good," Ms. Vervaine said, turning away to fiddle with a remote control. I glanced around. A couple of girls were eyeing me, but with no more than the usual amount of interest.

I angled the metal lid of my pencil case, trying to use it as an impromptu mirror. I couldn't get a decent look at my reflection, thanks to the glare of sunlight streaming in through the window behind me.

Sunlight. Now I really was being backlit. The light must be strong enough to drown out my own glow. If I was still glowing. With a furtive glance to make sure no one was paying too much attention, I dropped my pen, then used the pretext of retrieving it to duck under the desk. Rippling light illuminated dry, ancient bits of chewing gum, and I cracked my still-haloed head on the wood in my haste to get out of the shadows.

Okay. I started to breathe a little easier. As long as the sun was behind me, no one would notice anything weird.

"Video lesson," Ms. Vervaine announced. She pressed a button on her remote control and all the overhead lights went out.

And now I knew why this class was so popular. I never thought there would come a time when I was dismayed by the prospect of a video-based lesson—or as I liked to call them, nap breaks—but now I found myself longing for a nice pop quiz. Still, although the room was dimmer, she hadn't turned off the sun. I was safe enough.

"Part one of fourteen," Ms. Vervaine continued as automated blinds clattered down over the windows. "No tests—pay attention, Mr. Angelos!"

"Dropped my pencil case!" I squawked from flat under the desk.

"What is that light?" To my horror, I heard footsteps start to walk toward me. "Are you—Miss Dante, can you *ever* be on time?"

"No," said Michaela's unmistakable smoldering voice. "I have more important things to do."

I was expecting Michaela to get rusticated—whatever that was—from now until next term for that bit of cheek, but Ms. Vervaine only growled. "Sit," she said curtly. "Silence."

The footsteps continued to get closer, and I found

myself at eye level with a pair of ankle boots. I nearly got impaled by the stiletto heels as Michaela slid into the seat next to mine. My glow shone up her short skirt, granting me a perfect view of leather straps—*wait, what?*—curving across smooth thighs, leading up to *oh, hell yes*—

My halo vanished, plunging me into darkness. And Ms. Vervaine gave me another detention for swearing.

Chapter 7

"Are you sure you're comfortable, Raffi?" Ms. Wormwood said as she put a fresh bucket of soapy water down next to me. She winked. "I know detention is still technically within school hours, but I'll turn a blind eye if you want to relax the dress code a bit more."

"Really, I'm fine." I swiped the back of my hand across my dripping forehead, then bent over the scrubbing brush again. Actually, cleaning spray-painted pentagram symbols off the final-year girls' dormitory was bloody hot work, even in the cool autumn air. My shirt stuck to my back.

Of course, that was mainly thanks to the previous bucket of water, which Ms. Wormwood had accidentally sloshed over me. At least, she said it had been an accident. Given that most of the girls from my year were surreptitiously watching me from the upper-floor windows, I strongly suspected bribery.

Or rather, I *hoped* it was bribery.

"Well, pet, if you get too hot, feel free to undo another button." Ms. Wormwood's gaze lingered on my throat. "Or two. Or four."

Oh, how I wished I hadn't taken my jacket and tie off. Or that I'd been able to do the evening's detention with Ms. Vervaine, like I had the lunchtime one. The History of Art teacher, who obviously hadn't wanted to supervise a detention any more than I wanted to be in one, had plonked me down in a comfy armchair in her overheated office and instructed me to pay close attention to a riveting documentary called *Sheep Breeds of South East England.* I'd been asleep in under five minutes. Ms. Vervaine was definitely my new favorite teacher.

On the other hand, Ms. Wormwood was rapidly becoming my new least favorite teacher. I paused again, glaring at the stubborn pentagram as I caught my breath. "This isn't really coming off, miss."

Ms. Wormwood peered over my shoulder. "Oh, that's much better, pet," she said, though I'd only gotten rid of a few lines. Still, at least the weird swirling optical illusion had been broken. "We mustn't spend too long on a single bit of graffiti. We've got quite a list to get through." She checked an item off on her clipboard. "The Headmistress wants you to tackle the library tower next. Come along."

I gathered up the cleaning supplies, making sure to casually lift the heavy bucket one-handed, and was rewarded by an appreciative murmur from the open windows above. Clenching my jaw, I just about managed to last until we were out of sight. "Ms. Wormwood?" I said, panting. "I kind of need some help."

"Of course, Raffi pet." The teacher gave me a warm smile. "I thought something seemed to be on your mind. As your head of year, I'm here for you. You can ask me anything. Anything at all."

I'd actually meant that my arms were about to drop off, but now that she mentioned it . . . I paused to both readjust my load and try to figure out how to explain what was preoccupying me. *Well, you see, last night this weird goth girl told me I'm an angel, and this morning I woke up with a halo. . . .*

"Raffi?" Ms. Wormwood touched my arm. "Something's clearly bothering you."

No. Krystal *had* to be playing some sort of practical joke on me. "Not something," I said instead. "Someone." Krystal wasn't the only girl acting strangely. "Miss, what does it mean when a girl seems to hate you but sits next to you in every class anyway?"

Ms. Wormwood's eyebrows rose. "Generally, it means she secretly likes you." She started walking again. "But if we're talking about Michaela Dante, I'd say it's because she hates you."

"But I haven't done anything to her!" My pickup attempt hadn't been *that* bad. "I was only trying to be friendly."

"I know, pet." Ms. Wormwood led the way in silence for a moment, as if needing time to pick her words. "Raffi, although the Headmistress says we must make allowances for Michaela's . . . unfortunate history, the fact remains that she causes a great deal of trouble at this school. I know how attractive you find her, but she's a very disturbed individual. It would be better if you avoided her, pet."

"Believe me, I plan to." Having Michaela's black eyes fixed longingly on my jugular vein wasn't exactly helping me to concentrate in class. "I'm not really into the psychotic type."

"I'm glad to hear it, pet." We were coming up to the library tower, its modern structure wildly out of place amidst the older stone buildings. Reflected in the mirrored glass, Ms. Wormwood gave me a long, considering look as she unlocked the door. "You know, you really are a very mature young man."

"Uh . . . thanks?" Was she sidling closer to me, or was that my imagination? *Please let it be my imagination.*

Ms. Wormwood steered me through the door with an entirely unnecessary hand on my back. "I'm so glad we have this time to . . . get to know each other." Her hand drifted downward, and I practically teleported two feet forward. "Properly."

"Right! Absolutely!" I brandished my scrubbing brush at Ms. Wormwood, along with a slightly panicked grin. "So where are those pentagrams again?"

Ms. Wormwood waved dismissively at a spiraling staircase. "Oh, on the roof. But you don't want to tire yourself out going up all those steps, pet. Why don't we leave those silly things and find something more productive to do down here?" Her teeth gleamed. "I won't tell the Headmistress if you don't."

"No need!" I yelped, already halfway to the next level. I accelerated, taking the stairs three at a time. "I'm *really* keen to scrub some pentagrams!"

I reached the top of the staircase out of breath but unmolested. A door led out onto the flat roof and, miracle of miracles, there was a key in the lock. Not waiting to see how closely Ms. Wormwood was following, I snatched the key on my way through, slamming the door shut and locking it behind me as fast as I could.

With a gasp, someone leaped up from her kneeling position at the center of the tower top. Moonlight silvered her streaming hair as she whirled to face me.

"Faith?" I said, still panting.

"Raffi!" Faith clutched at her chest as if my abrupt arrival had given her heart failure. "What are you doing here?"

"At the moment, hiding to avoid a fate worse than death." I took a step toward her. "What are *you* doing up here?"

Then I noticed the chalk in her hand and the swooping lines that curled around her feet.

"It's you!" Faith cringed back from my pointing finger. "You're the one drawing those pentagrams everywhere!"

"That's not me!" Faith looked as if I'd accused her of sacrificing first-years under the full moon. "My holy circles are nothing like those evil things!"

I stared at her half-finished pentagram. I had to admit, it didn't look like the others. For a start, it looked like it had been drawn left-handed by a five-year-old on a sugar high. But even leaving the wobbly lines aside, this was a different design from the ones I'd been scrubbing off walls all evening. Sure, it was basically a pentagram, but this had flowing symbols written all around the edge of the circle instead of angular glyphs in the middle of the five-pointed star.

But it still seemed familiar. I'd seen it before. Not as chalked lines, but engraved on metal . . . I groaned as it hit me. "Faith, please tell me that's not one of Krystal's idiotic angel-summoning things."

"No." Faith hung her head, her voice dropping to a bare whisper. "It's one of mine."

I remembered the jeers about being crazy that Suzanne had thrown at Faith in History of Art class, and I silently cursed Krystal. It was one thing to try her special-effects scam on me, but pulling it on Faith—sweet, gentle, possibly brain-damaged Faith—just in order to get *one* friend was reaching new lows of desperation. "You seriously believe Krystal's crap? Whatever she's shown you to convince you her angel-summoning stuff works, it isn't real. If you think some guy with wings is magically going to appear to sort out all your problems, you really are nuts."

Faith turned away, leaning her elbows on the low iron railing running around the edge of the tower. She rested her forehead on her folded hands as if praying for strength. "I know."

I wasn't sure if it was the soft, hopeless misery in Faith's voice, or the way her pose inadvertently showed off the riveting curve of her backside, but I couldn't help myself. "Look," I said, coming forward to lean on the railing next to her. "I've seen how bad things are for you here." Oh, I should so not be getting involved with this walking social disaster, no matter how pretty she was. What was *wrong* with me when it came to this girl? "But this isn't going to help. You're making yourself a target, being friends with a weirdo like Krystal and letting the other girls walk all over you. Ditch this bullshit. Just try acting normal."

Faith turned her head to look directly at me. "But I can't, Raffi," she said with an odd gentleness. "Because I'm not normal. There's a great evil under this school, and I'm the only one who can stop it. I have to keep trying. I have to keep fighting the darkness, no matter how strange it makes me seem. For the sake of my mother. For the sake of everyone." She looked down at our hands, side by side on the guardrail, and drew hers back from mine slightly. "But I don't expect you to believe me."

Well . . . if she *was* crazy, it looked a hell of a lot better on her than it did on Krystal.

On impulse, I laid my hand over hers—and caught my breath, everything I'd been intending to say knocked out of my head by the heat of her skin. Faith's head snapped up, her startled eyes fixing on mine. For an instant that stretched like an eternity, we just stared speechless at each other.

Then a thick, black tentacle burst out of thin air between us, and hurled Faith over the edge of the roof.

Adrenaline turned everything as sharp and clear as glass. On pure instinct, I flung myself after Faith. My entire world shrunk to her terrified face, her golden hair streaming behind her like the tail of a falling star.

I caught her. The impact knocked all the breath out of me, but I gripped her tight to my chest even as I wheezed. Her arms locked around my neck.

For a moment, Faith clung to me, her breath coming in hitched gasps. I could feel her shaking as if plugged into an electric current. She lifted her head to look into my face, her own barely a handsbreadth away. "Rafael," she whispered. Golden stars shone in the depths of her wondering blue eyes.

"Gck," I said. Black spots danced in my vision.

Faith blinked, then appeared to notice that she was throttling me. "Oh!" She unwound her arms from around my neck. "I'm sorrAAAIIEEE!"

The word turned into a scream as Faith plummeted yet again. In blind panic, I dove, flipping completely upside down and just managing to grab her flailing hand. My shoulder screamed in protest as Faith seized my wrist with her other hand, dangling from my arm.

Hang on.

What was *I* dangling from?

I stared past Faith's feet to the distant ground. It was definitely the ground. It was also definitely distant. The tower rose at our side, so close I could have reached past Faith and put my hand flat on the glass. Heart pounding, I looked at my reflection.

A blaze of white fire reflected in the black glass. My halo was back, shining as brilliantly as the midday sun.

And behind it, springing from my shoulders, were the wings.

Chapter 8

I am not an angel!" Krystal and Faith both ducked as my wings swept over their heads. We were hiding out in the old shrine Krystal had shown me yesterday—Faith had gabbled something about the "sanctified ground protecting us" before running to fetch Krystal. I didn't know what she'd meant, but at least the half-ruined building was deep in the woods and still had most of its walls and roof. The last thing I needed was for anyone else to witness my psychotic breakdown. "There's—there's a perfectly rational explanation."

"For crying out loud, Raf, you have wings and a halo!" Krystal grabbed hold of my jacket, forcing me to stop my frantic pacing. "What more do you want, to be handed a harp by God Himself?"

"I don't believe in God! I'm an atheist!" I checked over

my shoulder to see if my wings had disappeared in a puff of logic. They hadn't. I groaned, clenching my fists in my radiant hair. "I can't be an atheist angel!"

Krystal shrugged. "And I'm agnostic. So? I still managed to get you here."

"I can't believe he's really an angel," Faith said, sounding as shocked as I felt. "I wasn't expecting one to be so . . . physical."

Krystal smirked, flashing her pentagram pendant. "Computer-guided laser-etching machine in the workshop. Accurate to a hundredth of a millimeter. I told you it was better than messing around with chalk on a freezing rooftop."

"Angel-summoning is supposed to be done with holy reverence," Faith protested. From the way Krystal rolled her eyes, this was not the first time they'd had this argument. "Not in between cutting out gears for your mechanical engineering course work!"

"Excuse me, could we get back to the topic of my *giant, glowing wings*?" I snapped, waving them for emphasis. "I don't care how hard you wished. People make dumb wishes all the time. They don't cause innocent bystanders to suddenly sprout extra limbs!"

"I didn't wish," Krystal said, maddeningly calm. "I made a summoning charm." She shrugged. "Even if you know the right symbols to call the angel you want, it's not easy. As Faith found out, if you don't get every line spot-on, nothing happens."

"I'm not good at geometry, okay?" Faith said defensively. She turned back to me, her voice softening again. "But the important thing is that you're here. You're my angel, and you're finally here." She smiled suddenly, as brilliant as the rising sun. "And now everything is going to be fine."

"Everything is not fine! *Giant freaking wings!*" I took a deep breath, forcing myself to stop hyperventilating. "Look, I don't know what you're playing at here, but I am *not* an angel. I'm a normal guy! I mean, I have parents and everything. What do you want me to do, show you baby photos? Call up my dad as a character reference? Trust me, I'm human!"

"I've met your dad." Faith chewed on her lip for a second, looking pensive. "Raffi, what's your mother like?"

"Dead, thanks so much for asking," I snapped. Faith flinched, looking stricken, and I felt a stab of guilt. "Sorry," I muttered. "It's okay, it was ages ago. What do you mean, what was she like? She was my mum."

"Yes, but how would you describe her?"

I hesitated for a second, trying out and discarding a dozen adjectives in my head. In the end, there was only one that did her justice. "Perfect," I said, my voice going low. "She was perfect." Then my head snapped up. "Wait, what are you suggesting?"

"I think you're right, you aren't an angel . . . not entirely, at least." Faith pointed up at the star-filled sky. "I've read about nephilim. The children of earthbound angels, half mortal and half divine. Maybe your mother didn't die. Maybe she just went home."

"Now you think my *mum* was an angel? That's the stupidest—" The words died, half formed in my mouth.

My dad had always loved to tease my mum about their first meeting, at some bigwig general's party. My mum had been a guest while my dad had been working security. "I fell in love with you at first sight," he'd always said to her, "but with all the gold braid in the room, I thought I didn't stand a chance. Then you saw my tag, and did that double take, and started laughing your head off." My dad would poke her, grinning. "I think you fancied my name more than you did me!"

My mum had always just shaken her head with a small,

private smile. And she never would explain what had been so funny about my dad's last name.

Angelos.

I sank down to the leaf-covered floor, my wings obligingly refolding themselves behind me, and put my head in my hands. "Okay," I said after a moment. "So let's say I'm, I'm what you say I am. Why?"

"You mean, why did we want an angel?" Krystal asked. She jerked her thumb at Faith. "Your turn, Faith. This is your show, after all."

Faith knelt opposite me, her expression grave. "Raffi, how much school gossip have you heard about my father?"

"Huh? What's that got to do with anything?" I vaguely remembered Suzanne sneering something about Faith's "crazy, dead dad."

"Everything. He was trying to summon an angel too, before he died. My father was a member of a secret organization sworn to protect the world against the forces of darkness." She took a deep breath. "You see, Saint Mary's is built on a Hellgate."

It took me two attempts to find words. "This school is built on a *what?*"

"A Hellgate," Faith repeated, apparently completely

85

serious. "A place where demons can manifest in the mortal world."

"You have to admit, it explains a lot about this place," Krystal interjected.

She kind of had a point, considering the rampant bullying, but I shook my head. "There's no such thing as demons."

Krystal snorted. "Says the guy with the wings and halo?"

"Raffi, you saw that tentacle yourself," Faith said earnestly. "That was a demon. It must have been trying to stop me from awakening your angelic powers." She frowned, looking worried. "I've never seen one physically manifest like that before. It shows that the Hellgate is starting to open without my father here to hold it shut. Soon the demons will be able to break through fully. They'll be free to roam the world, spreading evil through people's hearts, unseen and unsuspected."

"Unseen? I should think people would notice giant, alien squid-monsters crawling around the place." My wings shuddered as I thought of that icy-cold tentacle curling out of nowhere.

"If only demons were that obvious," Faith said, the corner of her mouth twisting. "Raffi, Hellgates let demons approach our world, but in order to be able to stay permanently they have to find a human host. A demon will seek out a weak, foolish person inside the Hellgate's area, and infiltrate their dreams with visions of a pentagram containing the mystic symbols that spell out the demon's true name. When the person draws the pentagram, the demon manifests inside it, taking on a seductive appearance to better tempt its target. It will promise power, money . . . whatever it takes to make its target agree to the binding." She shook her head. "Demons don't lie. The host *will* get the promised rewards . . . while the demon slowly corrupts them with its evil. In the end, the host becomes as cold and heartless as the demon itself. And that's not the worst of it."

"It gets *worse* than demons turning people into monsters?" I said.

"Yes." Faith's face was set and pale. "Because once the host dies, and the blackened soul finally leaves the body . . . the demon moves into the abandoned flesh. And then it can act in the world directly."

I thought of all the things an evil alien entity wearing a human skin could do, and shivered. "So close the Hellgate already! You said your father kept it shut, why can't you?"

"Because I don't know how he did it! He only talked to

me about all this once." Faith's head drooped. "Just before he died, a year ago. He said that I finally had to learn the truth, because time was running out before my final year here, when I'd be able to attend the Masked Ball. He told me that there was something I had to do, and that he'd summoned help to make sure I'd be able to do it . . . but he didn't get a chance to tell me more. My mother overheard and interrupted us. She thought he was delusional. They had the biggest fight. . . ." Faith trailed off for a moment. Her hair hid her face. "She made him leave. I never saw him again. My mother said his sickness drove him to suicide, but I know what really happened. Away from his home, without his holy sword, the forces of evil caught up with him." She took a deep breath, squaring her shoulders. "But I rescued his notebooks before my mother could burn them, and I've been studying them ever since. I've sworn to finish his life's work. My father kept the Hellgate from opening. *I* am going to destroy it for good."

"Great," I said. "Super. How?"

Faith drew herself up to her full height. She practically glowed with holy righteousness. "At midnight at the Masked Ball, I will kiss my one true soul mate, and the power of our love will banish the demons forever."

The wind rustled the leaves across the stone floor.

At last, I spoke. "That is—and I am speaking here as the guy who just found out he's a winged, glowing mutant, mind you—the most insane thing I have ever heard."

"I'm glad I'm not the only one who thinks it's unlikely," Krystal muttered. She held up a hand to forestall Faith as the other girl opened her mouth. "Let me handle this one, okay? I at least get where Raf's coming from." She folded her arms across her chest, facing me square on. "Look, up until now, I wasn't convinced myself that Faith could be telling the truth." Krystal threw Faith an apologetic glance as she spoke. "I was just willing to give her the benefit of the doubt. After all, it wasn't like I had any popularity to lose by hearing her out." Krystal gestured at me. "And now here you are. Pretty conclusive evidence that the mystic stuff Faith's learned from her dad's notebooks does work, no matter how nuts it seems. Isn't it at least worth testing her theory about closing the Hellgate? All you have to do is make sure she has a date for the Ball. What have you got to lose?"

"Apparently, my mind," I retorted. I buried my head in my hands again. "Demons and angels and now magic kisses . . . I didn't ask for any of this."

"I know you didn't." I felt rather than saw Faith lean forward. Her fingers hovered hesitantly over my shoulder, as if she was afraid to actually touch me again. "I'm sorry, Raffi. But please. I really need your help. Please help me. Please be my guardian angel."

I looked into her face and knew that even if I had no idea what I was meant to do, I didn't have a choice about doing it. "All right. I will."

Faith's blue eyes met mine, shining with more than just the reflected light from my halo. She was so close. "Thank you," she whispered, her breath soft on my lips.

Krystal cleared her throat. "I hate to interrupt the moment, but Raf is setting the place on fire."

Wisps of smoke were rising from the dry leaves drifting around my shining feathers. I sprang to my feet, wings jerking straight upward. Faith scooted back out of my way as I stamped out the smoldering embers. "That's strange," she said, touching one of the scorched leaves. "You weren't hot before." She blushed. "I mean, your wings were touching things without them bursting into flame."

"Uh, yeah, well," I said, surreptitiously tugging my jacket down. "Very weird. No idea what happened there." I cleared my throat. "All right. So I'll help you. What the hell am I supposed to do?"

"Stop the sixth-year girls from being utter bitches," Krystal said.

I stared at her. "Are you sure you wouldn't like me to fight some demons instead?"

"You can't fight demons," Faith said, getting to her own feet. She was still faintly pink and avoided making eye contact. "In their natural state, they exist on a different plane than us. Even when they're possessing a human body, they're practically invulnerable to normal weapons. Anyway, I'm not trying to just drive them off temporarily, but to seal the Hellgate for all time. That can only be done with the power of true love. But I can't *get* my true love here unless I have a date for the Ball. It's the only time boys are allowed in the school. Were allowed," she corrected herself. "Anyway, only girls with the highest Peer Assessment results are allowed to take a boy to the dance." Her face was the very picture of woe. "And I'm the least popular girl in the year, thanks to the demons. They know full well what I'm trying to do. They're influencing the girls here, making them hate me."

Krystal must have read the skepticism on my face, because she aimed a kick at me. "She's actually got solid evidence on this one. Up until last year—before Faith's dad died—Faith was the *most* popular girl. She always has been. It was freaky how fast it all went bad. One minute everyone was tiptoeing around, feeling sorry for her because of her dad, and the next there were all these rumors flying around about him actually having gone insane and that Faith was just as crazy. Then someone drew one of those pentagrams—maybe under demonic influence, maybe just as a joke—and Faith completely flipped in front of the whole year group. That confirmed the rumors. Fast train to outcast town."

"I couldn't help it," Faith said in a low voice. "Those things . . . they're wrong and evil. I still can't believe you don't feel it yourself."

Krystal wrinkled her nose. "They're just lines, Faith. No one else finds them upsetting."

"I do," I said. "A few of them anyway." I still hadn't worked out why some of the pentagram graffiti I'd cleaned today had inexplicably made my stomach churn, when others didn't affect me at all.

Krystal's eyebrows rose. "Really? Well, you're the angel." She shrugged. "Anyway, Faith's spectacular fall from grace was another of the things that made me think she might be onto something with her Ball plan. Why else would demons want to destroy her popularity? That's why we decided to try to summon an angel, using the instructions in Faith's dad's notebooks. If demons *are* influencing the girls subconsciously, it makes sense that it could be counteracted by angelic influence."

"You have to spread your holy love over everyone," Faith said, nodding.

I was pretty sure a real angel wouldn't find that quite so dirty. "You want me to send soothing vibes at people? Looking like this?"

We all paused for a moment, considering my wingspan and incandescent glow.

"Good point," Krystal conceded. "You'd better go back to normal, Raf."

"If I knew how, don't you think I'd have done it already?" I waved my arms, sending up a draft as my wings echoed the movement. I still wasn't used to the bizarre sensation of the air pushing against them. I groaned as a thought struck me. "Oh, man, and this suit was custom tailored. My dad is going to *kill* me."

Krystal circled me, ducking under my outstretched wings. "Actually, your jacket isn't torn," she said, startled. "They're just hovering behind you. Not really attached."

"But I can feel them in my shoulders." I squawked as she tugged experimentally on my feathers. "Believe me, they don't come off! Quit it, Krystal!"

"Sorry." Krystal reappeared, frowning. "How small do they fold up? Maybe we can hide them."

"Under what, a tent?" Nevertheless, I tentatively flexed . . . something. The wings stirred. Trying to control them consciously was like wrestling with a couple of enormous and recalcitrant umbrellas. In a closet. In the dark. It was ridiculous, considering that I'd managed to fly with the things. I closed my eyes, letting instinct take over. My wings settled themselves on my back with a strange little *twist*.

Faith's gasp made me open my eyes again. "They vanished!" she exclaimed. "Into thin air!"

"Huh?" I waved my arm behind myself, encountering nothing. But I could still feel them, tucked up behind my shoulders, feathers ruffling in a warm wind. I opened them experimentally, and they popped into visibility again. "They're still here. Just . . . somewhere else."

"Well, that's one problem solved," Krystal said as I folded them up again. "At least we won't have to try to explain to the teachers why you're wearing a cloak."

"Just a hat," said Faith. "The halo's still there."

I swore. "And the teachers won't let me get away with that. I tried."

Krystal tapped her finger against her lips. "You started glowing last night, but you weren't today. I saw you during your detention. How did you turn it off?"

"I didn't do it deliberately. It just went away on its own when I—uh."

"After you what?" Krystal demanded when I didn't continue. "This is important, Raf!"

"After I, uh . . ." I glanced at Faith. "After I kind of . . . looked up Michaela's skirt."

There was a horrible silence.

"That makes sense," Faith said thoughtfully. "You can't have a halo if you're acting like a demon."

"Hey!" I protested. "I only looked!"

"Yes, but you were still, um, filled with lust, right?" Faith was going pink again. She cleared her throat. "That's one of the Seven Deadly Sins. It's not very angelic."

"But just now I was—uh, that is, you were kind of close to me, and you're very, um, pretty." I was certain that my blush had to be as visible as my halo. Clearly, Embarrassment wasn't a Deadly Sin. "And I'm still glowing."

Krystal frowned. "Lust is meant to be sinful. I don't think simply being attracted to someone is necessarily, you know, a bad thing. Maybe you have to actively be trying to take advantage for it to count, as it were."

There was another, longer silence.

Faith swallowed hard, the sound carrying clearly. "W-well, you're doing a lot for me," she said. Her hands went to the top button of her shirt. "S-so I suppose . . ." The shirt slipped, flashing a glimpse of bra strap. "I mean, I do owe you my life."

"You don't have to do anything you don't want to!" I spun around to face the wall, my wings briefly flaring out again before I got them under control. "And I can't just ogle you in front of an audience!"

"B-but if it's the only way . . . Krystal, can you, um, step outside?"

"Oh, bollocks. This is such a bad idea—"

A hand closed over my arm, yanking me around. Before I could object, I found myself pushed flat against the wall, head jerked down by my tie, being kissed.

Very . . . *thoroughly* kissed.

Not that I had a lot to compare it to, but I was pretty sure your standard kiss wasn't this intense. Tongue seemed to be getting involved. My hands slid down over warm, curved hips, her body melting against mine—

"Um," I heard Faith say, remarkably clearly. "I don't think it's working?"

I drew back—and found myself looking down at annoyed brown eyes. *"Krystal?"* I yelped, shoving her away.

"Crap," Krystal said, a little out of breath. She pushed her hair back. "Maybe we did that wrong."

"We?" I scrubbed my hand across my mouth, horrified. "I'll tell you what was wrong! You sexually assaulted me, that's what's wrong! When I don't even fancy you!"

Krystal flushed, and not in Faith's delicate roselike way. She looked more like an angry tomato. "Believe me, I'm fully aware of that," she spat. "But Faith didn't want to, and I thought that if I took you by surprise, I might be able to substitute!"

"Um, guys?" Faith ventured tentatively.

"Keep your bright ideas to yourself in the future," I snarled. "And your tongue!"

Faith bobbed at Krystal's elbow, hands fluttering. "Really, guys!"

"My tongue!" Krystal said, practically incandescent with rage herself. "I wasn't the one with the wandering tongue! Or hands!"

"Guys!" Faith shouted, the loudest I'd ever heard her soft voice. "Raffi isn't glowing anymore."

"I'm not?" I paused, caught somewhere between relief and indignation. "But I really, really, *really* am not into Krystal. Not even subconsciously. Trust me on that one."

"Thanks for that clarification," Krystal said sourly. "I was worried that a tiny bit of my self-esteem might survive the night uncrushed."

"Wrath," Faith said. "It's another Deadly Sin. And Raffi got angry. So that's another way to turn him off again."

"Yeah, well," I muttered, shooting Krystal a dark glare. "Won't be a problem getting rid of the halo in the future then, if it comes back." Krystal made a rude gesture at me, which I was pretty sure had to be sacrilegious under the circumstances.

"At least you can turn up to class now without founding a new cult," Faith said with forced brightness. "I'm sure your heavenly presence will free the other girls from demonic influence."

"Actually, I'm pretty sure it won't." Faith and Krystal both looked at me—one with perfect trust, the other with perfect irritation, both expectant. I set my shoulders. "But I know what will."

Chapter 9

So I was, for want of a better word, an angel, possibly with a holy mission to protect the world from the forces of evil. Obviously, there was one thing I had to do as soon as possible.

The next morning, I got up at the crack of dawn, liberated a helmet from the communal bike shed, and set off to learn how to fly.

A half-hour hike found me a nice wide clearing in the woods, well away from the school buildings. With a last glance around to check for onlookers, I shrugged my wings out. Early morning mist scurried along the ground as I lofted them to full vertical extension, the glowing pinions reaching for the sky like outstretched hands. I crouched, looked up, and took a deep breath.

"Okay," I said softly, and swept my wings down.

It was a good thing I'd worn a helmet.

"Right," I muttered to myself, spitting out dirt. "Less sideways, more up."

After another ten minutes of running, leaping, and rather unangelic swearing, I was still resolutely earthbound. I brushed the mud off my knees, scowling. Maybe what I needed was motivation. I'd certainly had plenty last night. Unfortunately, I didn't think Faith would appreciate her own guardian angel pushing her out a window, not even in the interest of science. And I wasn't quite confident enough in my wings to want to throw *myself* out of a window either.

I crouched down in a sprinter's stance and squeezed my eyes shut. Just think of all the things I'd be able to do once I mastered flight. I'd be able to save Faith if she fell again. I'd be able to sneak out in the evening and find the nearest pub—

"Oh my *God*," said a voice behind me.

I leaped into the air in alarm—literally. A short midteens girl in a baggy cardigan and unflattering glasses stood frozen in the bracken, staring up at me with her mouth hanging open. "You're . . . you're an angel," she said.

As I was hovering six feet above her on glowing, slowly

beating wings, this did not seem like something I could deny. The rising sun highlighted the girl's tear-tracked face and red eyes. She took a hesitant step forward, holding up a hand to shield herself from my light. "Who are you?" she breathed.

With my head backlit by my incandescent feathers, she must not have been able to make out my features. If only I could get away quickly, she need never know my identity. "Yes, I am an angel," I said in the deepest voice I could manage while frantically trying to work out how to go *up*. I wobbled dangerously in the air. "Sent from Heaven to, uh . . ."

"Smite the wicked?" the girl suggested hopefully. She sniffed, swiping her sleeve across her nose. "Because I can totally give you a list. Starting with that bitch Joanne."

"Er, no." What the hell did angels talk about? Half-remembered bits of the few Christmas services my dad had forced me to attend drifted up out of my memory. "I come bearing Good News! For unto you a child shall be born!"

The girl stared at me. She did not look like she considered this to be glad tidings.

"Hey, I just deliver the news, I don't write it," I snapped, most of my attention still occupied with wing-wrestling.

So this joint moved like *this* and then rotated like *that* . . . and to my unending and eternal relief, the ground fell away from beneath my feet. "Bye!"

"But I'm *fourteen!*" I heard her wail as I soared straight upward. I kept going until I was certain I must be no more than a distant dot in the sky.

"Phew," I muttered, hovering once more. That had been a close one. I glanced down to see if the girl had gone away yet—and wished I hadn't, as my stomach pitched at the sight of nothing but thin air between me and the inch-high trees below. I swallowed hard, focusing on the horizon instead. "Okay, Raf. You got up here, so you can get down again. Nice and slow."

I tentatively tried to bank, tilting my wings like I'd seen seagulls do—and nearly fell to my death. Heart hammering, I managed to hover again. My wings obviously didn't work like a bird's. I concentrated for a moment on them, trying to visualize their motion. It seemed to involve twisting in more directions than I had names for. I risked a glance over my shoulder and saw that feathers flickered in and out of view as they beat, as if they kept briefly flashing into wherever they went when I folded them up all the way.

"Huh." At least they seemed to function well enough,

if I didn't think about it. I fixed my eyes on the distant roof of the sixth-year girls' dormitory, as tiny as a dollhouse below my dangling feet. "Okay, wings, let's go *there*."

Without any effort, my body still upright as my wings churned gently away behind my shoulders, I slid down out of the sky as if on an invisible escalator. I parked myself directly above the dormitory, taking care to stay too high to be seen from the ground, and pulled out the pair of binoculars I'd borrowed from Faith. I had a hunch about who was behind all this. And I was going to find out exactly why she was always so late to class.

Five minutes later, my patience was rewarded. A dark figure emerged from the building, her head swiveling as she checked she wasn't being followed.

Michaela.

I kept pace with her, tracking her progress through Faith's binoculars. She was heading straight for the old shrine where I'd talked with Faith and Krystal last night. With one last cautious glance behind her, she disappeared into the ruined building.

I dropped silently next to the shrine, folding my wings the instant my feet hit the ground. With a quick check that my feathers were hidden and I wasn't glowing, I circled the old building, searching for a window. Finding one, I stretched on tiptoe to peer inside.

Lit by the flickering light of a dozen candles, Michaela was chalking an enormous pentagram on the stone floor, whispering under her breath in some arcane tongue.

It was so nice being proven right.

The death threats, the stalking, her complete lack of attraction to me . . . it all made sense now. She was being influenced by demons.

Faith had been dubious when I'd advanced my theory last night. "I don't think the demons would target Michaela, Raffi," she'd said, shaking her head. "They go after weak-willed people, who they can tempt into evil. Michaela's already beautiful and smart and popular. Why would she *need* to sell her soul?"

Even when Krystal had added her voice to mine, pointing out that it was suspicious that Michaela had arrived at the school mere weeks after Faith's father had died, Faith had remained stubborn. "It's a coincidence," she'd said finally. "She's never been caught drawing any pentagrams, even though I know for a fact my mother told all the teachers to keep a close eye on her."

Well, I'd been able to keep an even closer eye on her, and now it was obvious who the demon planned to have as its host. The question was, should I go tell Faith and

Krystal what I'd discovered or just confront Michaela here and now? I had heavenly glory on my side, after all, while she had some chalk. This whole thing could be over before breakfast.

While I was hesitating, Michaela drew a few final lines. Still chanting, she stepped into the pentagram . . . and her head snapped around. Her black eyes locked straight on mine. Reaching under her skirt, she pulled out two long, wicked daggers.

Warmth licked my hidden wings, as if something with burning-hot breath had exhaled down the back of my neck. Stifling a yell, I spun—but there was nothing behind me. Even though my spine was now pressed against the wall, I felt tentacles trail over my feathers, the touch light and curious.

There was something else in that mysterious space where my wings went. Something *alive*.

I ran for the school as if all the forces of Hell were after me. Which, just possibly, they were.

Chapter 10

Michaela can't be possessed." Faith tossed a basket-ball halfheartedly at me, her face whiter than her gym outfit. I was grateful that we had P.E. first thing today. Under the cover of warming up, I'd been able to drag Faith and Krystal off to one side of the playing court to fill them in on what I'd discovered that morning. "It can't be true."

"I'm telling you, she is," I said, bouncing the basket-ball back. I kept glancing around nervously, but Michaela hadn't appeared yet. Guess it took a while to commune with demons. "The Hellgate must already be open."

"No, I'm sure I'd know if it was." Faith twisted her hands together, the ball flying past her to smack straight into one of our classmates. "But my father told me there were more Hellgates in the world besides this one. The demon must have come through one of those, possessed her before she ever arrived here. She must have been tricked into it, maybe she agreed to the binding so the demon would get her out of that horrible orphanage. . . . Oh, poor Michaela!"

"I always knew she was pure evil." Krystal looked as if it was Christmas Day and she'd just unwrapped a pony. "Can I watch when you smite her, Raf?"

"When I *what*?"

"Smite her," Krystal repeated, a distinctly bloodthirsty gleam in her eye. She took aim at Suzanne, across on the other side of the court, and let fly. The blonde girl yelped as the basketball bounced off her back. Luckily for Krystal, our gym teacher, an enormous woman named Ms. Hellebore, hadn't noticed the deliberate foul. "Burn her up with your holy fire. Like you smote the Headmistress, only more so."

"You smote my mother?" Faith exclaimed.

"It was an accident," I said to her, then rounded on Krystal. "And I'm not going to murder her! What do you think I am?"

Krystal shrugged. "I think you're a guardian angel. Check out the Bible sometime. The angels in there aren't exactly nice." She paused to deflect an incoming basketball and flip off the girl who'd sent it at her. "And we have to do whatever it takes to stop the demon. Don't you see, Faith, this is why we could never find any hint as to how your dad was keeping the Hellgate closed! He *wasn't* doing anything—at least, nothing mystic. He was just stopping demons like Michaela from sneaking in and trying to open it up to summon more of her kind through. We've got to stop her."

I hadn't thought Faith could go any paler, but she did. "But my father said . . . once a demon is bound to a mortal, that's it. There's no way to exorcise it without, without—" She stopped, swallowing hard. "Without killing the host."

"We're talking about demons being set free to rampage all over the world, Faith!" Krystal retorted. "We can't get squeamish."

That was easy for her to say. *I* was the one who'd find himself trying to explain to the jury that the angels had made him do it. "Forget it. I'm not smiting anyone."

"Then you'd better think of another way to get rid of her," Krystal said, staring over my shoulder. "Fast."

The next thing I knew, I was sprawled on the ground, feeling as though my brain had been knocked out my ears. "Now that's just pathetic," I heard Michaela say, through the ringing pain. She strolled over to us, her brief gym shorts showing off her endless legs. "I thought it would be easy to defeat you, but I didn't think it would be *this* easy."

I scrambled to my feet, getting between her and Faith. "You just took me by surprise." Our classmates were too busy chasing balls to notice the confrontation, but I lowered my voice anyway. "I'll give you one chance. Leave this school, or I'll make you leave."

"I know what you are now, Michaela," Faith said. Her voice trembled, but she came to stand at my side. Krystal, I noticed with irritation, had buggered off at the first sign of trouble. "And Raffi's going to stop you."

"I'm terrified," Michaela said. "See me quake. Oh, no, wait." She folded her arms, her black eyes mocking. "See *Raffi* quake."

Hellfire breath licked my hidden feathers. I couldn't help cowering, my invisible wings clamping tight to my back as I was driven to my knees.

"Stop it!" Faith was cringing too as if she also felt the demon's hidden presence. "Leave us alone!"

"Never." Michaela leaned in close, staring directly into Faith's terrified eyes. "Now that you know about me, I'll give *you* one last chance, Faith. No matter what your little pet here says, you won't close the Hellgate. One way or another, I'll stop you from getting to that

Ball. Run away while you still can."

"Get away from her!" The demon was still breathing down the back of my neck, but the sight of Faith in danger was enough to get me back on my feet. I lunged for Michaela, but she swayed on the balls of her feet, effortlessly turning my momentum against me. I slammed against the wall of the court, Michaela holding my arm painfully twisted behind my back.

"You want to do this here and now?" Michaela snarled into my ear. She was inhumanly strong. She only needed one hand to pin me in place, her other tracing a pentagram on my back as she spoke. "Happy to oblige." She whispered something in a foreign language and I cringed . . . but nothing happened. Burning heat still washed over my wings, but I felt Michaela's grip slacken fractionally, as if she was surprised by something.

"Is there a problem here?" boomed Ms. Hellebore, looming over us. Michaela released me in a hurry. Evidently, not even a demon wanted to tangle with someone who looked like she swigged steroids for breakfast.

"Like I said, Michaela attacked Raf! Totally unprovoked!" Krystal bobbed at the teacher's side like a tugboat next to a battle cruiser.

"I know how hot teenage tempers can run, Michaela, but you must learn to channel your aggression productively," Ms. Hellebore said severely. A circle of girls was forming around us as the class sensed imminent drama. "We are not brutes, settling differences with mere fists." She pointed back into the gym. "Go to my office and fetch the disciplinary equipment. I think you need to spend this lesson on your own, practicing your self-control."

"Yes, Ms. Hellebore," Michaela replied dutifully, though her black eyes flashed with leashed rage. "This isn't over, Rafael," she breathed. She stalked back into the gym, the crowd drawing back hastily to let her through.

"Let's hear some balls bouncing!" Ms. Hellebore roared, nearly scaring my own off me. Our audience scattered. Under the sudden din of rubber hitting asphalt, she said to me, "I could give you some tips on combat techniques, if you wanted. Looks like you could use them."

"Thanks, miss." I got to my feet, brushing dirt off my grazed knees. "But actually, my dad's already taught me a load of self-defense stuff." Unfortunately, how to defend yourself from invisible demons hadn't been on the curriculum.

"Self-defense only?" Ms. Hellebore sniffed in disdain.

"Useless. The best defense is a good offense. I can show you how to take down your enemy before they even know you're there."

"Uh, thanks, but really I'm—SHE'S GOT A GUN!"

Faith squawked as I knocked her off her feet. I spun, intending to tackle Krystal as well—and discovered that she, along with everyone else, was staring at me as if I'd gone insane.

"Yes, of course she does," Ms. Hellebore said, glancing from me to Michaela. "What's the problem?"

"The problem?" I yelped. Behind Ms. Hellebore's back, Michaela was checking over the monstrous weapon with rapid, practiced movements. "No one else sees a problem with the fact that the school psychopath just wandered out with a damn AK-47?"

"Don't be ridiculous," Ms. Hellebore said. "That's not an AK-47. It's a Saiga-04 M3 7.62mm assault rifle."

Somehow, I failed to find this reassuring.

"It really is all right, Raffi," Faith said, getting to her feet as Michaela headed off without a backward glance. "She's taking it to the range. If you get a time-out from gym, you have to practice rifle-shooting instead."

"An excellent discipline for unsettled minds," Ms. Hellebore said happily. "It teaches control and focus." The fact that it also taught how to head-shoot a man at two hundred paces evidently had not occurred to her. The gym teacher blew her whistle. "All right, excitement over! Back to work, girls!"

Faith stared after Michaela's retreating form as the class drifted back to basketball practice. "Well, we've learned something important."

"Yeah, Michaela's not only a demon, she's a demon with a gun." My heart was still pounding from the adrenaline surge. "And she knows how to use it. Wonderful."

Faith shook her head. "Not that." Despite everything, she started to smile. "She's afraid of me getting to the Ball. She knows I *can* close the Hellgate with my true love. My father was right!"

"And so's Raf," Krystal said sharply. "Faith, this is not a good time to look on the bright side. Michaela knows we're onto her, and she's obviously *not* afraid of Raf. We're in deep trouble." She looked at me. "Reconsidered that smiting thing yet?"

"No," I said firmly. "I'm not a murderer." My gaze went to Ms. Hellebore, who was now exhorting girls to hurl their balls harder. "I think it's time to invoke the aid of a higher power."

Chapter 11

"ongratulations, Mr. Angelos," the Headmistress said without looking up as I entered her office. She turned another page in my school file. It already seemed to be quite thick. "Three detentions in your first forty-eight hours. You have set a new school record. We may have to commission a plaque."

"Um." I sat gingerly on the chair opposite her desk, trying to ignore the really disturbing scuff marks on the arms that suggested at least one previous occupant had been handcuffed to the thing. "I'm sorry. Things kind of haven't been working out as I expected."

"Yes, I am aware of that. Obviously." The Headmistress cast me a level look over the top of her reading glasses. "Is that a nervous tic, Mr. Angelos?"

"No, Headmistress!" I yelped, straightening up from

my surreptitious attempt to check that my wings hadn't slipped out. "Er, when you say that you're aware of my, um, issues . . . ?"

The Headmistress sighed. "Mr. Angelos, there is nothing that goes on in this school without my knowledge. Much as I would prefer to remain blissfully oblivious to the mind-bogglingly mundane dramas that so traumatize your teenage lives, it is my job to observe, guide, and—alas, all too occasionally—punish. So yes, I am fully aware of your problems."

"Actually, I don't think you are." I was pretty sure that not even the Headmistress would describe unexpected angelhood as "mundane."

"If I am not already aware, then I have no desire to know," the Headmistress said crisply. She flipped my file shut. "Now, while Ms. Wormwood has already complained to me about you absconding from your detention last night, I am not thinking of expelling you. Yet. So, Mr. Angelos, it is quite unnecessary for you to grovel before me. You may leave now."

I nearly launched myself out of the chair in sheer relieved reflex at being dismissed, before remembering that I was here about something else. I sank back down again, miserably. "Um, that's not what I wanted to talk to you about. It's Michaela Dante. I think she's dangerous."

"You have a remarkable talent for discovering the obvious, Mr. Angelos." The Headmistress steepled her fingers. "If only your grasp on the English language was so masterful. Let me repeat myself, in words of one syllable: I know all at this school. What exactly do you think *you* know about Miss Dante that I do not?"

"She's a demon!" I blurted out.

The Headmistress looked at me.

"Uh, that is, I found her doing black magic out in the woods. With pentagrams and candles and stuff."

The Headmistress looked at me some more. One hand reached out to pick up what on initial glance appeared to be the hollowed-out shrunken head of one of her past pupils, but on closer inspection was just a lumpy pottery mug. It had a blobby heart and *World's Best Mum* painted on it. Poor, poor Faith. The Headmistress took a long, slow sip, still regarding me unblinkingly over the rim. Then, "Come with me, Mr. Angelos," she said, putting the mug aside and rising. "I wish to show you something."

I was halfway convinced she was going to escort me to her *own* demon-summoning pentagram, but instead she led the way to a long corridor lined with framed photographs. "Observe, Mr. Angelos," the Headmistress said, standing back to let me go first. "What do you notice?"

Hesitantly, I walked down the corridor, eyes staring disapprovingly down at me as I passed. Deep crimson carpet ate the sound of my footsteps. The place had the hushed, reverential air of a cathedral or an art gallery.

All the photos were of women. I thought at first that they were previous Headmistresses, but then I recognized a Hollywood actress and realized they had to be alumni of the school. Farther on, there was a former prime minister; a couple of senior politicians I remembered seeing on TV; a prominent engineer who was always in the news for lobbying against environmental policies; a famous businesswoman who had her own show, crushing the dreams of aspiring entrepreneurs.

All the women bore the smug, sleek expressions of people who had everything. Just seeing their photos made me feel weak and unimportant. Trying to shake off the odd sense of inferiority, I looked at the brass plaques under the photos. Each one had a name and a number, and as I drew closer to the end of the corridor, the numbers got bigger. 15,000. 20,000. 120,000 . . .

"Donations?" I said, getting it at last.

"Indeed, Mr. Angelos," said the Headmistress from right behind me. I jumped. I hadn't even heard her move.

"These are all benefactors of Saint Mary's. Past pupils who have reason to express gratitude to their alma mater."

I summed up the amounts listed under just the closest five pictures, and got an eye-watering figure. Multiply that by the length of the corridor, and ... "You get all this *on top* of the school fees? Man, you should be paying us!"

"And have you take your education for granted?" the Headmistress said. "You will find in life, Mr. Angelos, that nothing concentrates the human mind quite so wonderfully as money. But I did not bring you here merely to demonstrate how extraordinarily fortunate you have been to be admitted to such elite company." She pointed to the very end of the corridor. "There."

A portrait hung in splendid isolation on the far wall— not a photograph, but a huge oil painting in an ornate golden frame. It was the only picture that showed a man. A stern-faced old guy, wearing weird black robes.

FATHER DANTE

2.5M

"So, let me see if I have this straight, Mr. Angelos," the Headmistress said as I stared at the figure in disbelief. "You wish me to expel the ward of the most generous benefactor this school has ever had, on the grounds that, while illegally stalking her without her knowledge, you came across her exercising her human right to free expression of her spiritual beliefs. Do you wish to add anything to this summary?"

"But she's a troublemaker, Headmistress," I said hopelessly. Krystal had told me that Michaela had been adopted by a rich family, but I hadn't realized they were *that* rich. "She's late to everything, and talks back, and doesn't pay any attention at all in class. And she gets away with it too. None of the teachers will punish her for anything."

"Two and a half million pounds," the Headmistress said. "Which I only receive if Miss Dante satisfactorily completes her education. It somewhat ties my hands. I cannot risk Miss Dante finding any reason to fault either her teachers or this school."

I paused, studying her face. The Headmistress wasn't looking at me, but rather at the painting. There was a certain sour twist to the set of her mouth. . . .

"*You* don't like her either, do you, Headmistress?" I said. "You'd rather she wasn't here too."

"I could not possibly comment, Mr. Angelos." She paused. "If, however, you were to discover something of rather more import than a few chalk lines and candles, I would of course be duty-bound to take the matter seriously. *Very* seriously."

119

"She's threatened to kill me. Is that serious enough?"

"Words, Mr. Angelos. Only words." She tilted her head to one side a little as if struck by a thought. "It does suggest an intriguing possibility, however. I have reason to believe that Miss Dante may indeed be carrying lethal weaponry around the school."

My mind flashed on the memory of the daggers Michaela had drawn in the shrine . . . and on the straps I'd glimpsed around her thighs when I'd looked up her skirt in History of Art. "She really is. I can testify to that."

The Headmistress sighed. "Mr. Angelos, I will need a little more evidence than your word alone. Your bloody corpse would be convincing, but alas, that presents certain logistical difficulties. Alternative proof is required. I do not have the power to demand Miss Dante submit to a strip search, but if *you* were able to liberate her weapons from her person, I would be able to expel her immediately. *And* demand the bulk of the Dante bursary as a penalty fee."

"I'll get you the proof, Headmistress." I lifted my chin, staring into Father Dante's painted eyes. He certainly looked like a leader of an evil cult, with his black robes and grim expression. No doubt he'd sent Michaela here to take over the Hellgate and summon more demons to do his bidding. But I wasn't going to be cowed. I was a guardian angel, and I was going to do whatever it took to stop the forces of Hell.

I was going to get into Michaela's pants.

Chapter 12

Y ou want me to help you do what?" Krystal stared at
me in horror over the lung we were meant to be dis-
secting.

"Seduce Michaela," I repeated in an undertone, leaning to peer past her shoulder. Michaela was staring at us
from the far side of the room, toying with a scalpel in a
rather disturbing way, but I didn't think she could overhear us. The rest of our classmates were fully engrossed
in attempting to make their animal organs fall apart into
neatly labeled schematics without actually touching them.
"It's the only way to get my hands under her skirt."

Krystal looked down at her gloved hands as if only the
fact she was covered in blood to the wrists was stopping
her from face-palming. "Raf, no offense, but you are the
worst guardian angel *ever*."

"No, he's a genius." Faith smiled at me from her lab stool, where she was perched making drawings of our offal. "It would be so much better to get rid of Michaela without hurting her. I think it's a wonderful plan."

"And that's your big, red warning flag right there, Raf," Krystal said with a sigh. "Look, leaving aside the problem of actually carrying out this idiotic idea, what makes you think we can trust the Headmistress to do her part? If she really wanted Michaela gone, she could have expelled her months ago just for the bullying."

"My mother can't do anything that would look like favoritism," Faith said. "She can't risk punishing Michaela just because of how she treats me."

"I wasn't talking about you," Krystal muttered, stabbing our lung with her scalpel.

Noticing Ms. Oleander's eyes on us, I passed Krystal another instrument. "Open up that bit next," I said loudly. "Let's get a closer look." I tried to appear deeply interested in the horrible roadkill splayed out before us. "Anyway," I said, lowering my voice again, "I have to get my hands on Michaela's daggers, but there's no way I can take her in a fight. I need a more subtle approach. I thought you could tell me the best way to go about it, Krystal."

"Oh, because I'm obviously the authority on seducing

123

girls," Krystal snapped, slicing at the lung with such force that the whole thing collapsed with a wet fart. "You of all people shouldn't listen to gossip, Raf. Just because I'm not obsessing like an idiot about getting a boy for the Ball doesn't mean—"

"What are you blithering about?" I finally managed to jam a sentence edgeways into the torrent. "I meant you're the one who told me all that stuff about Michaela in the first place, so I thought you might have some idea of what she likes. You know, what sort of approach I should take."

"Oh." Krystal's indignation deflated, rather like the lung. "Right. Of course." She frowned down at her scalpel. "Personally, I'd recommend a net and a big stick."

"Krystal," Faith said reproachfully. She looked at me. "I think the most important thing is to be genuine. Michaela's smart. She'll see through any act. But if you approach her sincerely with real feeling, I'm sure she'll respond."

"Uh," I said. "Are you sure flowers and chocolates wouldn't work better?"

"Imagine the possibilities," Faith continued, her face brightening. "You could redeem her! Turn her to the side of light with the power of your true love!"

Krystal groaned. "Faith, there are *wood lice* with more common sense than you."

"Yeah, I'm not going to actually fall for Michaela," I said. Faith's enthusiasm was starting to bug me and not just because it was patently insane. I hadn't expected her to be wild with jealousy or anything, but . . . it would have been nice if she'd been just a *little* dismayed at the thought of me making out with another girl. "You do get that, right?"

"But it's obviously meant to be!" Faith clapped her hands. "Just look at the way you two hate each other!"

"Could we have that again, this time in Earth logic?" I asked.

"You two are sworn enemies caught on opposing sides of the war between Heaven and Hell," Faith said patiently. "Clearly, you're destined to be soul mates!"

I stared at her. "You have got to be kidding me. I'm not even attracted to her!"

"Don't be silly." Faith gestured at Michaela. "Of course you are. Who wouldn't be?"

"Faith, Raf isn't going to have the hots for someone who wants to stab him in the kidneys," Krystal said in exasperation. "Michaela's not *that* gorgeous."

"Well, I think she is." Faith gazed across at Michaela wistfully. "I had the biggest crush on her when she first arrived."

My brain hiccupped to a halt.

"She was so beautiful, so strong and confident," Faith continued, apparently oblivious to my frozen state. "I was dazzled by her." She sighed. "Maybe it was just her supernatural powers, but it felt so real. All I wanted was to be with her, to join our—"

Krystal snapped her fingers in front of my eyes. "Faith, I think you've broken Raf."

The end-of-class bell rang, shattering my contemplation of a frankly arresting mental image. "Time, my sweets!" declared Ms. Oleander. She'd become my new favorite teacher for her habit of handing out toffees as rewards for answering questions. I'd gotten one for giving the correct answer to "And what's *your* name, my sweet?" Now she rattled the bag, smiling around at us. "You must all be ravenous after working so hard. Come and have a little something to sustain you on your way to the next lesson. Oh, and someone needs to stay behind to cut the organs into bite-sized pieces for proper disposal. Whose turn is it? Julia?"

"Faith said she'd do it for me," Julia said without looking up from packing her bag.

Faith blanched a bit, looking around at the quivering, bloody lumps scattered over the work tops. "Yes," she said faintly. "I'd be happy to."

"I'll give you a hand," Krystal said to her. She shot me an irritated glance. "Since I suspect this isn't the sort of thing that merits angelic intervention."

"Sorry," I said, already slinging my bag onto my shoulder. "Heavenly duties call."

I distinctly heard her mutter, "More like heavenly *bodies*," as I headed to intercept Michaela, who was loitering near the door. My palms were sweating. How was I going to start this conversation? *Hi, it's me, the guy you want to kill! Let's make out!*

"You," Michaela said in greeting. She dismissed her usual entourage with a flick of her wrist. "We have to talk." She leaned in a bit closer, body curving sinuously, and dropped her voice to a throaty purr. "In private."

Well . . . that was easy.

"I'm glad you've decided to stop attacking me on sight," I said as she led me away from the crowds rushing to get to the next class. She was definitely swinging her hips a bit more than was strictly necessary . . . not that I was noticing. I made my own voice darken with a hint of smoldering passion. "I've been thinking about you a lot."

"Not as much as I've been thinking about you," Michaela answered. We'd reached a deserted corridor, which, from all the dust on the floor, didn't see a lot of traffic. She opened a door to reveal a small, dim store-room, the walls lined with shelves of obsolete computer equipment. "In here." She licked her lips slowly, looking me up and down. "I don't want us to be disturbed."

"Right," I said, the word coming out as a bit more of a squeak than I'd intended. As nonchalantly as I could, I sidled past her. *Get in, get the knives, get out*, I chanted to myself. I could do this. "So you've been feeling the sparks between us too, huh? I mean, you're the queen bee here, I'm the only guy. . . . It makes sense for us to get together."

"Save your breath." Michaela shut the door behind her with a very solid-sounding *click*, her seductive attitude dropping away in an instant. "Your wiles won't work on me."

Belatedly, it occurred to me that I was in a small room, outside of shouting distance from anyone else, with my mortal enemy between me and the door.

Maybe this hadn't been such a good idea.

From the triumphant smirk on Michaela's face, she thought this was a *fabulous* idea. Her hand whipped around to the back of her waistband, pulling something out. "Take *this!*"

Bemused, I did. "Okay," I said, inspecting the index

card. It had a pentagram drawn on it, but not one of the eye-twisting ones. It was just lines on paper. "What am I supposed to do with it?"

"I didn't mean literally," Michaela snapped, plucking it out of my fingers again. She had a whole stack of the things in her other hand. With a small glare at the pentagram, as if the symbol had personally disappointed her, she tossed it aside, then flipped over the next one. "How about this?"

"*Gah!*" Shelves rattled as I recoiled into them. Okay, it was still just ink, but I could have sworn the thing was about to jump off the paper and bite me. "Get it away from me!"

Michaela's lips curved in satisfaction. "Oh, no," she said, moving closer, the card held in front of her like a shield. I couldn't help cringing away. "We're going to be here for a while, and it's going to get much worse for you than this. I'm going to go through every symbol, every possible combination until I find—"

"*Rafael Angelos!*"

I had never been so glad to hear my name in my life. An instant later, Ms. Wormwood wrenched Michaela away. The teacher's red hair was practically alight with the force of her outrage. "What are you two doing in here?"

I opened my mouth, but Michaela beat me to it. "Making out," she said coolly. The cards had disappeared under her skirt again. "We've got a free period."

"You may not spend it being lewd in private!" Ms. Wormwood stabbed a shaking finger at the door. "Go to your dormitory at once, Michaela! I will be speaking to the Headmistress about this. Not you," she added as I made a move to follow Michaela. "*You* stay."

That left me trapped in an isolated storeroom with a cougar rather than a demon. It really wasn't much of an improvement. "We weren't making out," I said quickly. "Michaela dragged me in here. She was acting really weird."

Ms. Wormwood's bristling hair seemed to settle back, like an animal's fur after a scare. "I did tell you not to get mixed up with Michaela Dante, Raffi. For your own good."

"I know," I said wholeheartedly. I really wished I *could* take Ms. Wormwood's advice. "Sorry, miss. Can I go now?"

"I think we need to discuss this at greater length. In more . . . congenial surroundings." Ms. Wormwood regarded me for a moment. "You still have a detention outstanding, don't you, Raffi?" I nodded, and she smiled, looking unnervingly like a cat with a mouse under her paw. "Then you can do it with me, this evening, between dinner and Peer Assessment." Opening the door, she cast me a last glance over her shoulder, a sly smile tugging at the corners of her mouth. "Don't even think of running out on me this time."

"No, miss," I croaked to the closed door. I sagged down the wall, feeling like I was under attack from all sides.

I was doing my best to be Faith's guardian angel. Now who was going to be mine?

Chapter 13

Krystal was still laughing as the two of us entered the sixth-year common room for that evening's Peer Assessment session. "Oh, shut up already," I growled, flopping down onto a chair next to Faith. "It wasn't that funny."

"Yes it was." Krystal nudged Faith, grinning ear to ear. "You should have tried to get a last-minute detention too. Totally worth it. You know how Ms. Wormwood likes to set lines as punishment? Guess what she made Raf copy from. Go on, guess."

"I don't know." Faith was obviously not in the mood for guessing games. She looked like a little kid waiting for a dentist appointment, huddled in her chair with her arms around her knees. She flinched as another group of sixth-year girls entered the room, pointedly ignoring her as they found seats. "What?"

"The K-k-kama S-sutra!" Krystal dissolved into laughter again.

"The woman is a sadist as well as a nympho," I muttered.

Faith mustered a weak smile, though it didn't really shift her drawn, anxious air. "Ms. Wormwood's a good teacher, Raffi. I'm sure she didn't mean anything by it."

"Yeah, right." I glared at Krystal, who was still helpless with mirth. "If Krystal hadn't been there, Ms. Wormwood would have been chasing me around the desks."

"You are so full of it," Krystal said. She wiped tears of laughter from her eyes, smudging her makeup. "Faith's right, Raf. Ms. Wormwood *is* a good teacher. Oh my God, she's an utter genius. Talk about effective punishment. You're going to be following every school rule to the letter now, aren't you?"

"Damn straight." I folded my arms, scowling. "Which is not going to make it any easier to thwart the forces of darkness."

"Speak of the devil," Krystal said as Michaela swept into the common room, surrounded by her usual cronies. She was as cool and collected as ever, but the other girls were talking in overloud voices, a distinct undercurrent of tension in their exaggerated gestures. The whole room had the nervous, electric energy of a locker room before a big match. Krystal stood up again, shouldering her bag. "And that's my cue to leave."

"I thought this thing was compulsory," I said.

"It is." Krystal shrugged. "And if it's a choice between an F minus for not showing up, and a D for sitting under a steaming shower of crap, I'll take the former, thanks." She looked at Faith. "You sure I can't persuade you to join me?"

Faith shook her head. "I have to try. Maybe Raffi will make a difference."

"Don't let the bastards grind you down." Krystal squeezed her shoulder, then punched mine. "You do your job, Halo Boy."

"Uh, what exactly were you hoping I would do?" I said to Faith as Krystal left.

"Help me get a good grade." Faith swallowed, squaring her shoulders. "We've only got a few weeks left before the Ball, Raffi. Time's running out. I *have* to meet my true love there. Or else Michaela wins."

I still didn't see how a kiss could close the Hellgate, but I wasn't going to argue with someone who looked on the verge of vomiting with nerves. "Okay," I said a little dubiously. "But I really don't see how I can help with your popularity. I mean, this is girl stuff. Not exactly my domain."

"You don't have to do anything." Faith wiggled her fingers by her forehead, as if to indicate a halo. "Just let your angelic light shine out, banishing the demons' darkness and filling everyone's hearts with peace and love."

While I was still trying to work out how to do *that*, Ms. Hellebore ducked through the door, followed by a little old lady in a fraying cardigan. The room instantly fell silent, all the girls freezing under the old woman's vague, clouded gaze like mice in front of a snake. "Good evening, girls," she said in a creaking but kindly voice.

As a nervous-sounding chorus of, "Good evening, Ms. Henbane," filled the air, I leaned over to whisper to Faith. "Why's Ms. Hellebore here?"

"Anger Management exercises," Faith replied under her breath. "And also to break up fights."

I stared at her, but didn't have a chance to ask what she meant by that. Ms. Henbane was addressing the class, a warm, grandmotherly smile on her wrinkled face. "Let's start with a little self-esteem exercise before we begin the feedback sessions, shall we? I call this 'Honest Admiration.'" She waved a stopwatch. "I want everyone to mingle for the next five minutes, with two constraints—tell the truth and only express admiration. Off you go!"

"I used to like this game," Faith said miserably, as girls started to mill around, a buzz of conversation rising up. "But now no one ever talks to me."

"Well, I will," I said, edging a little closer to her. I would have deployed one of my practiced smiles, but something about Faith made all my rehearsed moves fly out of my head. "I think you're pretty great."

Pretty great? Oh yeah, Raf, you silver-tongued devil. That'll really wow her. From the way Faith was looking at me, though, you'd think I'd just extemporized a sonnet. "Really?"

"Um, yeah, actually. In fact, I—"

"Raffiiii," trilled a girl, inserting her knockout curves between us. "I wanted to tell you that you are just sooooo good-looking."

I blinked. "Okay. Um. Thanks?"

"No, no, not like that, Rafael." Ms. Henbane had snuck up on us, like a geriatric ninja. "You need to echo the compliment."

"What, like, give one back?" I said, eyeing the girl. Unfortunately, the first compliment that sprang to mind was likely to get me slapped.

"No, no," Ms. Henbane said. "This is a

self-esteem-building exercise. You have to repeat Debbie's compliment."

"Uh, okay. Thanks, Debbie. I am indeed good-looking." And now I felt like a massive dork. This was supposed to raise my self-esteem?

"Good, good." Ms. Henbane patted my arm and wobbled off, leaving Debbie still grinning up at me. Behind her, Faith was making her radiating-goodness-and-light gesture again, her eyes imploring. With a mental sigh, I stared hard at the girl, trying to visualize angelic power beaming out from me.

"Raffi, are you all right?" Debbie said in concern. "You're looking kind of constipated." She slapped her hand over her mouth. "Oops. That wasn't actually meant to be a compliment. Let me try again. Is it true that you're a male model? Because you totally could be."

"Thank you," I said dutifully. "I could indeed be a model." Then I remembered the lies Suzanne had been spreading. "I'm not, though."

"None of that rumor is true," Faith said quickly. "We're just friends."

"Really?" Debbie's eyes flicked from her to Michaela—who was staring at us across the room—and back again. She bit her lower lip for a second. "You know, Faith, I've always really admired your . . . hair."

Faith's face lit up like a fireworks display. "Oh, thank you. My hair *is* beautiful. And I love your sense of fun, Debbie. I've really missed hanging out with you."

"That's right. I am a lot of fun." Debbie winked at me. "Maybe we could *all* hang out sometime?"

"Raffi, it's working!" Faith clutched my sleeve as Debbie sashayed away. On the far side of the room, Michaela's hands were twitching by her thighs like a gunslinger longing to draw. "Keep doing it!"

I had no idea what I *was* doing, but it certainly seemed to be working. As if Debbie had breached some invisible wall, Faith and I found ourselves surrounded by eager well-wishers. Most of the compliments were directed at me, but even the few halfhearted overtures dropped in Faith's direction had her practically glowing with joy. And it was all down to me. I was saving Faith. I could already picture her gratitude—

A hand closed like a vise on my arm, yanking me around. "I can't say what I admire about you," Michaela growled. Before I could jerk away, she'd grabbed my chin, forcing my face down to hers. "So I'll show you."

"Yes, yes." Ms. Henbane's testy voice was barely audible over the chorus of cheers and whistles. "This is meant to be a *verbal* exercise, Michaela."

Michaela released my mouth. "You were right," she murmured, her breath warm on my lips. Her eyes gleamed as she stepped back. "It does make sense for us to get together."

And here I'd been thinking Operation Demon Seduction had crashed and burned. I stared after Michaela in confusion, head spinning with more than just the passionate kiss. Surely, Faith couldn't be right about Michaela and me being soul mates? The demon had to be up to something. Even for someone who'd just made out with me, she was looking a little *too* pleased.

"Time to begin the assessments," Ms. Henbane announced. Behind her, Ms. Hellebore was now openly dozing. "We'll go in reverse order tonight." She consulted a tablet computer. "That means you first please, Faith."

Faith took the tablet eagerly, holding it, screen out, in front of her and flashing me a confident smile. Ms. Henbane shepherded the rest of us into a single-file line. I was a little way back from the front of the queue, but I could still make out the POSITIVE and NEGATIVE buttons displayed on the tablet's screen. It was clear that we were all going to take turns scoring Faith. I was still worrying about Michaela's newfound passion for me, so I wasn't really paying attention as the girl at the front of the line stepped forward. Then Faith's clear voice cut through my preoccupation. "Thank you. I am indeed conceited and self-centered."

"You what?" I said aloud. Debbie half turned at my outburst, casting me a questioning look. At the front of the room, Faith had her smile fixed on her face like a shield as another girl advanced on her. I didn't hear what she said, but I saw Faith flinch. Then, "Thank you," she said, with apparent sincerity. "I am indeed lucky that my mother is the Headmistress." Ms. Henbane said something to her, and Faith closed her eyes for an instant before continuing, "Because that's the only reason I'm here rather than in a mental institution."

"They're insulting Faith to her face? In front of a *teacher*?" I said in disbelief, as Faith agreed that she should indeed eat a sandwich once in a while. "A second ago they were sucking up to her!"

"A second ago we all thought you were single," Debbie said, shrugging one shoulder. "Now there's no incentive to risk going against Michaela."

Up ahead, Michaela glanced over her shoulder to give me a small, secret smirk. My fists clenched as she strode up to Faith, who for the first time lost her desperately eager-to-please expression. For a second, the two girls faced each other, eyes locked. Then Michaela said something, and for one heart-stopping instant I thought that Faith was about to take a swing at her. Ms. Hellebore even jerked out of her upright catatonia—but Faith took a deep breath, stepping back from Michaela. "Thank you," she said with only the barest tremble in her voice. "I am indeed wasting my life, just like my father did."

I realized Ms. Hellebore, with a teacher's unerring instinct for sensing trouble, was now scrutinizing me. I forced my fists to unclench. "You're not going to join in with this, are you?" I hissed at Debbie, remembering how she'd snapped at Suzanne in History of Art. She avoided my eyes. "Don't *any* of you have the balls to stand up to Michaela?"

Debbie huffed out a humorless breath of laughter. "Raffi, everyone knows how loaded her family is. And she's promised that her very closest friend will get 'something special' at the Ball. Half the girls here would happily *eat* the other half for the chance to win the mystery prize." We'd reached the front of the line. "If Michaela hates Faith, the rest of us have to as well." To Faith, she said, "Look, you're never going to make any friends here." The tablet made a rude buzz as Debbie touched the screen, giving Faith a negative score. "Your life would be a heck of a lot easier if you'd just accept that and leave."

Faith's smile twisted slightly. "Thank you," she said in return, for once sounding in wholehearted agreement. "It would indeed."

"Raffi?" Ms. Henbane prompted me.

It took a lot of effort to make myself step forward. If Krystal had handed me a sword in that moment, I would happily have stabbed Michaela then and there.

Something special. Oh yes, the chosen girl would get something special all right. Cold, black tentacles wrapping around her, a gaping maw opening to latch onto her soul like a monstrous leech . . . If Michaela succeeded in opening the Hellgate, she'd need bodies for her demonic buddies to possess. And here she had her pick of girls, all desperate to impress her, all willing to agree to do anything, no matter how strange or wrong it sounded.

The stupid, *stupid* cows were competing for the honor of becoming a demon's human hand puppet. And they were turning on the one person who was trying to save them.

Faith read my expression, and her own slid into outright alarm. "Don't, Raffi!" she whispered urgently. Behind her, Ms. Hellebore and Ms. Henbane had their heads together, their eyes fixed on me as they conferred. At the far side of the room, Michaela's air of studied indifference dropped away, every muscle abruptly taut and ready as she too stared at me. "I'm fine. Don't make a scene!"

It was excellent advice. Which I completely failed to follow, as the instant my hand closed on the metal body of the tablet, the device burst into flame.

Faith shrieked, dropping the tablet, which immediately set fire to the carpet. I jumped back from the spreading blaze, instinctively grabbing Faith and yanking her away too. The entire room erupted into pandemonium.

"Raffi, this way!" Faith linked her hand in mine, hauling me after her as she bolted for the door. Behind us, Ms. Hellebore was stamping out the fire with her enormous boots, barking at the screaming, ricocheting girls to stop panicking. The white flames were already dying down, but Faith didn't pause. She pulled me right out of the classroom and down the hallway.

"Faith!" I yelped as she ushered me into a bathroom. "I can't be in here!"

Ignoring my protests, Faith locked the door behind us, slumping against it. Her shoulders heaved as she panted. "Have to. Halo."

"What?" I checked myself in the mirror and was nearly

blinded by my reflected glory. "Oh. Shit."

"You smote my Peer Assessment results!" Faith pushed back her disheveled hair in order to glare at me. "After I *told* you not to make a scene!"

"I didn't mean to! It just happened!" I groaned as it finally hit me. "Metal. The tablet was metal. That's why I keep setting things on fire. When I'm pissed off, my wings get hot, and if I touch something metal it must conduct the energy down. Like a lightning rod."

Faith did not look impressed by this superpower. "Well, thanks to *your* temper, now *I* have to do my Peer Assessment all over again."

"Hey, at least I got pissed off!" My wings were starting to heat up again. I thrust my hands out to the sides before I could inadvertently immolate my belt buckle. "Rather than standing there like a brain-damaged parrot! Why the hell do you let those bitches do that to you?"

"Because I have to!" Faith flared up, as if finally releasing a reservoir of accumulated rage. "When will you and Krystal finally understand that nothing is more important than my popularity? Without good Peer Assessment scores, I won't have a date for the Ball, and without my true love I can't close the Hellgate! I *need* those bitches!"

"No you don't!" I yelled right back. "You don't need

stupid Peer Assessment to get a date for the Ball! You've got me!"

Faith paused, her mouth open. "Did . . . you just ask me out?"

I shoved my hands in my pockets. My fingertips encountered some loose change, but apparently angelic embarrassment wasn't a leading cause of forest fires. Which was a pity, because I could really have used the distraction. "Um, yeah," I mumbled at the floor.

There was a hideous silence.

"Look, I'm not saying I believe this stuff about the power of true love and all that," I said, because it was that or run away, and Faith was between me and the only door. "But, um, you know. I could help you out. At the Ball. Save you the hassle of importing some other guy. If you like."

"I honestly can't work out if that's incredibly sweet," Faith said, sounding bemused. "Or the least romantic confession of true love ever."

I'd jumped off a building for her. I'd faced down both a demon and Ms. Wormwood for her. Even in this dingy bathroom, she seemed brighter, more vibrant, than anyone I'd ever met, as if she stood in a permanent sunbeam. And her mere presence dropped my IQ through the floor.

Oh, hells. I *was* in love.

I swallowed hard, edging closer to her. "Maybe . . . it's both?"

"Oh. Oh dear." Faith held up her hands as if she thought I was about to lunge at her. "Raffi, um . . . I have a boyfriend."

I froze. "You do?"

"Well, you didn't think I was going to hope I happened to fall in love with whatever random Winchester boy turned up for me at the Ball, did you?"

I barely managed to stop myself from blurting out *yes.* "No, of course not," I said instead, weakly. "So you already know a guy at Winchester?"

Faith nodded, her whole face brightening with enthusiasm. "My mother put me in contact with him years ago, because she thought it would be helpful for me to talk to someone else who has a parent with a demanding, time-consuming job. I think his dad's someone really high up in government—he must be famous, because my boyfriend's not allowed to tell me his own last name, in case I was secretly a spy for the newspapers or something. Anyway, he texts me all the time. Wonderful, sweet words, telling me that everything will be okay and we just have to wait until we can finally be together." She touched her shirt

146

pocket. "I keep my phone next to my heart, to give me strength when things get really bad. He says—"

"Does he know about your plan?" I interrupted somewhat sharply. "About your dad, and the Hellgate and everything?"

Faith's happy glow flickered a bit. "Well . . . no. I don't want to scare him off. But he doesn't need to know. He just has to meet me at the Ball, and our perfect love will do the rest. He's my soul mate. I know he is."

I was the one protecting Faith from a damn demon, and some other guy was going to get the reward? Oh, *hell* no. And I had an ace up my sleeve. Or rather, behind my back. "Maybe. But I know what he isn't." The bathroom tiles reflected a thousand dazzling points of light as I spread my wings. "He's not an angel."

Faith did not swoon into my embrace. In fact, she took a sharp step back, as if I'd waved a spider at her.

"Raffi?" Her alarmed eyes were fixed somewhere over my shoulder. "Why have you got four wings?"

Chapter 14

"Why have I got four wings?" I demanded as I climbed through Krystal's window.

"Raf!" Krystal jumped, knocking over the stack of teen fashion magazines piled next to her on the bed. She grabbed at them before they could slide to the floor. "What the hell—" She stopped dead, blinking at me. "Raf," she said after a second. "Why have you got four wings?"

"That's what I asked you!" I waved the offending limbs, fluttering the pages of her magazine. "They just appeared out of nowhere during Peer Assessment. What the hell am I, a Swiss Army angel?"

"How should I know?" Krystal stared at me in fascination. "Wow, that looks topologically unlikely. Not to mention unaerodynamic. What happened?"

I briefly filled her in on the Peer Assessment debacle. "Then I spread my wings, and discovered I had too many. I mean, *more* too many." I slumped into her swivel chair, draping my wings over the back. "I am really getting fed up with sprouting extra body parts every night."

Krystal's forehead wrinkled in thought. "Your first pair appeared when Faith was in danger, and so did the second, kind of. Maybe some sort of instinct to protect her is unlocking your powers? Like, you know, leveling up."

"Wonderful," I said gloomily. I swiveled the chair back and forth. "So now I'm a Pokémon. Rafael has evolved."

Krystal snorted, a grin tugging at her mouth. Then she frowned. "The question is, will it *keep* happening? Did Faith have any idea?"

"No, she just freaked out. Aren't you two supposed to be the experts on this stuff?"

"All we've got are her dad's notebooks. Believe me, they're not exactly Angelology 101. It's like trying to learn addition from a postgraduate paper on number theory." She shook her head. "I'll see if I can find anything, but don't hold your breath."

"Great." With a sigh, I folded all four wings into invisibility. "At least they still disappear."

Krystal cleared her throat. "Which," she said, "your halo still doesn't. Unfortunately."

I kicked my chair back. "Don't even think about it, Moon!"

She glared at me. "Believe me, after your reaction last time, I wasn't." With a snap, she opened her magazine again, disappearing behind the glossy pages. "Your halo, your problem."

"Good!" So now I just had to find a way to sin on my own. Well, when it came to *that*, I was practically an expert. Scrunching my eyes shut, I concentrated very hard.

"If that's somehow meant to be stopping you from glowing, it isn't working," Krystal commented after a few minutes.

"Damn!" I opened my eyes again. "Guess it doesn't count as sinning if you're only thinking about it."

"I am *not* going to ask," Krystal muttered. "Go sin somewhere else, okay? I'm busy."

I looked pointedly at her magazine. "Yeah, I can tell."

Krystal lowered the magazine far enough to reveal her long-suffering expression. She turned it around to show me the article she was reading. It was rather denser than I'd been expecting. And apparently, this season pentagrams were the new black.

"Uh. Okay." I was pretty sure they hadn't started printing fashion advice in handwritten Latin. "Are those Faith's dad's notes?"

"Faith put them into old magazine covers, in order to hide them from her mother." Krystal looked at the cover, handling it between finger and thumb as if it was used toilet paper. "Personally, I'd be a lot more worried about any daughter of mine reading this crap than delving into the occult."

"My mum would have agreed with you. She always said those things were soul destroying." I'd thought that had just been because she knew what went on behind the scenes of the fashion industry, having started her career at a glossy style magazine, but now I wondered if she'd been speaking from angelic experience instead. "What are you looking for?"

Krystal rubbed her eyes. "Anything. Any clue as to how he actually intended to close the Hellgate." She dropped her hand again, looking frustrated. "I knew Mr. Jones, you see. He was quiet and reclusive and always seemed kind of sad, but he was *smart*. I used to run into him sometimes. We'd talk math. Higher-dimensional geometry, mostly. So I have to believe he had a sensible plan to deal with the threat here." She flipped a few pages. "Problem is, he never intended anyone else to read this stuff. Half of it's incredibly technical notes about angels and demons, and the other half is just mundane observations about Faith. He was obsessive about recording her life as she grew up."

"I guess that's why she's so convinced she's special and part of his plan somehow."

"Yeah. But alternatively Gabe Jones was just really proud of his daughter, like any good dad." Krystal blew out her breath. "The only thing that *is* clear is that he was absolutely desperate to attract an angel. He keeps going on about wishing he knew how to summon one . . . and then, suddenly, he did." She turned to the last page in the magazine, handing it to me. There was my name, *RAFAEL ANGELOS*, in neat, precise block-lettered capitals, underneath a set of weird, swirling symbols. There was an intricate pentagram drawn on the opposite page, with arrows marking where the symbols were meant to go. "That's his last journal entry. No comments, no explanations how he found it, no hint as to what you're supposed to do once you got here. Nothing. And then he was gone."

I stared at the symbols representing my name. I was pretty sure I recognized the first one—it had been on one of the index cards Michaela had brandished at me—but even the ones I'd never seen before sparked an odd sense of recognition. I could almost hear them whispering in my mind. I closed the magazine, repressing a shudder. "Well, at least *someone* thought I was needed to close the Hell-gate." I couldn't help the hint of bitterness that slid into my voice. "Faith sure doesn't."

Krystal looked at me. "Ah. This must be about her boyfriend."

"You knew about him?" I glared at her. "And you didn't think to warn me?"

"I thought you'd heard the school gossip. Anyway, why would you even care? Most the time you act like you're as exasperated by her as I am."

"Believe me, I am! It's just—she's just—I can't explain it." I ran a hand through my glowing hair. "It's like when-ever she's around, I can't see anyone else, you know?" I sighed. "It doesn't matter. I made a total ass of myself."

"I'm shocked." Despite the sarcasm, Krystal's expres-sion softened. She gave me a friendly sort of prod with her foot. "Hey. Cheer up. You can't possibly be a bigger ass than Faith's boyfriend."

"He is?" The world was suddenly a much brighter place. "You don't like him?"

Krystal wrinkled her nose. "The bit from his latest text, the one that Faith keeps mooning over? Totally cribbed from *The Bavarian Billionaire's Bought Bride.*"

"Ha! Wait, how do you know?"

"Never you mind," Krystal said hastily, with the briefest of glances at the ebook reader sitting on her bedside table. "Faith said I was just jealous, and that his words didn't have to be original to reflect his true feelings. But I reckon he's either lazy or a jerk. For what it's worth, I think she'd be much better off with you. At least you . . . aren't . . ." She trailed off, staring at me.

"What?" I glanced over my shoulder, just in case I'd sprouted any further freakish additions, but couldn't see any change. "Why are you looking at me like that?"

"*Raf!*" Krystal bounced to her feet, scattering magazines everywhere. "I could kiss you, if you wouldn't dive out the window. Don't you get it? You and Faith! Her dad keeps saying in his journal that light drives out darkness, and that the greatest light is love. That's why Faith's so fixated on the idea. But he also writes that divine love is greater than anything mortals can comprehend. And he was trying to summon an angel. What if Faith's right, but it's not *her* love that's important?"

I sat bolt upright, my wings twitching open before I got

them under control again. "You think Faith's dad meant for an angel to fall for Faith?"

"Well, it's nuts to think ordinary love could defeat demons, but you aren't ordinary, are you? And Faith, for all that she makes me want to scream, is pretty damn virtuous, going through what she does. If anyone could make an angel fall in love, it would be her."

"But I already do, uh, like her. And it doesn't seem to be doing squat to close the Hellgate."

Krystal chewed on her lip. "Maybe . . . maybe you both have to be in love. In order for it to be effective. Like reflecting a light between two mirrors to make it brighter."

"Great. So I'll just tell Faith that her dead dad wanted her to fall in love me, so if she would kindly do so straightaway, we can get on with the more important business of demon-banishing?" I could picture how well *that* would go down. "You know how much she's into romance. This feels more like an arranged marriage."

"You have a point." Krystal tapped her finger against her chin for a second. "Look, I'll help you. I'll talk to her, make her see your good side. You just . . . do the best you can. Be yourself. Only less arrogant."

"Thanks for the vote of confidence." I started for the window—and then groaned, catching sight of my reflected light in the glass. "I forgot. How the hell am I going to get rid of this stupid halo? I've had enough Lust and Wrath for one day. What other Deadly Sins are there?"

"Sloth?" Krystal suggested. "On second thought, don't try that one. The last thing we need is for you to draw attention to yourself by being late to class. We really don't want you to get expelled." She frowned. "What about Envy?"

"I'm the only guy around," I pointed out. "I haven't got anyone *to* envy."

Krystal gave me a Look. "And considering I have no idea how you could manage to be any more full of yourself, I guess Pride is out too. That leaves Avarice and Gluttony."

"Gluttony," I said, seizing on the word I actually knew. I was already practically starving on the girl-sized portions of salad and vegetables that the canteen offered. I looked around, my mouth already watering at the thought of stuffing my face with real food. "Great. Where do you keep your chocolate?"

I thought I'd seen the full spectrum of Krystal's glares, but this one was dark enough that it should have put my halo out on its own. "What, exactly, makes you think *I* have a stash of chocolate?"

"Well, you know," I said, starting to gesture at her—and then my survival instinct kicked in. "Uh. No reason. I mean, you're obviously very healthy. It's just that I've only got you and Faith I can scrounge from, and obviously *she* doesn't—"

"Keep going, Raf," Krystal said in tones of doom.

I shut up.

Krystal glowered at me for a moment longer, then sighed. "It's okay. I really don't have any chocolate, though. I don't know anyone who does. Everyone's permanently dieting here."

"You girls and your stupid weight obsessions," I muttered.

"If you had a public weekly weigh-in, you'd be obsessive too," Krystal said sharply. "Particularly when your success at 'maintaining a healthy figure' is graded."

I stared at her. "You have got to be kidding."

"Believe me, I wish I was."

"This place," I said from the bottom of my heart, "is nuts. Whose brilliant idea was it to put a school on a Hellgate anyway?"

Krystal shrugged. "Faith insists it's *good* that the school encourages us to eat well and exercise." Her lip twisted. "Of course, she's thin and blonde. Anyway, I doubt there's anyone here past puberty who's so much as looked at chocolate for years, let alone eaten any. I don't know anyone who can get their hands on food that's actually appetizing."

"Maybe you don't," I said slowly. "But I do."

--- ✗ ---

The second-year dormitory was on the third floor of the east wing. This was not a problem. The problem was that evidently individual rooms were a privilege reserved for the final-year students. Through the crack in the curtain, I could see four bunk beds. Even if I'd wanted to try my luck at sneaking past them all while glowing like a light-bulb, the window was locked.

I should have abandoned my plan. I *knew* I should have abandoned it. Krystal would have told me to. But Krystal wasn't there, I still had no idea what Avarice was, I was cold and hungry, and I just wanted some goddamned bacon.

I knocked.

The girl who pushed back the curtains looked some-what startled to find a winged glowing guy hovering outside her window.

"Hi," I said with a friendly grin, trying to look as though all this was completely normal. "Can I talk to Lydie, please?"

Chapter 15

Why," Faith asked at break the next day, staring in a perplexed way at the fleeing form of my latest admirer, "do little girls keep running up and giving you sandwiches?"

"No idea," I said, quickly cramming the greasy package into my already overflowing bag. My chances with Faith would not be improved by her discovering that her sacred family secret was now common knowledge amongst the misfits of the second year. "Mysterious female minds. No doubt some prank. Aha-ha."

"Raffi?" My next worshipper turned out to be Lydie herself, her eyes wide with admiration and her hands full of bacon rolls. "I brought you—"

"Yes, *thank you*," I snapped, snatching the rolls away from her. With a nervous glance at Faith, I took Lydie to one side, dropping my voice to a whisper. "Look, I'm really grateful and all, but can you guys knock it off?" I gestured at my no longer haloed head. "The problem's sorted out for now. And you're starting to attract attention." It wasn't just Faith I was worried about. "I don't want Michaela realizing you know about me. I've got my hands full just trying to watch out for Faith, let alone all you lot."

"Okay," Lydie said, her expression wistful. She caught my sleeve as I started to straighten. "I wish you were *my* angel."

"Did she . . . call you an angel?" Faith said as Lydie bolted.

"She's, uh, just got a crush." Definitely time to change the subject. "Hey, has Krystal managed to catch up with you yet?" Last I'd seen her, she'd been cornered by a couple of Lydie's roommates, begging her to teach them how to summon their own angels. The look she'd given me over their heads had informed me I was a walking dead man. "I think she wanted to talk to you."

"Actually, yes." Faith bit her lip. "Raffi, can we talk? Privately, I mean. There's something I really need to discuss with you."

My heart started to pound, but I managed to maintain

a nonchalant tone. "Sure." We'd been loitering in front of the chapel-turned-assembly-hall, as the drafty courtyard wasn't a favored hangout for Michaela's gang. Now I followed her through the arched oak doors and into the cool, silent building. It might not be a place of worship anymore, but the huge space with its soaring vaulted ceiling still had a hushed, reverent air. I swallowed, feeling small and out of place. "What's up?"

"That little girl isn't the only one with a crush on you." Dappled colors from the stained-glass-angel windows made patterns over Faith's serious face. "But this one's much more important. This one could change everything." She moved closer, putting one hand on my sleeve. "I need to ask you to do something. Something very important."

Was it sacrilegious to make out in a deconsecrated church? And damn it, why hadn't I flossed this morning? "You know I'll do anything for you."

"Good." Faith's hand tightened on my arm. "Because I need you to date Krystal."

"Yes, of cou—wait, *what?*"

"She's crazy about you." From Faith's face, you'd have thought she was telling me that the cancer was inoperable. "She didn't talk about anything else while she was helping

162

me serve breakfast this morning. Raffi, I'm so, so sorry, but do you think you could, um, indulge her? Just a little," Faith added hastily as if anticipating a violent protest. "To keep her happy. For me?"

"I . . . think you might be misinterpreting that conversation," I said, resisting the urge to beat my forehead against the stone wall. "Look, it's nice that you want to look out for your friend, but Krystal doesn't want to date me. Trust me on that one."

"You didn't hear her! She's never talked like that before." Faith's eyes were wide and worried. "Raffi, she may not be much help, but Krystal's the only ally I've got. I can't afford for her to get offended and stalk off. Please at least try to be sweet to her. For me?"

I stared at her, a dozen objections crowding in my head. For some reason, the one that found its way to my tongue first was, "I think Krystal's a lot of help, actually. I mean, she got *me* here."

"Yes, with an unorthodox summoning charm that obviously went wrong!" Faith gasped and covered her mouth. "Oh, Raffi, I'm so sorry," she said through her hand. "I didn't mean that the way it sounded. It's not your fault you're a little . . . " She gestured at my shoulders to indicate my hidden wings. "Um. Defective."

The world was saved by a discreet cough from behind us. At least, if Krystal's theory was right, it had been, considering that the response I'd been about to make would have destroyed any tiny remaining chance I had with Faith. "Are you two in search of some spiritual guidance?" Ms. Henbane tottered toward us between the rows of chairs. She smiled hopefully at us. "I'm the chaplain as well as the counselor, you know. It's outside of my usual office times, but I'm always open for any students having a crisis of faith."

"Thank you, Ms. Henbane," Faith said politely. "Normally, I'd come straight to you with any problem." Her shoulders slumped. "But I don't think these are ones you can help with."

"Well, I *do* have a Faith problem," I said, folding my arms and glaring at her. "And maybe you can help me out, Ms. Henbane. You do Religious Education sort of stuff, right?"

"I do indeed." Ms. Henbane cocked her head at me. "Something on your mind, Rafael?"

"Yeah." Faith was never going to want to get with an angel she thought was "defective." Which meant I had to prove that I wasn't. I summoned my best charming

164

smile, aiming it at Ms. Henbane. "Know anything about angels?"

--- ✗ ---

"I knew you'd come to confide in me eventually." Ms. Henbane fussed with a teapot. "When we first met, I thought: now there's a young man after my own heart. Do make yourself comfortable."

"Uh, thanks." I gingerly lowered myself into the velvet depths of an antique armchair, unable to shake the impression that I was violating some sort of museum exhibit. Ms. Henbane's room looked more like a Victorian parlor than an office. "But I think I should tell you straight off that I don't do God."

"Ah, I knew we were kindred spirits." Ms. Henbane offered me both an encouraging smile and a rose-patterned teacup. "Neither do I."

"You don't?" I took a gulp of tea, nearly swallowing the dainty slice of lemon floating in it. "But you're the R.E. teacher. Aren't you a Christian?"

"Goodness, no." Ms. Henbane fussed with something on a side table. "Technically, I'm a Satanist. Macaroon?"

I sprayed tea all over the proffered plate. "Sorry?"

"It's quite all right," Ms. Wormwood said graciously. "Let me get you a ladyfinger instead."

"No, I mean—you're a *what*?"

"A Satanist," Ms. Henbane said with perfect equanimity, as she discreetly hid the now-soggy macaroons under a doily. "Oh, I don't mean that I go out sacrificing goats in the dark of the moon," she added, catching my surreptitious glance around to try to spot any demonic altars amidst the china shepherdesses. "I believe in a supreme deity, but I also believe that He is doing such a terrible job that He doesn't deserve our worship. By strictest definition of the word, that rejection of the Creator of the universe makes me a Satanist." She sniffed in disdain as she seated herself on a wingback chair. "Not that I'm convinced that Satan would do much better. If you want something done right, you have to do it yourself. Can I tempt you to an iced ring?"

I stared into the box of assorted biscuits. They were pink. Pink biscuits did not seem very Satanic. "So . . . you don't go around trying to summon demons?"

"My word, why on earth would I need to summon a demon?" Ms. Henbane said, raising an eyebrow. "Now, you wanted to know about angels?"

I guessed Ms. Henbane was the Satanic equivalent of people who only go to church at Christmas. Nonetheless, I found myself clutching my teaspoon, just in case I needed to defend myself against sudden demonic attack. "Uh, yeah. Have you ever heard of angels with more than two wings?"

"Certainly." Ms. Henbane went over to a large oak bookcase and plucked out a leather-bound tome. "They're categorized in *De Coelesti Hierarchia*, the foremost authority on angelic matters. As a matter of fact, multiple wings are one of the identifying traits of the highest orders in the celestial hierarchy."

I perked up. "Really? You mean like archangels?"

"Actually, archangels are part of the lowest sphere." Ms. Henbane turned pages as she spoke. "Ordinary angels, archangels, and principalities are all in the third sphere. Above them in the second sphere are the types of angels called powers, virtues, and dominions. And above *them*, highest of all, are the angels in the first sphere. Thrones, seraphim, and cherubim. They all have multiple wings, as you can see." Turning the book around, she showed me a woodcut.

"Uh," I said, squinting. "I don't see any angels."

167

"Right there," Ms. Henbane said, pointing to a freaky thing that looked like a couple of spoked wheels jammed together and set on fire in some horrific bicycling accident. "That's a throne."

"Riiight." Were those *eyes* all around the wheel rims? "I'm pretty sure that's not what I am. I mean, what I'm looking for."

"In which case, let us go on to the seraphim." Ms. Henbane turned a few pages, displaying another illustration, this one entirely consisting of folded wings. "The highest of the high, the mightiest of the mighty. They radiate burning light and continually sing praises to the Creator. They cover their eyes with one pair of wings, their feet with another, and fly on the third pair."

"Too many." And unless seraphim were meant to sing *really badly*, I was pretty sure I wasn't one of those either. "Don't suppose you've got anything with exactly four wings?"

"Why, yes," Ms. Henbane said. "The cherubim. They're warriors and protectors. In fact, it was a cherub who was sent to guard the Garden of Eden with a flaming sword."

I sat up straight. That sounded more like it. "And they've got four wings? You're sure?"

"Certainly." Ms. Henbane flipped to yet another woodcut. "In fact, they're the only type of angel that do."

I took the book from her eagerly. "Great! That's just what I'm—"

I stopped dead.

"They also have four heads," Ms. Henbane said happily, as I stared at the illustration in horror. "Ox, eagle, lion, and man. Oh, and they're covered in eyes."

Chapter 16

R af, you're a guardian angel!" Krystal looked like she wanted to smack either her own forehead or, prefer-ably, me. "You can't just quit because you're worried about sprouting extra heads!"

"It seems like a bloody good reason to me!" I lowered my voice as a couple of girls went past, heading into Ms. Wormwood's classroom. We were meant to be in there ourselves, but I'd yanked Faith and Krystal aside to give them the bad news. "You didn't see the picture. I am *not* risking turning into a monster."

Krystal rolled her eyes in exasperation. "I can't believe you're taking some stupid old book this seriously."

"Actually," Faith said, "I'm pretty sure my father had a copy of *De Coelesti Hierarchia*. He used to tell me bedtime stories about the angel hierarchies, saying that seraphim and cherubim were watching over me." She frowned. "I admit he left out the bit about all the eyes and heads. He probably didn't want to give me nightmares."

Krystal groaned. "Faith, you are not helping."

"Oh. Right." Faith turned her big blue eyes on me, summoning up a reassuring smile. "Raffi, no matter how many heads you grow, we'll never think of you as a monster." She reached out to pat my hand.

I recoiled from her. "Don't touch me!" Faith looked hurt. "Sorry," I muttered. "Nothing personal. It's just that every time I've gotten close to you I've ended up with weird new body parts."

"But you have to close the Hellgate with her!" Krystal practically yelled. "This is too important for you to get squeamish now!"

"He has to what?" Faith said.

"Just a stupid theory Krystal came up with," I said quickly. "Look, I'm not abandoning you, okay? I'll still try to get rid of Michaela. But that's *it*."

Faith smiled at me, though she still looked a bit perplexed. "That's all I ever asked, Raffi."

"Getting rid of Michaela won't solve anything, you idiots!" Krystal yelled, her hands balling into fists. "The Hellgate will still be here, and a new Michaela will come along to try again once we've left the school. We have to close the thing!"

"That's what I'm going to do," Faith said, brow furrowing. "You know I am. Why are you so upset?"

Krystal moaned, running both hands through her hair in agitation. "We," she said, seizing Faith's wrist, "have got to talk." She shot a glare at me over her shoulder as she dragged Faith into the classroom. "And then *we* are going to talk, Rafael Angelos."

"Not if I can help it," I muttered. I slouched after them, pointedly taking the seat farthest away from Krystal's corner. She was whispering urgently to Faith, with many hand gestures that left little to the imagination as to what she was talking about. I was glad I couldn't see Faith's expression. I slumped farther down in my seat. I wasn't sure which would be worse: if Faith didn't believe Krystal's theory or if she did. One way, I would continue to be rejected in favor of some dick with a smooth writing style. The other way . . .

I wanted to be with Faith. I really did. But I wasn't willing to get mutated into some freak-show attraction. The wings were bad enough, but at least I could fold them up. What would I do with extra heads?

Of course, if Krystal was right, and I *didn't* get with

Faith . . . it could mean the end of the world. I didn't know exactly what demons would do if they got loose, but I was willing to bet it wouldn't be good. A demon possessing a St. Mary's girl, most of whom came from rich, power-ful, well-connected families . . . it could end up anywhere. Imagine a demon in charge of the police, or the stock exchange, or the government. Or—I thought of my dad, and my stomach contracted—the army.

My morose contemplation of the wall was abruptly interrupted by a close-up of Michaela's cleavage. "What are you up to?" she demanded in a tone that did not go at all with her flirtatious expression. "Why was Krystal Moon yelling at you just now?"

"Get out of my face," I growled. I was so not in the mood for Michaela at the moment. "You may have sur-prised me in Peer Assessment, but you can't keep up the pretense that we're dating. I'm not going to let you under-mine Faith that way again."

"You'll do as I say, or—," Michaela started.

I slammed a hand down on the desk, making her jerk back. "No! I have had it with girls telling me what I have to do!" I'd spoken too loudly. I flushed under our classmates' stares, sinking back down into my seat. Nonetheless, I folded my arms and glared at Michaela, still filled with rebellion. "You can't order me around," I muttered. "Not you *or* Krystal."

Michaela's eyebrows rose at my tone. Then she froze. Slowly, her head turned from me toward Krystal, who was still arguing with Faith in the back corner. Without another word, she made her way over to her own seat next to Suzanne, though she kept glancing back at Faith and Krystal.

I groaned and buried my head in my arms. That was all I needed, Michaela deciding that if she couldn't dominate me, she should go after easier targets. I had a nasty feeling I'd just painted a bull's-eye on Krystal's forehead. Even if it wouldn't solve the Hellgate problem, I had to get those knives off Michaela and get her expelled. Stat.

Problem was, I still had no better plan than trying to seduce her. And, in a fit of temper, I'd just ruined my best chance of doing *that*. Lifting my face an inch from my arms, I cast a glance around the classroom, wishing there were someone I could talk to about this besides Krystal and Faith. I needed help. I needed advice. I needed—

"Sex education!" Ms. Wormwood declared, striding into the classroom and beaming around at everyone.

No. NonononoNO.

"I know, pets," Ms. Wormwood said as a chorus of

mixed groans and sniggers filled the air. "But this is part of the curriculum, and some of the most important knowledge you'll learn at this school." She clasped her hands, gazing at us all earnestly. "I hope you'll all help me make this class a warm and supportive environment in which to explore your developing bodies."

I fought an intense urge to take cover under my desk while the entire class, as one, looked at me. Even Michaela did it, with a raised eyebrow and slight amused twist to her lips.

"Ms. Wormwood?" Krystal had her hand in the air. "I don't think I'm comfortable discussing this with a boy present."

I was going to buy her a dozen red roses.

"Krystal isn't comfortable with having a boy present for *any* of it," Suzanne stage-whispered to her friend. "Just as well, really." Krystal went scarlet but didn't back down. Make that *two* dozen red roses.

"I thought some of you might feel that way, pet," Ms. Wormwood said to Krystal. "I know that this is a difficult subject to discuss in mixed company, which is why," she gestured at the door, "I've asked Ms. Vervaine to join us."

The cadaverous teacher stepped in, looking as if she

175

was being forced at gunpoint. She held a DVD case in front of her like a shield. "Film," she croaked, brandishing it at the class. "You will watch it."

"Indeed you will," Ms. Wormwood said. "While Raffi comes with me."

"What?" I yelped. "I mean, please, can't I watch a video too?"

"Pet, Saint Mary's was a girls' school until this term." Ms. Wormwood was already halfway out the door. "Our educational videos are rather useless if you don't have a uterus. Come along now, don't be shy!"

A video on Things Man Was Very Definitely Not Meant to Know or a private date to put condoms on cucumbers with Ms. Wormwood? Talk about a rock and a hard place. But I didn't really have any option other than to follow her. The door swung closed behind me, cutting off Ms. Vervaine in the middle of saying, "Anyone excused on religious or—"

I wondered if Ms. Wormwood would buy a sudden conversion to strict Catholicism. Then again, the thought of corrupting the virtue of a good religious boy might excite her even further. I took a deep breath, commanding myself to get a grip. Krystal and Faith were right. I was reading way too much into Ms. Wormwood's over-friendly manner. Okay, this was no doubt going to be excruciatingly embarrassing, but she wasn't *actually* going to risk her job by getting inappropriate with a student.

"Here we are!" Ms. Wormwood proclaimed, holding a door open and waving me through. "We'll have our lesson in my office."

My attention was instantly riveted by the item of furniture that dominated the small room. It was a sofa. With a leopard-print fake-fur blanket.

"Nice and informal," Ms. Wormwood purred, closing the door behind me with a very ominous-sounding *click*. "And very private. Completely soundproofed, in fact. Don't worry, everything that happens in here is in *complete* confidence."

I scrambled to put the sofa between us. "Uh, Ms. Wormwood, actually I've done lots of sex ed lessons before, at my old schools."

"Oh, I'm sure there's plenty more for you to learn," Ms. Wormwood said, seating herself and patting the cushion next to her invitingly. "Especially from an . . . experienced woman."

My back hit the window.

"I mean that your previous teachers were probably all men, pet," Ms. Wormwood said with a slight smile. "And there are some things that need a female perspective." She crossed her legs, her long split skirt falling away down one side, and patted the sofa again. "Don't worry. I don't bite."

Given she'd just revealed she was wearing thigh-high leather boots with steel stiletto heels, I wasn't so sure about that. I reluctantly perched on the sofa, as far away from her as I could get. "Now, Raffi, there's no need to be shy," Ms. Wormwood said earnestly. "I know that adolescence is such a difficult time for young men. Your body is changing in so many unexpected ways."

"Man, you have no idea," I muttered to myself. Desperately embarrassed, I stared out the window. A flash of brightness over by the edge of the woods caught my eye, morning sunlight glinting from long, gold hair. *Faith?*

I stifled a yelp as Ms. Wormwood patted my knee. "And with hormones raging through your veins, I can understand why you're so attracted to Michaela Dante."

"What?" I said, distracted. That was definitely Faith kicking through the fallen leaves, with her distinctive hair rippling behind her. What was she doing out of class? "I'm not attracted to Michaela. Actually, I'm interested in someone else."

"How wonderful." Ms. Wormwood's face lit up. She

edged a little closer to me. "Tell me, who's the lucky girl, pet?"

I didn't say anything. I didn't have to. Ms. Wormwood followed the direction of my gaze, and her expression froze. "Not . . . Faith?"

"I know it's a bad idea," I said wretchedly. "In fact, it's a really terrible idea, for more reasons than just her mother." Oh, what the hell. I needed to talk about this with *someone*. "Ms. Wormwood . . . do you believe in true love? I mean, that it's a sort of magical power that can defeat any darkness?"

Ms. Wormwood put a hand over her eyes as if praying for strength. "No," she said forcefully. "It can't. There's no such thing as love at first sight, no mystical bonds, no soul mates. You have to forget about her, Raffi."

I looked out the window again, though Faith had disappeared by now amidst the trees. "I know I should," I said softly—and then stiffened. "Oh, no."

Michaela was striding rapidly across the lawn, her long legs flashing like knives as they devoured the ground. Even at this distance, I could see she was pissed off, her entire body one tense line. Within seconds, she'd disappeared down the same path as Faith.

In that moment, I discovered something. I might be ambivalent about saving the world. But I damn well wasn't about saving Faith. I didn't care how many extra heads I sprouted. I was not going to leave her in danger. My mind spun, generating horrific images of what the demon might do with her knives if she caught Faith alone—

Which was nothing compared to the horrific situation I abruptly found myself in as Ms. Wormwood tackled me.

"Let me help you forget Faith, Raffi," she breathed into my ear, her body pressed against mine. How could one skinny woman be so damn heavy? "You know I can. Can't you feel the heat—"

My flailing hand found the steel heel of her boot. White fire shot down my hidden wings, blasting Ms. Wormwood off me as if a rocket had gone off between us. She hit the wall and crumpled into a heap.

"Sorry!" I yelped as I shot to my feet. Remembering the Headmistress, I waved my hands vaguely in her general direction. "Uh, be thou raised up! Bye!"

I didn't have time to see if it had worked. Flinging the window open, I streaked into the sky. I hoped everyone was really paying attention in class for once. I arced high over the woods, frantically scanning the canopy.

There. A glint of gold through the bare branches. I dove.

Faith gasped as I snatched her up, flailing at me for a second before realizing who I was. "Raffi! What are you—*eeeep!*"

Her arms nearly crushed my rib cage. "Not—so—tight!" I managed to get out. I didn't stop climbing. "Relax! It's okay, I've got you! What are you doing out here?"

Faith was trying to find a platonic way to cling to me, without much success. "My father's notebooks say you have to be pure and virtuous to commune with angels, so I begged my mother to let me skip sex ed classes. What are *you* doing here?"

"Michaela was following you. Didn't you see her?"

"No, not a sign—"

A dozen cold, thick tentacles closed around my wings like a gigantic hand, squeezing them shut.

"Raffi!" Faith screamed as we plummeted. I struggled against the invisible grip, but it held my wings tight. The world spun toward us. We were going to smash like eggs—

The tentacles jerked back. My wings exploded out like a supernova. For a second, the lower pair brushed something icy chill, while the upper encountered fiery heat—and then both demonic presences were gone.

Breathing hard, I managed to bring us to an

almost-controlled landing back in the clearing where I'd first practiced flying. We collapsed in a heap. For a second, all I could do was lie there, my head hanging and my wings splayed out behind me.

"Raffi." Faith's hand touched my face. My halo reflected in her wide eyes. Despite our near-death experience, she smiled. "You have six wings. You're a seraph."

Chapter 17

I was a seraph.

Oh, *hell* yes.

"Raf," Krystal said as the two of us patrolled the corridors that evening, "would you give it a rest? That is getting *really* annoying."

I broke off from my hummed rendition of "U Can't Touch This." "I'm a seraph," I reminded her happily. "I'm supposed to sing constant praises."

"Not to yourself!"

"*Doo do be do—demons can't touch this!*" I sang again, spinning in a little impromptu dance. I moonwalked backward, grinning at her. "C'mon, lighten up, Krys. Or do you need me to do it for you?" I flicked my wings out momentarily, their glow illuminating her irritated face like a strobe light.

"Oh, how I wish you'd turned out to be a cherub," Krystal said under her breath. "Though on second thought, I bet you'd manage to be even more insufferable if you had four mouths." She paused to peer into yet another darkened classroom. "Not here either." She chewed her lip for a moment, then shook her head. "I don't know where Michaela could be."

"She's probably hiding somewhere to lick her wounds." Michaela had been missing in action ever since sex ed. Rumor had it that she'd claimed illness and gone to her room, but she hadn't been there when we'd checked. I reckoned the demon had been hurt by the blast of heavenly fire when I'd broken her grip on Faith and me. "In fact, maybe she's already packed her bags and fled the school. She must know she can't take me now that I've unlocked my seraph powers. Come on, I'll walk you back to your room."

We headed out of the main building, back toward her dormitory. Krystal slouched beside me with a scowl, her hands deep in her coat pockets. "I don't like it," she burst out after a few minutes. She kicked through the dried leaves on the path as if she had a personal grudge against every one. "What if you're right, and Michaela's entire family *are* a demon-summoning cult? She could be reporting back to Father Dante even now. Summoning reinforcements."

"Bring it." I extended all six wings again, striking a majestic pose. "I can handle any mere demon."

Krystal cast me an exasperated glance—and then stopped to study me more intently. "Raf, what's up with your wings?"

"Huh?" I swept a couple of my wings forward to look at them myself. The edge of each feather still shone as brightly as ever, but now they darkened toward the middle, with the central quills as black and glossy as obsidian. "That's weird," I said, angling a few of them to check it wasn't just a trick of the light. "They were all white when I rescued Faith earlier."

"See, Raf, this is exactly why you can't get complacent!" Krystal waved at my two-tone feathers. "We still have no idea how your powers work, or how you can control them, or even what you can do! This could be perfectly normal or it could be deadly corruption from the demon's touch."

I beat my wings experimentally, making her duck. "Still seem to work okay," I said from two feet off the ground. I dropped back down and shrugged, folding my wings out of sight again. Privately, I thought that the silver-edged black suited me a lot better than that dorky

Christmas-card white. "They're fine. You worry too much."

"That's because neither you nor Faith worry at all!" Krystal practically wailed. She looked on the verge of throttling me. "You don't know they're fine. We don't know anything at all about how this stuff actually works!"

"So what, as long as it does? I defeated Michaela today, right?"

Krystal ground her teeth. "That's beside the point."

"Hey, you summoned me to fight evil, and you can't deny that I've got the demon running scared. So chill out and leave things to me." I smiled beatifically at her. "After all, I am a seraph. The highest of the high, the mightiest of the mighty."

"The cockiest of the cocks," Krystal muttered.

"It's not arrogance when you actually *are* the highest form of life in all creation."

"God, I hope a demon eats you," Krystal said with feeling.

"I shall forgive your blasphemy." I patted her head in benediction and jumped back from her answering shove. We'd reached her window, so I held out my cupped hands to give her a boost back up into her room. "I'm going to go check on—whoa, what happened here?"

"Just the usual," Krystal said sourly, barely sparing a glance for the wreckage of her room. All her clothes had been pulled out of the closet and trampled on the floor. Drifts of paper covered every surface like an indoor snowstorm. "Someone thought it was funny to come in and mess up all my stuff this morning while I was in class. It happens. At least whoever it was didn't tip a bucket of pond water over my bed again."

"I think I know who it was," I said grimly, thinking of Michaela striding away from sex ed. Then I blinked. "What do you mean, again? Michaela only got interested in you today."

"You think it was Michaela?" Krystal considered this for a moment. "Well, if it was, I don't see what good it did her. Whoever it was didn't find the notes hidden in the magazines. Faith's dumb disguise actually worked." She frowned. "The only thing missing is my jewelry box. That had my old angel-summoning charm in it, the one I used to call you. But the only thing that would tell Michaela is that there's an angel named Rafael Angelos here, which is hardly news to her." Krystal shrugged. "So no harm done. And like I said, I'm used to girls trashing my stuff."

I folded my arms on the windowsill, resting my chin on them for a moment as I watched her move about the room, putting things to rights. "Hey, Krys . . . tell me if there's anything I can do to help, okay?"

"Close the Hellgate?" Krystal cast me a half-wry, half-resigned smile over her shoulder. "No matter what Faith says, I still think it's influencing the students, making them act like complete fiends from Hell. It's got to be the reason behind the bullying." She sighed. "At least, I hope it is," she added, so quietly I almost didn't hear it.

"I'll work on it, I promise. And in the meantime, if you do ever want me to smite someone with angelic wrath, just say the word."

Krystal snorted with a more genuine look of amusement. "Tempting. But considering that so far you've mown down more teachers than demons, maybe you'd better keep your cool." She waved me off. "It's okay. See you tomorrow."

With a quick glance around to make sure that nobody else was looking out of their windows, I spread my wings and took off. Rather than head for my own dormitory, I flew toward the Headmistress's house. Krystal was right. The Hellgate had to be closed. And that meant I had to talk to Faith.

I was halfway to Faith's house when I realized that my feathers were brilliant white once again. It was kind of inconvenient, given that it meant I was now about as subtle and unnoticeable as a second moon.

"Great," I muttered sourly, diving back to the ground again. I trudged the rest of the distance on foot, getting a new collection of scratches and bruises from the undergrowth on the way. My caution proved worthwhile, though—despite the late hour, light glowed from the front window, and two silhouettes were clearly visible through the closed curtain. I guessed the shorter figure had to be the Headmistress, but I couldn't immediately identify the other one. Then she turned, showing an unmistakable profile of short, spiky hair, and my heart skipped a beat.

Ms. Wormwood.

On the one hand, it was a relief to know I hadn't killed her outright. On the other hand, she could even now be getting me into deep trouble. I was pretty sure that striking down a teacher with holy fire was grounds for expulsion, even if it wasn't actually listed in the school rule book. The window was cracked open, the edge of the curtain fluttering in the cold night air. Holding my breath, I skulked closer.

"—Reckless and irresponsible!" the Headmistress was saying. I had a sinking feeling she was talking about me.

"Throwing yourself at the boy like that! What were you *thinking*?"

I blinked. Then, slowly, I grinned. I wasn't the one getting bollocked.

"I'm sorry, Headmistress! I've simply never encountered a male like him before!" Ms. Wormwood pleaded. "I didn't anticipate his reaction. Then I panicked—"

"Yes, yet again! This is not the first such incident. Do you think I had not noticed your incompetence? You endanger this entire school with your lack of thought!"

I silently blessed Faith as I edged away from the window. I could never have brought the matter to the attention of the Headmistress myself—what could I do, complain that a woman wanted to have her way with me?—but I guessed that Faith must have told her mother about Ms. Wormwood's behavior. Now, even if the teacher *did* remember me smiting her, she couldn't bring it up without it sounding like the flimsiest of excuses. Feeling even more lighthearted, I made my way around the house and flapped up to Faith's bedroom.

"Hey, Faith?" I whispered, peering through the half-open window. "It's me, Raf." Duh. As if anyone else was going to be standing on thin air outside her bedroom. "You in here?"

"Raffi?" Faith pulled the curtain aside, and I nearly bit through my own tongue. She was obviously dressed for bed, in a man-sized T-shirt that looked an awful lot more interesting on her than it would have on a guy. The way the thin, white material skimmed her thighs was particularly riveting. "Is everything okay? Why are you here?"

"Guh." I dragged my eyes back up to discover that she was looking worried. "Everything's gorgeous. I mean good! Everything's good." I tried giving her my best slow, sexy smile. "I wondered if you'd like to come flying with me. It's a beautiful night."

Faith looked past my slowly beating wings to the twinkling stars above, temptation showing in her face. Just as I was getting my hopes up, she sighed, shaking her head. "Thank you for the offer, but maybe it's not such a good idea."

I maneuvered myself closer to her window so that I could gaze deep into her eyes. "You don't have to be worried about Michaela anymore, you know. I'm a seraph."

"Yes, so you keep mentioning." Faith hesitated. "Raffi, you know I like you."

"Yeah?" That sounded promising.

Faith fidgeted with the edge of her nightshirt, avoiding my eyes. "And I understand why Krystal thinks my father might have meant for us to get together." *Uh-oh.* "But . . . we haven't known each other for very long. True love takes *time*, time and trust. It means getting to know someone on the inside, how they think and feel. We haven't had that. And then there's Billy-Bob."

I stared at her for a second, then let out a whoop of laughter, losing two feet of height in the process. "Billy-Bob?" I spluttered, clawing my way back up to her window again. "Your boyfriend's name is *Billy-Bob*?"

"Yes," Faith said coldly. "Is there something wrong, *Rafael*?"

"I know, I know." Though personally, I thought that Rafael Angelos was a hell of a lot cooler than Billy-effing-Bob. Just thinking the name made me wobble in midair with suppressed mirth. Folding my wings, I managed to drop onto her windowsill, straddling it. "Sorry. Man, poor guy. He needs to get a nickname, like BB or something."

Faith looked slightly mollified. "He's never said anything about getting teased because of his name. Anyway, I think it's cute. It probably suits him."

"Probably? What do you mean, probably?" Faith abruptly found something very interesting about the carpet, and my jaw dropped. "Bloody hell. You've never actually met this so-called boyfriend, have you?"

"We don't have to have met physically to know that we're perfect for each other. We've been corresponding for years. I know all about him!"

"Except for what he looks like? You haven't seen him on webcam? Or even in a picture?" Faith's silence was all the answer I needed. "Then he's fat. Or has acne. Or he's horribly deformed. Or all three."

"I wouldn't care if he was!" Faith flared up. She raised her chin, her long, blonde hair rippling like a battle flag. "I'm not shallow! How he looks isn't important. I *know* him. He won my love over time, with words, not just with good looks and flashy powers. We *will* close the Hellgate together with the power of that love! Just like my father wanted!"

"Okay, okay!" I held up my hands in surrender. Man, had I ever cocked this one up. "It was Krystal's theory, not mine."

"Krystal overthinks things. And she doesn't understand true love." Faith calmed, her voice reverting to her usual soft tones. She dropped her gaze, a faint blush rising in her cheeks. Her bare toes dug into the carpet. "I do really like you, you know. As a friend."

"Yeah," I mumbled, as I ducked back out the window.

"Great." Spreading my wings, I hovered in midair. "Faith?" I called back.

"Yes?" She leaned out to look up at me.

I tilted down to catch her hand. With my wings glowing around me and the stars shining above, I softly pressed a kiss to her palm. "No matter what, I'll always be your angel."

Before Faith could respond, I released her. I shot into the air like a fallen star returning home.

Ha. Beat *that*, Billy-bloody-Bob.

--- ✗ ---

I drifted up from a dream of flying Faith through an endless golden sky to discover real sunbeams slanting through my fluttering curtains, promising a beautiful day ahead. I stretched luxuriously, rustling the chocolate bar wrappers still littering my bed from my latest de-haloing. I was a seraph. Not some freaky multiheaded thing, but a mighty being of fire and awesome power. Even Michaela and all her demonic strength hadn't been able to bind my six powerful wings. I didn't need to be afraid of her anymore. There was nothing to stop me from going after what I really wanted.

Faith.

Get the girl, save the world. Simple. She *had* said she'd liked me. All I needed to do now was show her that she *really* liked me. I grinned up at my ceiling. Poor Billy-world's-dumbest-name-Bob didn't stand a chance. Already planning how to tempt Faith into my arms, I opened my eyes.

Hang on.

I blinked, which somehow seemed to involve a great many more muscles than usual. I was looking at the ceiling. I was also, at the same time, looking at my pillow, my alarm clock, my curtains, the walls, the darkness under my bed, and, most disturbingly, *my own face*.

I sat up in bed. My many points of view shifted with me, spinning like a kaleidoscope. From the confused, multifaceted jumble of images, I managed to pick out my reflection in the mirror . . . and my eyes widened in shock.

All of them.

Including the ones orbiting my head.

Chapter 18

Krystal swallowed hard. "Okay." After her initial scream, her voice was now very calm in a very forced sort of way. "Let's not panic. I'm sure everything's okay."

"No it isn't!" I grabbed her shoulders, shaking her. My eyes whizzed about the small clearing like a silent swarm of agitated bees. I'd waylaid Krystal and Faith on their way to breakfast, dragging them off into the woods before anyone else could see me. "This is not okay! This is as far from okay as it is possible to be! This is the exact opposite of okay! I am COVERED IN EYES!"

"Are they . . . functional?" Faith tentatively held out a hand as if trying to entice a pet bird to come down. "Can you control them?"

"Yeah." Concentrating, I managed to land the nearest eye on her palm. She bit back a shriek, but didn't drop it. I was treated to a close-up view of her half-fascinated, half-disgusted expression as she examined the eye. I made it blink at her, all my other eyes blinking at the same time. My individual control wasn't that great yet. "I can see out of all of them at once. You don't want to know how hard it is to walk in a straight line."

"They're the same blue as your actual eyes," Faith said, inspecting my face. She turned the eye around in her fingers. "Actually, once you get past the fact that they're, you know, disembodied eyes, they're sort of pretty." A shiver ran down my spine as she stroked the metallic gold "skin" that wrapped the back of the eyeball. "Sparkly. Like jewels." Her forehead furrowed. "What does that remind me of . . . ?"

"I am seriously disturbed that this can remind you of anything," Krystal said. She was clutching at the collar of her coat as if afraid I might drop eyeballs down the back of her neck. "Maybe Michaela cursed you. Or you're a cherub after all."

Faith's expression cleared. "That's it!" She dug around in her bag and pulled out a copy of *Vogue*. I assumed it was hiding more of her dad's notes, unless fashion this season had taken a *really* odd turn. "I went searching for anything related to seraphim," she explained, flipping through pages. She turned the magazine around to show us a color illustration that looked like it might have originally come from a medieval manuscript. "This wasn't labeled as a seraph, but you agree it looks like one, right?"

"It's got the right number of wings, I guess," Krystal said, examining the three pairs of folded wings that hid most of the figure from view. "So?"

"So look at the gold sparkles." Faith pointed at a ring of dots circling the seraph's form, which I'd assumed were just indicating a halo. "And now look at Raffi."

I twisted one of my eyes around to inspect myself. The way that the sunlight flashed from my hovering eyes *was* similar to the illustration.

"And my father wrote something underneath this," Faith continued. "*Each of the four living creatures had six wings and was covered with eyes all around, even under its wings. Revelation 4:8.* That's got to be referring to seraphim." She shut the magazine, looking triumphant. "So there you go. You're meant to be covered in eyes!"

"Great," I snapped. "That's a tremendous relief. Apart from the fact that I am *covered in eyes*. I can't wander around looking like this!"

As if to underscore my predicament, the bell for first lesson rang. The sound of stampeding feet drifted through the bushes to our clearing. My eyes tightened nervously, drawing together into a swirling, basketball-sized swarm. Krystal bit her lip, looking up at them. "I guess you can't make them disappear, like you do your wings."

I glared at her. At least my multitude of eyes was useful for something. "I fold my wings. You tell me how I'm supposed to fold bloody eyes."

"Well," Faith said slowly, her gaze traveling up and down me in a way I would normally have appreciated, had I not been too busy freaking out about my monstrous new additions. "In that case, we'll just have to hide them."

--- ✗ ---

I stared glumly into my jacket. I stared glumly back out at myself.

I'd dreamed of having Faith's hands under my clothes. I'd never imagined it would be in order to stuff them with eyeballs. Something had gone terribly wrong with my life.

"What are you looking at?" Michaela slid into the seat next to me.

I jumped, pulling my jacket closed. "Nothing!" It was mostly true. I kept feeling like I was wearing a blindfold, even though my regular eyes were uncovered. "What do you want?"

Michaela's eyebrows arched. "Sounding a bit tense there, *Rafael*." I didn't like the gloating undertone to her voice. "Something worrying you? Discovered something missing?"

"Believe me," I said, "that is exactly the opposite of my concern at the moment."

Michaela looked momentarily baffled by that, but then her lips curved in a smile that was even more predatory than usual. "Don't worry. Your problems will soon be over." She straightened, turning to take up her English book with an air of dismissing me from her reality entirely. "Enjoy your last day on earth."

Maybe Michaela *had* done something to me. She certainly looked smug. As if all her plans were finally coming to fruition . . . which meant she had to be on the verge of opening the Hellgate. And, given that there was no chance I was going to be able to get her expelled in the next twenty-four hours, I had to stop her myself. By any means necessary.

I felt sick at the thought. I didn't even like killing spiders. Michaela might be possessed by ultimate evil, but she still looked like a human being. How could I burn her alive?

But if I didn't do it, Michaela would open up the

Hellgate and start bringing her buddies through. Suzanne and the other mean girls were bad enough *without* being possessed by demons. And it wasn't just girls like Lydie and Krystal who were in danger from them. The whole *world* was, if the school turned into a production line for a demonic army. If stopping that from happening meant killing Michaela, then I damn well had to man up and do the deed.

I had a nasty suspicion that none of this logic was going to help when it came down to me, Michaela, and a sharp piece of metal.

Of course, given that Michaela wasn't exactly quaking in fear of my seraphic might, it was possible I was worrying about nothing. I slumped with my elbows on the table, burying my face in my hands. Last night everything had seemed so bright and simple. Could my day get any worse?

"Attention, class!" The Headmistress stalked into the room. She glowered at us all as if she didn't want to be there any more than I did. "Ms. Wormwood is indisposed, so I shall be substituting for her today. Get out your books." She waited impatiently as we all did so. "Open your books." Pages rustled. "You may now commence reading your books."

There was a short pause.

"Uh, Headmistress?" One of the girls put her hand in the air. "Aren't you going to give us a lesson?"

"This is English Literature class!" the Headmistress barked, and the entire front row cringed. "In it, you read English Literature! No further activity is requi—Mr. Angelos, is that a gumball?"

To my horror, I realized that one of my eyes had fallen out of my trousers and rolled into plain sight. I scooped it up. "Yes. Yes, it is. Definitely. Sorry."

"Did you bring enough for everyone, Mr. Angelos?"

"Actually, yes," I said miserably. I drew my jacket a little closer around my body. "I really don't think they'd want them, though."

The Headmistress snatched the wastepaper bin from beside the teacher's desk and stalked toward me. She held it out commandingly. "Empty your pockets, Mr. Angelos."

"But—"

"Now."

I had no choice. I dropped a double handful of eyes into the bin, thankful that the swinging lid concealed what I was actually depositing. I could only hope that I'd have a chance to reclaim them before the caretakers came around this evening.

"See me after class, Mr. Angelos," the Headmistress

said darkly when I'd finished. She started back to the front of the room.

I felt a weird pull deep inside my body, which intensified as she moved away. Uh-oh. Previously, my eyes had never gone more than a couple of feet from the rest of me, and I hadn't tested how far they could actually roam. Now I was discovering that limit. The Headmistress didn't seem to notice anything, but it felt like she was pulling on elastic strings embedded in my bones. I had to grab onto the edge of my desk to stop myself from being yanked after her like a hooked fish.

"What are you doing?" Michaela hissed. She wound her heels around the legs of our table to hold it in place as I leaned against it. "Sit down!"

I could only manage a pained grunt in response, the hard edge of the desk nearly cutting me in half. The Headmistress had to be as strong as a rhino.

With a sensation like a snapped rubber band, my eyes *pinged* free. I thought for a second that the Headmistress must have yanked them straight off—but I could still feel them, bobbing upward like released balloons. In fact, all my eyes seemed to be floating outward, no longer confined by my clothing. My jacket hung loose and empty at my sides.

Shit. Apprehension gripped my stomach. I opened my eyes, expecting the screaming to start any second.

It did, but the sound came from my own throat.

Dimly, I was aware of the classroom erupting into chaos around me. My normal eyes were still back there with the rest of my body. But my angelic eyes had gone ... somewhere else.

A brilliant, terrifying space, where the very air seemed to be burning with white fire. *Now* I could see the tendrils connecting my eyes to the rest of me. They sprang out from under my wings, which were folded at my back in a brain-meltingly alien geometry.

But that wasn't what made me scream until the noise echoed in my head, blocking out everything else.

That was the thing hovering above Michaela.

Chapter 19

You *saw* the demon?" Faith hugged herself, as pale as my sheets. She and Krystal had snuck in through my window around midnight, Faith not having been able to get away from her mother earlier. "What did it look like?"

"All . . . fiery wings and eyes, and these sort of tentacle things, all hooked around Michaela." My hands moved vaguely, trying to sketch the demon's shape in the air. "It was right on top of her. Well, not exactly on top." I blew out my breath in frustration. "I haven't got the right word. That place was sort of alongside everything else. I could still see the normal world, but I could also see in this other direction, where the demon was. And my wings. That's where they go when I fold them up out of sight. I just managed to twist my eyes in the same way by accident."

"Can you do it again?" Krystal asked. She sat

cross-legged on my bed, shoulders hunched, resolutely not looking up. My angelic eyes bobbed over our heads like the world's worst party balloons. "Now? Please?"

I reflexively drew my eyes down a little closer, a couple nestling in my hair like a gruesome tiara. "No way. I don't want to see things again that way. It wasn't just that other place I could see—I could see everything around me too. And I mean everything. It was like having X-ray vision combined with an out-of-body experience. I could see under everyone's clothes. Under their *skin*." I shuddered at the memory. I'd had to clamp all my eyes shut, unable to make sense of it all, and the second I was alone in my room, I'd yanked my angelic eyes back down into the normal world. "I nearly decked the Headmistress when I came to. I thought she was some horrific creature like the demon. I could see her guts churning, her bones clicking together . . . everything. I don't want to see things like that again."

"No, I guess not." Faith was looking rather queasy. "My father wrote in his notebooks that angels can look inside human hearts. I didn't realize he meant it literally. That sounds—"

"*Awesome*," Krystal breathed. Her own eyes were alight with sheer glee. She actually bounced up and down on

206

the edge of my bed. "Raf, let me do an experiment." She pulled a coin out of her pocket and palmed it behind her back. Then she held out both her closed hands. "Do your eye thing, okay?" At my hesitation, she thumped me in the arm with the side of her fist. "Come on, this is important!"

Reluctantly, I gave my eyes that odd little twist that popped them free into that other space. Immediately, my perception widened. I could still see the everyday world stretching out around me, but I could see over and through things, as if I'd stood up from lying flat in long grass. "Above" me stretched that incandescent white sky, cloudless yet somehow growing foggy and vague higher up. Occasional twists of eye-searing flame roiled soundlessly across it, like horizontal lightning. Even though they looked distant, the effect was still unnerving. I huddled down, feeling horribly exposed in the barren, alien landscape, and pointed my eyes back toward the plane of the normal world. A sort of diffuse black fog shrouded everything, but the glow from my folded wings let me see through it well enough. I tried to concentrate just on Krystal, but my expanded field of view was too wide. I couldn't help but see the rest of the room—man, I was going to have to find a broom, because the dust bunnies underneath the wardrobe were *revolting*—including Faith.

My jaw dropped open. "Oh, wow," I breathed, staring at her.

Faith went a deep pink. She crossed her arms in front of her chest. "Stop looking through my clothes, Raffi!"

"But . . . you're beautiful," I said, still dazzled. Faith went even redder. "No, I didn't mean—I can't see your body, there's this sort of shimmery white stuff wound around you." I reached out as if I could touch the glowing, tightly furled petals veiling her form. "It's like you're wrapped up in a cocoon or something."

Faith looked taken aback, but pleased. "It must be my spiritual armor. My father's notebooks talked about cultivating a shield of virtue, to ward off demonic attack. I do the meditations every morning, after my workout."

"Huh," Krystal said. "Maybe I should start doing that too. Though preferably not at six a.m." She shook her fists at me. "Back to the experiment. Raf?"

"The coin's in your left hand," I said, cocking a few eyes in her direction. Unlike with Faith, I could see straight through Krystal, but now that I was prepared, it wasn't so bad being able to see all the squishy bits. Actually, it was kind of cool how much insane complexity was packed into her skin. "And it's a penny. From

2003. Kind of tarnished. So?"

With a startled look, Krystal examined the coin her-self. "You're right." A slow, triumphant grin spread over her face. "Which means I know what you are!"

"Brilliant, Sherlock." I twisted a few eyes back into the normal world just to give her the scale of withering look she deserved. "We already knew I was a seraph, remem-ber?"

"Not that," Krystal said dismissively. "You're some-thing much more interesting. You're *four-dimensional!*"

"I thought the fourth dimension was time," Faith said after a pause.

That was a lot more intelligent than the thing I'd been about to say, which was "Huh?"

"That's Einstein's dimensions," Krystal said to her. "In physics. I mean four spacial dimensions, like in geometry." She took in our identical blank expressions. "Oh, wonder-ful. Am I the only person here who's read *Flatland*?"

"Do we look like total geeks?" I said.

"Faith, you've got to know what I'm talking about. It was your dad who lent me the book." Faith shook her head, and Krystal sighed. "Okay," she said, rubbing her forehead in thought for a second. "We see our world as being three-dimensional, right? Things have depth, width, and length. So imagine a two-dimensional world. It would have width and length, but not depth. It would be like a piece of paper." She smoothed out a section of my sheet in demonstration. "Two-dimensional beings would be like drawings on a flat surface. They wouldn't be able to lift off the sheet or even know that there was such a direction as 'up' or 'down.' And a line would be like a wall. They wouldn't be able to see past it." Taking a ball-point pen from her pocket, she drew a circle on my sheet, then a smaller circle inside it. "So, for instance, if a two dimensional being was standing here," she marked a spot outside the bigger circle, "they wouldn't know about this small circle, because they wouldn't be able to see through the big circle. Okay so far?"

"I think so," Faith said, forehead furrowed in concentration.

"No," I said. "You just *drew* on my *bed*."

Krystal brushed aside this objection with an airy flip of her hand. "So imagine one of us visiting a two-dimensional world—like standing on the paper. The two-dimensional people would just see the outline of our feet, where we made contact with their plane, and to them we'd just look like another drawing. But we'd be able to look down from our greater height and see the whole world spread out beneath us. *We* could see the little circle inside the big circle. To the two-dimensional people, it would seem like magic. Like we could look through solid walls. So a three-dimensional being in a two-dimensional world would appear to have amazing powers." She pointed at me. "I think Raf here is a *four*-dimensional being, in our three-dimensional world."

"So," Faith said slowly, "he can see inside and through things in our world, just like we'd be able to see into things in the two-dimensional world."

"Right! Part of his body, the normal part, is here in 3-D space just like us. But his wings and eyes can reach into a fourth dimension. As well as up and down, left and right, backward and forward, they move . . ." Krystal stalled, searching for a term.

"Hellward," I supplied, rotating my eyes to glance at the flaming sky. "Believe me, this extra dimension is not a nice place."

"Hellward and earthward, then." Krystal tapped her pen on my sheet. "And the demon must be four-dimensional too. That's why you can see it, and we can't. It's hovering hellward, not touching our three-dimensional world. Maybe it can't come fully earthward, like Raf—"

"Okay, this is obviously all very thrilling for you," I

interrupted, as Krystal looked dangerously close to doodling on my bed linen again. "But it's all just theory."

"Oh, no it isn't." Krystal grinned. "Don't you see, Raf? A normal three-dimensional person can't fight a demon. We can't reach them, up there in four-dimensional space. That's why Faith's dad wrote that the only way to get rid of them is to kill their host. But you can fight the demon directly! You can drive it off!"

Faith's mouth and eyes went round. "You mean . . . we don't have to kill Michaela after all?"

"Exactly." Krystal pointed at me, practically vibrating with excitement. "We are going to do some experiments. Learn how your powers really work, and what you can do in four-dimensional space. And then"—her grin widened until she looked like a happy shark—"we are going to exorcise Michaela. With *science*."

Chapter 20

"Again," Krystal demanded.

"Krystal, I have already blown up a pencil case, a coat hanger, a doorknob, a hubcap, and a toilet this evening." That last one had been an accident. I'd still been a bit wound up when I'd taken that bathroom break. I gestured with Faith's sword at the still-smoking wreckage cluttering up the old shrine. "I've mastered channeling heavenly fire, okay?"

I'd spent all of Saturday practicing my smiting technique. Faith had been dragged off by Ms. Wormwood before lunch, to do some unspecified chore for the Headmistress, but Krystal had been tireless in scrounging up targets for me. Maybe a little *too* tireless. I rubbed my aching shoulder. "How long are you going to keep testing me? It's almost midnight."

"I'm not testing you. I'm testing materials." Krystal jerked a thumb at the sword. "We still don't know why that's the only metal that doesn't melt when subjected to your energy. What if you need to give Michaela a long blast to fully shake the demon off her? What if she wrestled the sword away? We need to find you a backup weapon, just in case." Krystal grinned as she exchanged my sword for a can. "Plus, of course, I just like watching things go boom."

"I need to stop enabling your pyromaniac tendencies." I glanced at the label as I stripped it off the can. "Lima beans?"

Krystal shrugged. "If you're going to smite a foodstuff with angelic wrath, might as well make it an evil one."

"Can't argue with that." I tossed the can into the air. As it arced up, I visualized a now-practiced mental image of demons threatening my friends, rousing my defensive instincts. In Hell-space, white flames crackled over my feathers. I caught the can as it tumbled back down. The instant my skin touched the bare metal, lightning flashed down my wings, through my hand, and into the mortal world.

"Krystal," I said a moment later when the smoke had cleared. "That was not one of your better ideas."

"Okay, I should have predicted that." Krystal combed exploded lima beans out of her hair. "But at least now we know aluminum isn't what we're looking for."

"What *I* am now looking for is a shower, thanks." I took Faith's sword back from Krystal, shoving it through my belt. "Let's call it a night."

"But I've got thirty-six more metallic alloys to try!" Krystal waved a plaque at me. "Look, I stole Ms. Worm-wood's nameplate! You must want to smite that!"

"Good *night*, Krystal."

I left her gathering up her specimens and muttering darkly to herself about lazy angels with no respect for the scientific method, and headed back toward my dormitory. The sword bumped at my hip. This late in the evening, the main school building was deserted. Nonetheless, I kept several dozen wary eyes out as I crossed the courtyard in front of the chapel, alert for any patrolling teachers. After my promise to the Headmistress to get Michaela's dag-gers, it would be beyond ironic to get expelled for carrying weaponry around the school myself.

I blew out my breath as I levered open the trapdoor that led into the old crypts. A flickering line of candles made a path down the worn stones of the ancient spiral stair-case. I hadn't forgotten Michaela's ominous threat about my "last day on earth" yesterday. At least her unknown countdown had lasted long enough to let me develop my own powers, but I had no idea if my newfound smiting prowess would be enough to counter whatever she was preparing. I shook my head as I ducked to avoid the heavy cobwebs curtaining the low, narrow passageway. I really wished I knew what she was doing.

Hang on.

What was *I* doing?

I stopped, right where the candles did, on the threshold of a pitch-black archway. Not only were the old crypts that ran under the chapel *really* not on my way home, they were out-of-bounds to all students. I had absolutely no reason to be down here.

No reason . . . except for a subliminal, bone-deep instinct that this was where I had to be. Now that I thought about it, I'd felt that sort of subconscious compulsion once before.

When Krystal had summoned me to the school.

The nagging urge grew into a roar as I tried to step back. I might as well have tried to walk through a wall. An irresistible force shoved me onward. As if in a nightmare, unable to control my own body, I felt my traitorous feet take that last, fatal step.

Into a pentagram.

"Fiat Lux!"

White fire flared around me, running down the intricate lines painted on the floor as if they'd been drawn in oil. I flung up my arms to shield my eyes, blinded by the sudden light. It wasn't just on the mortal plane—a glowing web flared around me in Hell-space as well, completely enclosing me in a prison of fire.

"You arrogant fool!" Michaela's voice rose in triumph above the roar of the flames. "I was almost convinced it couldn't be this easy, that you must have planted a fake summoning charm in your little witch's room in order to fool me." She crouched at the far side of the room, just outside the pentagram, the tips of her daggers touching the painted lines. Fire poured continuously down the blades. "But you really are using your true name! Your pride will be your undoing, Rafael Angelos. *By your name, I command and abjure thee!*"

I wrenched out my sword, answering fire blazing down the blade. I could see the demon hovering Hellward above Michaela, its many wings arched like some heraldic beast as it channeled power down to her. If I could only reach it—but the heat of my prison drove me back. Its eyes gleamed, bright as my own, as if it was mocking me. Just like Michaela had always mocked me. She was laughing at me right now. All that time I'd spent agonizing over whether I'd have to hurt her, all that time working my butt off to find an alternative way, all that effort and sweat, and she was *laughing* at me.

I was abruptly, coldly, utterly furious.

"Stop. Laughing." My rage ran down my sword, freezing the flames. Chill mist steamed from the blade as if I'd dipped it in liquid nitrogen. Heedless of the wall of fire, I thrust straight at the demon's burning core—

The pentagram shattered like a sheet of ice.

The demon shot up into Hell like a startled pigeon as I crashed through the barrier. Michaela threw herself backward, crossing her daggers to catch my sword between them—but the instant my steel connected with hers, frost ran down her blades. The daggers clattered from her numb, frozen hands. A second later, I was on her, pinning her beneath my weight.

"Back off!" I yelled at the circling demon as I fought to keep Michaela from writhing free. I spread my wings over her, in both normal space and Hellspace. Our breaths steamed in the suddenly freezing air. The demon's burning tendrils brushed my black, ice-sheeted feathers, and it recoiled as if it too had been frost-burned. "She's mine now. She's *mine*. BACK OFF!"

Hot wind buffeted me as the demon spread its wings wide in a blaze of fire. I crouched in my bubble of cold, refusing to so much as flinch, matching it eye for eye, glare for glare.

The demon beat its wings down, once, hard, and soared high into Hell. In the space of a breath, it was gone.

Michaela gasped and went limp, like a puppet with cut strings. "What have you done?" Her voice was as bereft as a lost child. *"What have you done?"*

"I've won." It was delicious to see *her* confused and helpless for once. Let *her* be alone and afraid. "I've won, and you've lost. Your little friend can't take me. If you try to summon it again, I'll kill it."

"If you can defeat her, so easily . . ." Tears ran down Michaela's face. "What *are* you?"

"More powerful than you could possibly imagine." I got to my feet, throwing her contemptuously aside, and scooped up her daggers. "I'm taking these as insurance. You give me any trouble, and I'll show them to the Head-mistress. You know she's just itching for any excuse to throw you out."

Michaela struggled to her knees. She was trembling with more than just cold. "Please," she said, turning her beautiful face up to me. "Please. Not Faith. Take me instead."

"I don't even like you," I said, annoyed that she could *still* think I was shallow enough to be bribed by a flash of cleavage. I snapped my wings shut. "It's over, Michaela. Stay the hell out of my way from now on."

Whistling jauntily, I left her alone in the dark.

Chapter 21

I deliberately slept late the next morning, for two reasons. Firstly, because I had to de-halo myself—if *halo* was the right word for the weird black aura that clung to my hair after my confrontation with Michaela—and since I couldn't face yet another binge-eating session and still had no idea what Avarice was, Sloth was my new sin of choice. Secondly, because I reckoned that I deserved to sleep in after smiting down the forces of evil.

Unfortunately, it didn't seem to have much effect on my weird anti-halo. In the end, I had to give up and jam Lydie's pink hat on my head once again.

"Hey, Raffi!" Suzanne waved at me as I strolled into the dining hall. Michaela was conspicuously absent from their table. Suzanne glanced at the empty chair, then gave me a knowing smirk. "Sooo . . . where's Michaela?"

Of course. They still thought we were dating. Aware that I had the full attention of every girl in earshot, I gave a careless shrug. "How should I know?"

"Isn't she with you?" another girl said. "She didn't come back to the dormitory last night, so we thought . . . ?"

"What, that she was with me?" I finished for her, when she didn't. "Nope." I leaned casually against the wall, examining my fingernails. "Actually," I said in tones of complete boredom, "we broke up."

I couldn't have caused more consternation if I'd jumped on the table and manifested my full angelic glory. Michaela's gang stared at me with wide eyes and dropped jaws while whispers started to spread through the tables around us.

"Well, I say we broke up," I continued, appearing oblivious to the way heads were turning all across the hall. "To be more accurate, I dumped her."

Suzanne looked like I'd hit her upside the head with my flaming sword. "You . . . what? She—you—" Apparently, my act was so outrageous it had broken her ability to form coherent sentences. Michaela's closest hangers-on were still looking stunned, but some of the less favored flunkies were starting to eye me with an air of speculative calculation. "Why?"

I pushed myself upright, straightening to my full height so that I loomed over them all. "Because," I said, speaking very clearly and loudly, "she's a manipulative, evil bitch who doesn't care about anyone except herself. No guy in his right mind sticks with *that* sort of girl." The girls shrank back as I swept them with a disdainful look. "Now, if you'll excuse me, I'm going to go join my friends."

I'd expected the buzz of gossip to start up immediately, but the entire hall was dead silent as I strode away from the popular girls. I caught a glimpse of Lydie through the crowd, frozen with her spoon halfway to her mouth, and gave her a little nod of acknowledgment; a mass intake of breath echoed through the hall, then gusted out again as I passed by her table without pausing.

In the hush, the *click* of my tray dropping onto Faith and Krystal's table sounded as loud as a gunshot.

Then the gossip started.

I winced as the wall of sound hit me, then grinned at Faith and Krystal. "Well, that was fun," I said, nonchalantly pouring milk over my cornflakes. "What are we doing today?"

Krystal found her voice first. "Are you *out of your tiny mind*? Michaela is going to go ballistic!"

"No she won't." I took a gulp of tea. "Ding-dong, the witch is dead." Faith dropped her fork, looking aghast, and I hastily added, "Not literally. But we had a show-down last night, and . . ." I tried to look modest over the rim of my mug. "Well, let's just say that she won't dare to bother us anymore."

Faith clapped her hands together in delight. Krystal looked at her spoon as if she really wanted to beat me to death with it. "You stupid idiot, you went to face her alone?" she hissed. "Without any backup? Without even *telling* us? You could have been killed! You could have—"

"Won," I interrupted. "Which I did. She was no match for me. I was right, Krystal, she *was* the one who broke into your room. She stole your charm in order to discover my true name, and used it to trap me in a pentagram. But I—"

Krystal kicked me under the table, eyes widening in warning as she stared pointedly over my shoulder. I turned to see a girl I didn't know sidling over to our table. "Oh, hi, Faith," the girl said, doing an exaggerated double take as if she'd only just noticed us sitting there.

Faith looked startled. "Hi, Julia," she said somewhat cautiously. "Can I help you with something?"

"Actually, I've been meaning to catch you," Julia said,

supremely unconvincingly. She tugged at a beaded bracelet on her wrist, holding it out to Faith. "I accidentally picked this up yesterday in Physics. It isn't yours, is it?"

"Why, yes it is." Faith's tone had turned even milder, which appeared to be the closest she got to withering sarcasm. "I took it off for the experiment. I *thought* I'd put it in the pocket of my bag."

Julia at least had the decency to go red. "I guess it fell out," she mumbled at the floor. She shoved the bracelet into Faith's hand. "Anyway, here."

Faith fingered the beads for a moment, regarding Julia coolly as the other girl fidgeted and looked anywhere except directly at her. Then Faith smiled. "Thanks, Julia," she said in her usual sweet voice. "You want to pair up in Latin later?"

From the look of vast relief on Julia's face, you'd think she'd been expecting Faith to have her hauled off in handcuffs. "Sure!" she chirped. "Catch you later."

"You do realize she stole that, right?" I said in an undertone as Julia hurried off.

"Of course." Faith slipped the bracelet over her own hand. "But only because she was trying to impress Michaela by harassing me. Julia's nice, really."

"If by 'nice' you mean 'two-faced shameless weasel,'"

Krystal muttered into her tea.

Faith frowned at her, opening her mouth, but before she could defend Julia's character, another girl plopped herself down at our table. "Hi, Faith!" she said brightly. "This seat isn't taken, is it?"

"No," Faith said, blinking. "It's . . . been a while, Kate."

"Yeah, well, you know how it is. All the schoolwork and stuff, I've been so busy I haven't had time to just chill out with friends." Kate was a much better actress than Julia. I'd seen her hanging hopefully around the edges of Michaela's outer circle. "Hey, speaking of activities, are you playing in the league this term?"

I coughed loudly. "We were having a private discussion here, you know."

"Oh . . . just a minute, Raffi?" Faith said. "Because actually, I was getting kind of worried about the league. The first game's only a week away, and I was starting to think I wasn't going to be able to play at all." She smiled hesitantly at Kate. "I was trying to get on a team, but everyone I asked said they didn't have any spaces left—"

"You can join us!" Kate interrupted. "Oh, please say you will. You're so good at the game. Remember in second year?"

"Yes, when we won the league," Faith said, brightening.

"I'd forgotten we were on the same team. You remember all that mud in the final match?"

"Heya, all." I grabbed at my bowl as Debbie slid her tray onto our increasingly crowded table. "Faith, can I sit here? I can't find a free place."

"Something wrong with the *one you came from*?" Krystal said pointedly, jerking her thumb at Debbie's recently vacated spot near Michaela's table.

"Yeah, the company," Debbie said without a hint of shame. She put her elbow on the table, leaning over to smile at me in a way that made it clear she knew perfectly well that her pose gave me a great view straight down her shirt. "Hiiiiii, Raffi. I always thought you could do much better than that cow."

"Debbie," Faith said, breaking off from her reminiscing long enough to give the newcomer a reproving glance. "It's not nice to be mean about people behind their backs."

"Sorry, Faith. I'll try to be a good girl," Debbie said, still leering at me. "Even if I find it . . . *very* difficult."

I hoped Faith noticed how nobly I was ignoring Debbie's assets. "It's getting crowded in here," I said to Faith. I could already see several other girls abandoning their places to make a beeline for our table. I lowered my voice, aware of all the curious ears surrounding us. "And I haven't had a chance to tell you about last night yet."

"We'll talk about it later," Faith murmured. "Right now, I need to catch up with my friends." Her foot nudged mine under the table. "You know why."

Oh. Faith *still* thought she needed her stupid Peer Assessment votes, of course. I looked around to share an eye roll with Krystal and discovered that she was no longer sitting next to me. "Hey, where'd Krystal go?" With my angelic eyes, I caught sight of her slipping out the door. "Faith? I think she's upset."

"I haven't got time to worry about that now, Raffi," Faith said, distracted. She turned back to her newfound best buddies. "I'm sure she's fine."

Leaving Faith to it, I wriggled my way through the converging crowds until I reached the exit. I caught up with Krystal slouching along the path outside the dining hall, kicking at stones. "Hey," I said as I jogged up to her. "What's up?"

"Nothing," Krystal muttered, hunching her shoulders. "Won't you be missed at court?"

"What do you mean?"

Krystal shrugged. "You just crowned a new queen. And now everyone's hurrying to suck up to her so they can get a shot at you." She thrust her hands deeper in her coat pockets. "I thought you'd be in there lapping up the adulation."

My spluttered protest was cut short by a tap on my elbow. "Raffi?" said a hesitant voice. "You okay?"

"Oh, hey, Lydie." I nodded to the couple of girls with her, recognizing them as her roommates and fellow sandwich conspirators. "How's it going?"

"Same as always." Lydie glanced around, then tugged me down closer to their level. "Did you really defeat Michaela?" The other girls huddled around us, gazing up at me in wide-eyed worship.

Typical. The only girls I could inspire awestruck devotion in were prepubescent.

"Yeah," I said dispiritedly. Somehow my big moment of glory wasn't turning out quite the way I'd imagined. I pulled my hat off to run my fingers through my sweaty hair, then remembered—too late—the reason why I was wearing it in the first place. None of the girls so much as batted an eyelid. I guessed my black halo had finally gone away, though I was stumped as to how I'd managed to sin in the past five minutes. "Something like that."

"Does that mean you're going to fly back to heaven?" one of the girls asked, apparently in total seriousness.

Krystal made a strangled noise that sounded a lot like a

stifled guffaw. I shot her a dirty look. "I come from Milton Keynes," I said. "Believe me, it's not heaven."

"But are you going back there now that your task is done?" Lydie asked. She and all the other girls looked up at me with anxious faces, hanging on my next words.

"My task isn't done," I said firmly. "I'm just . . . between jobs at the moment."

It was true. Faith still needed me. She just didn't know it yet. It was obviously me who had to help her seal the Hellgate, not Billy-probably-got-hooks-for-hands-Bob. Why else would I turn into such an idiot around her? We were meant to be together.

Now I had to think of some way to convince *her* of that fact.

A mass sigh of relief broke my train of thought. I glanced around to find that all the girls were now eyeing me speculatively. "What?"

"So, Raffi," Lydie said slowly, "if you're a guardian angel without anyone to guard at the moment . . . are you taking applications?"

Chapter 22

A week later, things were getting ridiculous.

"Raf, this is getting ridiculous," Krystal said, having tracked me down to my hiding place in an unused classroom. Scowling, she dropped a bundle of envelopes onto my desk. "Why are people shoving letters for you under my door? What do they think I am, your personal secretary?"

"No." I waved morosely at the notes already spread out in front of me. "They just can't fit any more under *my* door."

"What are these?" Krystal peered over my shoulder with an expression of bemusement. "Love letters?"

"Worse." I slouched lower. "Prayers."

What started as a trickle had turned into a deluge. Every time I went back to my room, I had to fight to get the door open past the letters that had been jammed under it in my absence. They were always crumpled, soggy, and smeared from being clutched in nervous, sweaty palms. Some of them were practically illegible from tearstains. Some of them were barely a few words long. Some of them went on for pages, a pent-up torrent of words spilled onto the paper.

. . . I should be grateful, at least I'm being left alone but it's been a week since anyone spoke to me and I'm so lonely. . . .

. . . I'm a fat, disgusting pig because I ate it even though I KNEW what she'd done to it, but she'd been stealing all my food for three days and I was just so hungry. . . .

. . . Everyone thinks I'm so smart and that everything comes easy to me, but really I'm exhausted from getting up at 3 a.m. to study. . . .

. . . If you're really what they say you are, then please, please help me. . . .

It was a relief to finally be able to show it to someone who was actually interested. Krystal's expression slowly changed from grumpy to gob-smacked as I explained.

"You've become guardian angel to the whole school?" she said incredulously.

"Feels like it." I raked both hands through my hair, staring glumly at the letters. "I started off just trying to help out Lydie and her friends, but somehow word got out. I had no idea there were this many unpopular girls here. Or that they had so many problems. What the hell am I supposed to do? Go around smiting the mean girls with my flaming sword?"

"You'd make a lot of us very happy if you did," Krystal said, reading over my shoulder. "But I take your point. I don't think there's much anyone can do about this stuff."

"Thanks. That actually makes me feel a little less like crap." I rubbed at my eyes. I hadn't been getting a lot of sleep recently. "I've been trying my best, but apart from using my angelsight to find stolen stuff, and occasionally freaking out bullies with unexpected eyes, I've made zero difference. Mostly the only thing I can do is listen. My suit is permanently damp from girls crying on it."

"So that's why you haven't been around." Krystal was looking at me with a weird expression I couldn't quite interpret. "I thought—never mind."

"Yeah, sorry I haven't been able to hang out. Between this and all of Faith's new friends hanging all over me, I've been completely swamped." Something occurred to me. "Hey, where have *you* been? Why don't you hang out with Faith anymore?"

Krystal's gaze slid away from mine. "Well, you know, Faith wants to regain her popularity. She doesn't need someone like me dragging her down." She shook her head. "What does she say about this?"

I blew out my breath in irritation. "Faith says that the Hellgate can't possibly be leaking anymore, now that the demon's gone and Michaela's stopped drawing penta-grams, so I should stop wasting my time worrying about the bullying and concentrate on more important things like who's wearing what and where everyone's sitting at dinner." I sighed. "Is it normal to want to throttle your true love sometimes?"

"You're asking the wrong person," Krystal said rue-fully. "I want to throttle everyone most of the time." She sighed herself. "So much for closing the Hellgate then."

"But we have to, Krystal. Look at all this." I spread my hands to indicate the pathetic scraps of prayers. "It was never like this at any of my old schools. Okay, they were boys' schools, but still. This can't be normal. Not even for girls."

"For what it's worth, I agree with you. Why do you

think I believed Faith about the Hellgate in the first place?" She was quiet for a moment, flicking through papers. "But I don't see what we can do. You can't force yourself to be in love just because you think you should."

"But that's the thing. I *am* still crazy about Faith. I mean, she drives me nuts, but whenever I'm actually with her, somehow none of that matters. But I can't even tell her how I feel. Either she's surrounded by other girls, or a teacher is dragging her away to do some chore. I can't get a minute alone with her." My shoulders slumped. "Not that it would do much good if I did. All she cares about is Billy-bastarding-Bob and his stupid text messages."

Krystal's forehead furrowed in thought. "Maybe if I helped you write a poem or—" She broke off as I groaned and thumped my head on the desk. "Hey, it was only an idea."

"A good one, actually, and I'll take you up on it later. But at the moment, angel duty calls." I stood, jerking a thumb at the ceiling. "Someone's crying in one of the bathrooms again."

Krystal's eyebrows rose. "Raf, there's *always* someone crying in the bathrooms."

"Well, there shouldn't be. I'm gonna go check it out." I was already gathering up my stuff. "Can you cover for me with Ms. Oleander if I don't make it to Biology in time?"

"Always asking for favors." Despite her words, Krystal smiled. She gave me a clumsy, friendly shove. "I'll think of an excuse. You go be a hero."

I took the stairs two at a time. Ms. Oleander, usually good-natured, had been getting a bit snappish with me recently, so I didn't want to be *too* late to her class. Hopefully, it wouldn't take long to console the sobbing girl. From my experience over the past week, I knew that mostly all the social outcasts wanted was to know that they weren't alone.

Then again, maybe this particular girl didn't need me, because by the time I reached the second floor, another girl had already joined her in the bathroom. I hesitated, focusing my angelsight on them, trying to work out if I should just leave them to it . . . and realized exactly who it was crying her eyes out in there.

Michaela.

I hadn't seen her at all lately, apart from in our shared classes. Even there she now sat alone at the back and kept her head down, never speaking to anyone. No one spoke to her either. The school rumor mill was still buzzing with stories of how Michaela had totally flipped and driven all her former friends away with unprovoked, vicious insults.

I'd kept silent through all the speculation, hiding my smug grin.

Yet here was Suzanne, rubbing her back and trying to calm her hiccuping sobs. Was Michaela's defeated behavior just an act? Was she secretly rallying her forces? Keeping watch in all directions to make sure no teachers were approaching, I tiptoed to the bathroom door and put my ear against it.

"—don't care," Suzanne was saying. "Put on a big, fake smile and beg that airhead Faith to let me join her Cult of Nice? As *if*. You're worth ten of her."

Michaela pressed her palms against her eyes. "I told you, I can't give you anything. Not anymore. Just go away and leave me alone."

"What, you think I only hung out with you for your money? Stupid cow. My mum could probably *buy* your family." Suzanne mock-punched Michaela's slumped shoulder. "I like you because you don't give a shit about anyone. It's not like you to be so soggy. So what if your boyfriend dumped you? He's a moron."

Thanks, Suzanne.

"He's dangerous," Michaela said in a low voice. "Stay away from him."

"Raffi?" Suzanne sounded bemused. She scrutinized

Michaela in concern. "If he's slapped you around, then I'll beat him up myself. Anyway, you don't need to worry about me panting after him like the rest of those idiots. He may be pretty, but I'm not going to suck up to that bimbo Faith just to get near him." She handed Michaela a wad of tissues. "Now stop sniveling and put your game face on. You gonna let that idiot Faith swan around like she owns the place? You gonna let her *win*? Come on. You can still take her out. I know you can."

Michaela took a deep breath, straightening. She stared at her own reflection. Under her drying tears, her face had gone cold and hard. Her black eyes were as blank as a shark's. "Yes," she said. "I can."

Chapter 23

"Loosen up, Raffi." Faith bounced on her toes, which—given that she was wearing a skintight cropped running vest and very, *very* brief shorts—was tremendously unhelpful in loosening any part of me. "Ms. Hellebore always keeps a close eye on the league games. It would be silly for Michaela to try anything this afternoon."

She had a point, but not even the watchful, looming presence of Ms. Hellebore could ease the knot of tension between my shoulder blades. "I still wish you'd let me hand those knives in to your mother yesterday. I'd feel a lot better with Michaela locked up and awaiting expulsion."

"I don't want Michaela expelled. I want to redeem her. I'm sure once she's recovered from the trauma of being possessed, she'll let me become her friend—oh, look,

239

there's our team! Kate, Debbie, over here!"

A small group of girls loped toward us, all wearing the same looks of eager anticipation as Faith herself. They did a bit of a double take when they saw me standing next to her. "Hi, Raffi," Kate said, sounding uncertain. "Are you playing in the league this term, then?"

"Yeah, last-minute decision." Normally, there'd be no way I'd voluntarily give up my precious free time for some dumb sports league, but until I knew what Michaela was up to, I wasn't leaving Faith unguarded for even a second. Still, at least this "voluntary extracurricular activity" was worth a lot of extra credits. The way my grades were going, I needed them. Apparently, so did a lot of other people, as practically the entire year group had gathered on the playing field. I scanned the crowd. "Hey, where's Krystal?"

"Krystal Moon?" said a girl I didn't know, wrinkling her nose as if I'd asked for the location of the nearest sewer. "Who knows? Or cares?"

"She never participates in the league," Faith said to me. "It's pretty impossible to compete without a solid team behind you."

"Ooh, that reminds me!" Debbie tore herself away from her rapt contemplation of my biceps to look eagerly around at everyone. "Guess who *is* competing alone this year?"

"Michaela," I said with utter certainty.

Debbie looked a bit disappointed at such a flat reception to her juicy piece of gossip. "Oh. You heard?"

"Lucky guess." I caught Faith's eye. "I told you it was a good idea for me to come and watch your back."

"Wait, you want to join *our* team?" Kate said. All the girls exchanged rather dubious glances.

"Trust me, Raffi will be brilliant," Faith said, with touching if totally misplaced confidence in my innate masculine prowess. "With him on our side, we'll definitely win. Right, Raffi?"

"Er," I said. Every memory of being picked last for teams came flooding back. "I'll—do my best." It wouldn't be so bad, I told myself. This was a girls' school, after all. I probably had way more experience at team sports than any of them, no matter that said experience mainly consisted of being ritually humiliated by other guys. "So, uh, what are we actually playing—"

An earsplitting whistle cut me off. "Ladies and gentleman!" thundered the deep voice of Ms. Hellebore from the other end of the crowded field, making us all wince at the volume. Just as well she didn't have a megaphone.

"Attention, please! The first game is about to begin. Let us all take a moment to review the rules." She lifted her hand above her head, one finger extended. "What is the first rule?"

"NO RULES!" all the girls yelled back at her.

I blinked.

Ms. Hellebore unfolded another finger. "What is the second rule?"

"NO MERCY!"

I . . . was starting to get a bad feeling about this.

"What is the third rule?"

"NO PRISONERS!"

Ms. Hellebore clapped her hands together like a crack of thunder. "The territory consists of the south side of the school grounds! The game lasts until sunset, and the last team standing takes all. Remember, there are no prizes for second place!" She waved at a stack of boxes behind her. "Come collect your starting equipment and then get your butts in gear! MOVE OUT!"

Girls converged on Ms. Hellebore as if it was the opening day of Christmas sales. Faith too made a beeline for the teacher. Fighting my way through the maddened crowd, I caught up with her as she rummaged through a crate. "What sort of game *is* this?" I yelled into her ear.

Faith turned, an utterly gleeful grin on her delicate face and a very large gun clutched in her hands. "The name of the game," she said, handing me the weapon, "is War."

--- ✗ ---

Scantily clad girls, mud, and me.

Throwing paintball guns into the mix just made it even more of a fantasy scenario. I was certain that most guys would have chewed off their own right arm for the chance to be where I was. At the moment, I would gladly have traded my own right arm *not* to be where I was. If I still had a right arm. I wasn't quite certain on that point.

"What the hell are those pellets made out of, lead?" I snarled under my breath, clutching at my shoulder. "That bloody hurt!"

"Well, of course it did," Debbie hissed back at me. "How else would you know if you'd been hit? Shut up, you'll give away our position!"

"Doesn't matter. Kate just head-shot one, Faith took out the other, and the last one's run off," I said absently, still trying to shake the numbness out of my hand. "And Faith's on her way back."

Sure enough, a second later, Faith slithered into our

243

hiding space under a fallen tree. "Did they get Raffi?" she said anxiously.

"Just winged him." Debbie nodded at the bright orange dye splattered down my bruised arm. "He's still in the game. Thank God." She gave me a new sort of appreciative look, one that said I had more qualities than merely being decorative. "You were right, he is a natural. I swear the dude has eyes in the back of his head or something."

"Something like that," Faith murmured. "Debbie, Kate needs backup on point. We'll take rear guard. Is it clear, Raffi?"

"Yep." My angelsight did give me a huge advantage in this situation, although it still wasn't much use when, as had just happened, *three* snipers decided to converge on your location. I scanned the patch of woods ahead. "Circle around. There's a girl hiding in the ruins just beyond Kate. She's alone."

Not questioning my knowledge, Debbie wriggled out from the ditch, grinning like a wolf. "I'm gonna slaughter her. Give me five, then follow." She loped off, calling back over her shoulder, "We're totally taking the trophy this term!"

"This is so great!" Faith was practically glowing with happiness through her generous coating of mud. "Thanks to you, we're easily going to win."

"Can't be soon enough. How much longer have we got?" I glanced at my watch. "We've only been out here an *hour?*" I groaned, thumping my forehead down onto the earth in despair.

Faith looked at me in surprise. "Aren't you having fun?"

"I'm cold and dirty and bloody terrified! No, I am not having fun!" With a heroic effort, I managed to get my emotions back under control before I accidentally channeled heavenly fire down the metal barrel of my paintball gun. "Sorry," I muttered. "I know it's just a game. But it's too realistic. And Michaela is still out here somewhere—we've got to move," I interrupted myself, angelsight showing me a whole crowd engaged in a running battle that was headed this way at speed. I slid out from under the trunk, then turned to offer Faith a hand. "Anyway, seeing even pretend guns being aimed at you gives me heart failure."

Faith's expression softened. "That's really sweet," she said, taking my hand. I'd been frozen to the bone, but the mere touch of her skin on mine warmed me to the core. "*You're* really sweet, Raffi." She caught her foot on a root as she scrambled up; I grabbed her other arm to steady her, and we ended up nearly toe to toe. For a long moment, we looked into each other's eyes.

Faith let out a forced laugh. "Oh, I'm so clumsy," she gabbled, a pink flush rising in her cheeks as she stumbled back. "I'm sure I must be holding you back. Maybe it would be better if we split up. I'll—I'll just head this way, okay?" She practically sprinted away from me.

Straight into the line of Michaela's gun.

The world congealed around me in one moment of pure horror that stretched into eternity. A split second ago, I'd only had eyes for Faith; now, too late, every tiny detail of our surroundings hit me like an arrow. Faith, far out of my reach across the clearing, facing the wrong way to see the threat. Michaela, out of breath, tears streaking her cheeks. Her rifle, pointed at Faith's heart, rock steady. The bullet inside, real.

Michaela's finger tightened on the trigger.

I threw myself forward—not with my legs, but my wings. One powerful beat lifted me out of the world entirely. For the barest instant, I arced through Hell, my human eyes blurring with impossible colors—and then I crashed back down into the mortal world, landing between Faith and Michaela. The *bang* of displaced air caused by my reappearance sounded simultaneously with the *crack* of the gun. I had only time for one last thought—*Oh man, angels better be bulletproof—*

Chapter 24

As it turned out, we weren't.

It hurt. A lot. Somewhere very far away, there was a great deal of running and shouting going on, but I was more interested in blinking at the sky at the moment. Something was wrong with my eyes; my normal vision was going dark around the edges, while angelsight seemed to be getting brighter and brighter.

"If you die, Mr. Angelos, I shall be greatly inconvenienced." Where had the Headmistress come from? Her hand felt like a cement block on my chest, stopping me from flying away. Even though her fingers were flat against my skin, I had the weirdest feeling that they were somehow under my ribs, holding me together. "Kindly refrain from doing so."

There was a point of light, high above her head, like

a star hung too low. The Headmistress looked up as if she could see it too. For the briefest instant, her impassive expression cracked, revealing—regret? Welcome? Or maybe just recognition . . .

"Yes," the Headmistress said. Not to me. "Come."

Wings, a storm of wings, hurtling down out of the swirling sky. They spread wide, revealing a burning core of fire studded with eyes like a million suns. The Headmistress drew back her hand, making way for the wings, and pain washed over me. I was going to drown in it—

The brilliant feathers settled over me soft as snowfall, and I lost myself in blissful, blank whiteness.

Chapter 25

"Raf, you look *awful*," were Krystal's first words to me on my return, two weeks later. Her note had asked me to meet her outside the old shrine at midnight, but now that I was actually here she looked like she wanted to pick me up and carry me back to bed. "Are you sure you're fit to be back at school?"

"Oh, don't you start too." Having arrived late in the evening, the only people I'd seen so far had been teachers, and all of them had told me I should leave immediately. I was sure the fussing was meant well, but I was starting to feel positively unwelcome. "Believe me, I would have liked to stay in my nice, comfy, completely Hellgate-less hospital room." I scowled. "Damn Dantes. If it wasn't for them, I'd still be enjoying my holiday."

The first thing I'd seen when I'd woken up in the

hospital was a very large ornamental cactus squatting on my bedside table. The card prominently displayed on the side had read: *With sympathies on your unfortunate accident. The Headmistress.* "Accident" had been underlined. The cactus had been extremely spiky. I'd gotten the message.

Problem was, since the official story was that Michaela's paintball gun had suffered a catastrophic and mysterious malfunction—and that there was thus no need for a lengthy and expensive investigation into the school's health and safety policies—the Dantes were fighting tooth and nail to prevent any blame from being assigned to her. They were also insisting they wouldn't pay a penny of the promised bursary money if Michaela was expelled. And apparently, the Headmistress found that of greater concern than the fact that I'd been shot in the chest. Thanks, Headmistress.

Which reminded me . . . "Thanks for the updates, by the way." Krystal had sent me a letter every day, along with a bundle of homework assignments. I'd pored over the former and ignored the latter. "Especially the bits about Lydie and my other girls." Without even a half-assed angel around to watch out for them, they'd been getting bullied worse than ever. "That certainly motivated me to get better fast."

Krystal bit her lip. "I didn't mean to make you stagger up from your sickbed and race back here. I mean, you're hardly fit to fight demons. You really do look like death."

"I have to admit, I could have done without late-night hikes." I adjusted the bulky bandages wrapping my torso under my shirt. Getting shot point-blank in the chest was no joke. "Don't get me wrong, I'm really glad to see you but couldn't this have waited until the morning?"

"*I* think it could have," Krystal said sourly. "But I'm not Faith. Come on. She wants to talk to you. Urgently."

My stomach lurched sideways. "Is she okay?" Krystal had already set off into the dark woods, her flashlight beam bobbing. I put a hand on the sword thrust through my belt to stop it from tripping me as I hurried after her. "Did things go downhill for her again while I was gone?"

"No, it's okay, she's fine. Still queen bee and all." Krystal shot me an odd look over her shoulder. "Didn't she keep in touch with you?"

"Not really. Sent me a nice card, though." I was quiet for a long moment. "You know what the weird thing is?"

"Apart from the fact that apparently you're not offended that she thinks your taking a bullet for her is only worth a single stamp?" Krystal muttered. She stomped through the dry leaves with rather more force than necessary.

"Actually, that's it exactly." I shook my head. "I didn't mind that she didn't write. I didn't . . . I didn't *want* her to write. I didn't miss her. I missed *you*." I nearly ran into her as she stopped dead. "Uh, and Lydie and everyone too, of course," I added quickly, grinning to cover the sudden awkward moment. "Hell, I even started to miss Ms. Wormwood."

Krystal snorted but started walking again. "Okay, now I know you must have been on some serious drugs."

"Felt more like I was coming off a drug. Like I'd been addicted to Faith and had kicked the habit. That can't be right, can it? Aren't you supposed to want to be with your true love?"

"When your true love is Faith, I can kind of see why absence might make the heart grow fonder," Krystal said. She punched me on the arm and looked mortified when I winced. "Sorry, I forgot. Seriously, Raf, don't worry about what love is 'supposed' to be like. Who says it has to be one particular way or it doesn't count? Only you can know what's right for you."

"That's the thing," I said very quietly. "Even though I *have* to be in love with Faith in order to seal the Hellgate . . . I don't know if I really am. While I was away from her, all the feelings I thought I had just faded, like a dream." I sighed. "Maybe Faith has the right idea after all. Maybe she should stick with Billy-Bob. Maybe I'm not the one for her."

"Maybe," Krystal echoed softly. She cleared her throat, reverting to her much more usual brusque voice. "In which case, I'll tell you what Faith has also got." She stepped aside, revealing a small clearing in the woods. "Absolutely *terrible* timing."

Dozens of small candles made a firefly circle in the short-cropped grass. Faith knelt in the center, head bowed as if in prayer. White petals were scattered around her. She rose at our arrival, her long, white dress flowing like water over her slim body. Her hair was braided away from her face, revealing her solemn expression.

The sight of her felt like a fishhook through my heart. Or a hole in my head. I could practically feel my brain dribbling out, along with all my doubts. "Hi," I blurted out.

"Hello," Faith said softly without smiling. She glanced at Krystal. "Thank you for bringing him."

Krystal glared at the petal-strewn lawn. "Your mother is going to be royally pissed about those flowers."

"I said *thank you*, Krystal." When Krystal continued to

fidget without actually retreating, Faith added with a hint of steel, "It's late and you must be tired. You should go to bed."

"*I'm* not the one with a chest wound," Krystal muttered. "Raf . . ." She looked at me, and her mouth twisted. She turned abruptly, heading into the woods without looking back. "Don't be stupid." I wasn't quite certain whether she was talking to herself or me.

That left me, Faith, and the awkward silence.

Faith took one of the flowers from her braided hair, holding it out to me. "I wanted to thank you for saving my life."

"Uh." I stumbled on my way into the circle of candles, nearly setting fire to my own trousers, and took the flower from her. What was I supposed to do with it? Stick it in my own hair? I settled for wedging it through my belt, next to the sword. "Thanks. For the thanks."

Faith looked down at her bare feet. "Are you mad at me?"

"What? No!" My whole body yearned toward her as if I was a plant reaching for the sun. "Why would I be?"

"For the way I've treated you." Faith took a deep breath, straightening her spine like someone about to charge into battle. Her blue eyes met mine steadily. "For the way I've kept pushing you away, refusing to accept what you've always known."

"Right." My mind struggled to work in the face of her beauty. "Er. What would that be, again?"

"That it's you." I stood frozen as she moved closer, until I could feel the heat of her body all along my own, only inches away. "You're the one, Raffi. You would have died for me. If that's not true love, what is?"

It was the hardest thing I'd ever done, but I put my hand on her shoulder, stopping her. "Faith." I gently pushed her back a little. "That's what I feel for *you*. It's okay if you don't return it."

"But I do." Faith put her own hand over mine. "I've always felt drawn to you, Raffi. I buried it because I thought it was just attraction. I hated myself for being shallow, telling myself that I had to be loyal to Billy-Bob. But everything that's happened, everything you've done for me . . . it's fate. It has to be fate. I don't have to wait for the Ball to meet my soul mate. He's here now." Her free hand found the back of my neck. "Close the Hellgate with me."

Weirdest euphemism *ever*. My stomach roiled with instant performance anxiety. All I could think about as she pulled me down to her exultant upturned face was whether she was about to get the disappointment of her life, and if she'd hate me if she did, and . . . and . . .

And then our lips met, and everything went white.

Literally.

With a strangled yell, I flung myself backward, breaking the kiss. The fire surrounding Faith didn't die down. It outlined her head in curling, eye-searing flames. Panicking, I reached for her, but had to jerk my own hand back from the heat. "Faith!"

Faith's eyes opened slowly. Her expression was as serene and remote as the moon. Her hair lashed about her head, whipped by an invisible wind. "Rafael," she whispered.

With a noise like tearing silk, her wings unfolded.

Chapter 26

I stared at Faith, newly revealed in all her heavenly glory, and could only think of one thing to say. "Oh . . . *shit*."

It was an STD. I'd given Faith a bad case of angel.

Faith blinked, her eyes dimming back to their usual clear blue. The flames wreathing her sank back into her skin, although her halo still outlined her head. "Wow," she said, sounding a bit dazed. "I didn't think it would feel like that." Anxiety crossed her face as she stared around at the unchanged night. "Did it work? Is anything different?"

Mutely, I pointed at the wings springing from her back, flexing a little with every breath she took.

Puzzled, Faith looked over her own shoulder—and froze. "Oh," she said again, just the tiniest squeak of air. "Oh my."

"I'm really sorry!" I gabbled as Faith extended one wing to stare at the glowing pinions. "I didn't know it was contagious! I'm so, so sorry!"

"I'm an angel?" Faith said wonderingly. She turned in a circle, as if she could somehow inspect her own back. "This explains everything! My father must have been an angel in disguise, just like your mother. That's why we're so drawn to each other—we're alike! Krystal was right, it's our combined powers that can close the Hellgate!" She flung herself into my arms. "Oh, Raffi! It's all part of a divine plan!"

"You're okay with this? You don't mind?" I said anxiously. The fact that she was squeezing me hard enough to crack a rib seemed like a good—if painful—sign, but I wasn't sure she'd fully appreciated the potential drawbacks yet. "I mean, you might get the eyes. I'm really sorry if you get the eyes."

"I *want* the eyes," Faith said, muffled by the way she had her face buried in my chest. Her wings arched above our heads. "I want everything! I want to smite evil! I want to fly! I want—"

There was no warning. One moment she was in my arms, the next I was thrown backward by an icy tentacle. I hit a tree trunk hard, the impact jarring my half-healed wound. Pain made the whole world tip sideways and go black.

"Stay away!" Faith was shouting. I blinked up at her wings, spread protectively over me. She'd grabbed the sword from my belt, holding it ready in a practiced, expert grip. "I'm warning you. I know what I am now! You can't touch us, Michaela!"

"Michaela?" A low, cold chuckle twisted around us like a snake. "Whatever gave you that idea, my pet?"

The figure stepped into the circle of light cast by our combined halos . . . but darkness still clung to her, as if she bent and broke our angelic radiance. Through that shadowy aura, her hair gleamed as red as freshly spilled blood.

"Ms. Wormwood?" Faith said uncertainly. The point of her sword wavered.

"Hello, pets," said the teacher. The endearment no longer sounded affectionate, but a literal description of what we were to her. There was something wrong about the way she moved, as if she was a badly controlled puppet. She didn't quite make contact with the ground as she stalked jerkily toward us. She seemed to have to fight against the brightness of our combined light as if against a strong gale. "I see you've managed to make a mess of everything as usual, Raffi. We should have ripped your heart out the day you arrived."

Black tentacles unfolded from thin air around her.

Faith gasped, whipping the sword around to slice at the reaching limbs. They didn't dodge—middle sections just *disappeared*, the blade whistling through thin air. She danced back, nearly tripping over me. "Raffi, I don't know how to make it flame!"

"Give it here!" The pain had receded enough to let me struggle upright again. I snatched the sword from Faith—but even as my fingers closed around it, Ms. Wormwood hissed, a tentacle lashing out to wrap around the tip of the blade. The suddenly frost-covered metal ripped a layer of skin off my palm as she yanked it out of my hand.

"You're not the only one who moves in mysterious ways, Raffi," Ms. Wormwood said, flicking the sword away. It stuck point-first into the ground behind the possessed teacher, well out of reach. "And now, it's time for you to die."

"Faith, fly!" Even as her mouth opened in protest, I shoved her away from me. "Just don't think about it, you can do it!"

Faith leaped into the air and hovered there for a second,

looking rather startled. Before I could even attempt to spread my own wings to follow, icy bands clamped them shut. "Not this time, Raffi," Ms. Wormwood snarled. Her tentacles wrapped around me like an octopus embracing its prey, winding through both the normal world and Hell-space. Their chill sapped what little strength I'd managed to regain. I was frozen, even my halo dimming, unable to resist at all as Ms. Wormwood hauled my limp body toward her. "You aren't getting away from me again."

"Raffi!" Faith dove, her halo blazing around her head with the force of her fury. "Let him GO!"

"No, don't—!" I was too late. Without angelic vision, Faith couldn't even see Ms. Wormwood's tentacles, let alone avoid them. A contemptuous slap from one of them knocked her spinning out of the sky. She hit a tree with a heart-stopping *crack*.

Ms. Wormwood seemed to gain strength, her movements once again smooth. She even smiled her usual flirty, let's-all-be-best-friends smile as her tentacles dumped first me, then Faith at her feet. "At least there's one good thing to come out of all this mess," she said in satisfaction. "I get to kill someone. It's been too long." She tapped her finger against her chin. "But do I dare . . . oh, why not.

The Prince will be furious, but *she* can take the blame. She's the one in charge of this debacle." She hauled Faith's limp form up, one hand around her neck. "And I am sick of your stupid, sappy love letters."

"Don't!" I croaked, grabbing at Ms. Wormwood's boots. "Please!" I scrabbled to think of something to offer her. "I'll be your—your willing sex slave! Anything! Just let Faith go!"

"Sex slave?" Ms. Wormwood dropped Faith like hot potato. *"Sex slave?"* She stared at me for a moment as if unable to believe her own ears . . . and then burst out laughing.

Okay, that was adding insult to injury.

Still chuckling, Ms. Wormwood lifted me up effortlessly with one tentacle. "Little boy," she crooned as I dangled, feet kicking. "I'm a succubus. I've done things your sweaty mind can't even imagine. And you actually think I want *you*? Believe me, you were just a job—if I hadn't been ordered to distract you from the precious princess here, I would never have tried to seduce you. Not that it worked. You're the most oblivious, obdurate male I've ever had the misfortune to encounter." She pursed her lips. Her fingers tightened around my neck. "Actually, you spoiled my perfect record. For that, I think I'll kill you first."

I choked, clawing desperately at Ms. Wormwood's iron grip. Her vicious, delighted eyes filled my vision. "Struggle, Raffi," she purred. "Extend the agony. No one's coming to rescue you this time."

"Sancte Michael Archangele, defende nos in proelio!"

Water hit me in the back of the head. It splashed onto Ms. Wormwood too, and she screeched like a thousand nails running down a blackboard, flinging me aside. For a second, all I could do was wheeze, both my hands clutching at my bruised throat.

"Contra nequitiam et insidias diaboli esto praesidium," continued the strident voice. The veil of black stars clouding my vision finally cleared, just in time for me to dodge out of the way as Ms. Wormwood stumbled back. *"Imperet illi Deus, supplices deprecamur!"*

Next to me, Faith's eyes fluttered open. "Michaela?" she said dazedly, looking around in confusion.

Michaela didn't spare either of us so much as a glance. She had an empty plastic bottle in one hand, with a tiny amount of liquid left sloshing at the bottom. Ms. Wormwood eyed it, and her wary expression twisted into a sneer.

"Really, Dante? Taking me on with just a cupful of holy water? After all your caution?" Ms. Wormwood's tentacles darted at Michaela, who twisted with perfectly timed precision to avoid them. The two circled each other like fighting cats, Michaela always keeping her own body between the demon and Faith. "You can't bind me. You don't know my name. You don't have a circle. You don't even have your sacred weapon. You have nothing."

"I have the only thing I need." Michaela's voice was rock steady. She never took her eyes off the demon. "Faith."

"Also this," I added. *"Michaela, catch!"*

I flung her the sword. Ms. Wormwood grabbed at it, but Michaela was faster. She snatched the spinning sword out of midair, twisting to redirect the momentum. In one smooth, fluid movement, she drove the blade straight through Ms. Wormwood's chest.

The demon spat blood into Michaela's face. "That all you've got?" she said, grinning.

Michaela's mouth curved in an answering feral smile. "Not quite," she said—and then, speaking so fast the syllables all ran together, *"Princeps militiae Caelestis, Satanam aliosque spiritus malignos qui ad perditionem animarum pervagantur in mundo divina virtute in infernum detrude* and for God's sake don't get in the way, Rafael, *Amen!"*

Michaela's demon plummeted out of the Hell-sky like an air strike. I flung myself flat, throwing a wing over Faith to press her down too, as it screamed over us in a white-hot blaze, invisible to normal eyes but blinding my angelsight. A bolt of lightning leaped from the burning feathers, haloing Michaela and running down the blade still embedded in Ms. Wormwood's chest.

She blew apart into ash.

Dead demon was probably not a healthy thing to inhale, but none of us had much choice about it. We all spent a moment coughing before the cloud started to settle. "Thank you," Faith said, waving a hand in front of her face. "I think. What on earth just happened?"

Michaela was bent double, leaning on the sword as she panted for breath. I answered for her. "Her demon destroyed Ms. Wormwood."

"My *what*?" Michaela wheezed. She straightened, holding the sword so that the blade pointed directly at my heart.

"Sorry!" I held up my hands in surrender. "Sorry to you too," I said to the apparently-not-a-demon, who was now hovering in the Hell-sky above Michaela's head and looking, if a huge burning ball of eyes and wings could be said to have an expression, mortally offended. "Uh, no insult intended. I just don't know the politically correct term for whatever the hell that thing is."

"Not hell," Michaela said icily. "Heaven." She lowered the point of the sword. "And the correct term is *guardian angel*."

Chapter 27

Let me get this straight." Krystal pushed her glasses farther up her nose, squinting through them at Michaela. She'd been in bed when I'd turned up at her window and flown her to my room with a quick, garbled explanation. She was still blinking myopically and looking as if she suspected this was all a dream. "You're a demon hunter?"

"I'm from the Order of Dante." Michaela sat next to Faith on my bed, her daggers resting in her lap. From the way she kept fingering them as she eyed me, I was beginning to regret giving them back to her. Her guardian angel hovered on motionless wings above her in Heaven, its burning eyes half-lidded and lazy. "We're dedicated to seeking out and destroying any demons that manage to escape from Hell."

"Well, you guys suck." I gestured at my still-glowing head. I was steadily munching through chocolate bars as we talked, but I hadn't yet been sufficiently gluttonous to put out my halo. "How could you mistake me for a demon?"

"You turned up out of nowhere and started acting suspicious!" Michaela retorted hotly, her fists closing on her daggers. "And you reacted to my warding pentagrams. It was only when you managed to defeat my guardian angel that I started to suspect you weren't just a demon possessing a human body. But I never dreamed what you really were. Nephilim—half-breeds—are incredibly rare." She gestured from me to Faith. "To encounter two at once is unthinkable."

"You knew I was a nephil too. Even if you suspected Raffi was an agent of Hell, you can't have thought *I* was!" For once, Faith was actually, genuinely, completely pissed off. Her own halo flickered and died as she glared at Michaela, her hands balling into fists. "I wondered how the rumors about me and my father got started. It was you, wasn't it? You made everyone think I was crazy, when you *knew* I wasn't. You made my life a living hell for an entire year!"

Michaela's air of cool superiority slipped a little. She

268

avoided Faith's eyes. "I'm sorry. But I had to drive you away from here, or at the very least stop you from meeting your boyfriend at the Ball." She took a deep breath. "You're right, I do know your father's plan for you. Gabriel Dante told the Order everything in his letter."

"Who's Gabriel Dante?" I asked, my voice slightly muffled by caramel.

"Faith's father." Michaela put one of her daggers down next to Faith's sword, which was resting between them on the bed. The resemblance between the two weapons was obvious. "Gabe Jones used to be Gabriel Dante. He was expelled from the Order for heresy. He thought he'd discovered a way to close Hellgates."

"He did." Faith straightened up, lifting her chin proudly. "I've read his notebooks. He meant for me to close one at the Ball, with my one true love."

"I know what he intended for you," Michaela said grimly. "And it had nothing to do with the Ball or ridiculous notions about love. You see, we Danteans learn how to channel a tiny fraction of our guardian angel's light in order to banish demonic darkness. But Hellgates are a deeper and darker darkness than we can illuminate, flawed mortal mirrors that we are. Gabriel thought nephilim would be able to channel an angel's *full* power."

"Can we?" I asked. "Would that really work to close the Hellgate?"

"Possibly." Her mouth twisted. "If you didn't mind dying to do it. Nobody, human or otherwise, could withstand that much power."

Faith went white. "No. My dad would never have meant to hurt me. If he thought I could do it—"

"He was wrong, Faith." Michaela shook her head. "In order to channel an angel you have to become like them. Perfectly selfless, acting only for the greater good. We Danteans train for *years* to be able to attain that pure, egoless state of mind, and it's dangerous even for us. An untrained, unprepared person, full of ordinary doubts and sins . . . at the very best, you'd have been crippled for life, terribly burned. That's why Gabriel couldn't persuade an angel to come help him, no matter how hard he prayed. They aren't like demons, who'll happily trick people into binding with them. No angel would ever channel light through someone who hadn't accepted the link willingly, in full knowledge of the risks."

"If Faith's dad was kicked out of your club, why'd he send you a message about where he was?" Krystal asked. "He must have known you guys would try to stop him."

"Because, as I said, he couldn't summon an angel

himself. He was growing desperate. He knew that even if we didn't help him in his heretical scheme, we'd at least make sure Faith was safe." Michaela's hands clenched on her daggers. "You see, the forces of Hell have their own plans for you, Faith. Plans that come to fruition at the Masked Ball."

"Plans?" Faith said blankly. "What do you mean?"

"You're being groomed to accept demonic possession," Michaela said flatly. "And not for just any demon. A Demon Prince, one of the seven Lords of Hell, so powerful that mere mortal flesh would be destroyed by its touch. Demon Princes can only possess nephilim. That's why Hell needs you."

Faith jerked back. "I would never agree to bind to a demon!"

"Yes, you would. Willingly." Michaela's voice softened. She shifted position, leaning toward her. "There's nobody at Winchester called Billy-Bob, Faith. We checked."

"But . . . he texts me. All the time. We've been friends for years."

"You've been communicating with a demon already here on Earth, in possession of a mortal body. It's been acting as the Prince's harbinger, preparing the way for his arrival. It would have drawn a pentagram for him at the

Ball, so that he could appear as a beautiful young man for you. And you, expecting to meet your true love, would have immediately pledged your eternal devotion to him." Michaela stopped, swallowing. "You wouldn't have been giving your heart away at the Ball. You'd have been giving away your soul. And setting unimaginable evil loose on the world." Michaela's self-possession cracked for a moment, betraying the shame and fear underneath that cold mask. "I was ordered to stop that from happening, at any cost. Even if I had to kill you to do it."

"For God's sake!" Krystal yelled in exasperation, as Faith looked as if Michaela had just shot her through the heart then and there. "Drama queen much, Michaela? Why did you grab a gun when you could have just opened your mouth? Why didn't you *tell* us any of this stuff earlier?"

"Because I didn't dare. Not even Gabriel dared to tell Faith the whole truth." Michaela's black eyes were fixed on Faith, steadily. "Faith, do you know what nephilim are?"

"Of course," Faith said, brow furrowing. "We're half angel."

Michaela let out a bark of startled laughter. "Don't be absurd."

"What? *My* mum was definitely an angel." I reached for another chocolate bar. "Don't look so skeptical, Micheala. If you'd ever met her, you'd have seen straightaway how amazing she was. Hell, maybe you did meet her. She died rescuing kids from your old orphanage."

"The Circle of Trust," Michaela whispered, going very still. "So that's how you knew that name. But you said you knew the truth about that place."

Something about her tone made me stop in midbite. "What truth?"

"The Circle of Trust orphanage was a Hellgate." Her face was absolutely expressionless. "Controlled, as they always are, by a single powerful demon. It would occasionally summon one of its brethren through, when it managed to groom a child to accept demonic possession. The embodied demons would go out into the world, but had to return periodically to pay a tithe to the master of the Hellgate." There was no emotion at all in her voice. She might as well have been reciting ancient history or the weather. "Father Dante himself led the cleansing mission. *He* rescued me from that hellhole. He and his guardian angel destroyed all the demons with holy fire."

There was a long, long silence.

Krystal's hand crept into mine. "It doesn't matter," she

said angrily. Her fingers tightened, a sole point of warmth against my blank, cold numbness. "I don't care what you say about Raf's mother. *He's* not evil."

"And anyway," Faith said, "even if Raffi's mother was a demon, that has nothing to do with me."

"Yes it does," Michaela said. "Faith, angels don't possess people like demons do. They're too pure, too powerful. They can't have children." Her face was set and grim. "The Headmistress is a demon."

Chapter 28

"H ey, Raffi!" Debbie plunked her dinner tray down next to mine uninvited. She glanced at the empty chair on my other side. "Why's Faith been avoiding you all day? I thought she'd be excited to see you again. Have you two had a fight or something?"

"Something." I moodily stirred my bowl of lentil sludge, elbow on the table and my head propped on my hand. My eyes stayed fixed on the teachers' table, just in case the Headmistress conveniently decided to reveal her true nature. Unfortunately, at the moment, she was just demonically eating some peas. "We had a disagreement. About our families."

"Oooh. That's tough." She ran her tongue over her top lip. "Well, you know, if you're not chasing around after her anymore . . ."

"I am." I sighed, dropping my spoon into my now cold soup with a *clink*. "I mean, I have to. It's kind of a higher calling."

"Pity," Debbie said, though her expression softened as if I'd just produced a fluffy kitten out of my jacket. She nudged me with her elbow. "Well, don't wait too long to make up with her, 'kay? The lists go up tomorrow!"

"Lists?"

"You know, for picking your partner for the Ball." Debbie sounded as if nothing in the world could possibly be of more interest than this. I was pretty sure she'd still have held this view even if she *had* known there was a demon sitting twenty feet behind her, now demonically spooning sugar into a cup of tea. "God, I hope my Peer Assessment results are good enough to get me a Winchester boy. According to what the older girls used to say, they're always *super*hot and totally romantic. So if you want Faith, you better get groveling. She's going to have her pick of the Winchester studs."

I could hardly explain that I had bigger worries than who was going with whom to some stupid dance. Faith hadn't spoken to any of us since she'd fled my room last night in tears. Judging from the way the Headmistress was calmly eating dinner, at least Faith hadn't gone straight to her to tattle on us . . . yet.

I stared down at my untouched food, anxiety churning my guts. If *my* mother had still been alive, and I'd found out what she really was . . . I knew, in my heart of hearts, that I'd have gone over to her side. No questions asked. Sure, my mum had been special, while the Headmistress had the maternal instincts of a frozen haddock . . . but she was still Faith's mum.

Movement caught my eye. The Headmistress had stood up. Any normal person would have had to call for attention to quiet the room, but all she had to do was sweep her gaze over the crowd, and the entire hall went dead. "I have an unfortunate announcement to make," the Headmistress said into the waiting silence. "Due to unforeseen circumstances, Ms. Wormwood is, as of last night, no longer employed at this school. A replacement will be found as soon as possible. In the meantime, I will personally be taking over her role as form tutor. Any final-year students with personal difficulties should report to me directly." She turned to address the rest of the teachers at the top table, who were collectively looking uneasy but unsurprised. "There will be a meeting for all teachers in the staff room in one hour's time to further discuss this issue. That is all."

The Headmistress reseated herself, as the hall filled with astonished whispers. "What happened to Ms. Wormwood?" Debbie asked me, echoing the question that everyone was asking everyone else. "Do you know?"

I pushed my bowl away. "I've got to go. You're right, Debbie. I've got to talk to Faith."

As I headed for the door, my angelsight showed me the Headmistress's head turning. A chill ran across my skin. She'd seemed unaware of my previous scrutiny, but now her cool, blank gaze fixed on the back of my neck. The crawling sensation of being watched persisted even once I'd put a solid stone wall between us.

Shivering, I turned my angelic eyes away from the hall, peering instead across the flat expanse of Hell. Or Heaven, I guess I had to start calling it, although the word *really* didn't suit the inhuman, burning space. I could see the fierce flame of Michaela's guardian angel hovering over the girls' dormitories, keeping watch over Krystal and Michaela. They were holed up in Michaela's room, poring over Gabriel's notebooks in search of anything that might help us fight the Headmistress.

Apparently, all the pentagrams Michaela had been scrawling over the school had been a trial-and-error way to discover the demon's true name, so that she could create a pentagram to bind it. Each of her pentagrams had contained a different symbol, and the idea was that a demon would flinch from the ones matching its true name, but not be affected by ones that didn't. Unfortunately, the Headmistress had been pretty good at avoiding Michaela's traps, and Ms. Wormwood had been even better—Michaela had never even suspected the presence of a second demon, given that they tended to be territorial.

In any event, Michaela wasn't keen on facing the Headmistress without the safety of a pentagram, but she hadn't made much progress working out the Headmistress's true name herself. I fervently hoped that she could find some hints in Gabriel's notebooks, because any demon that could instantly stop three hundred teenage girls midgossip was not even going to break a sweat slapping down one and a half angels. With or without the help of her own nephilim.

Faith wasn't with them or in her house. Straining my eyes, I made out the soft glow of her folded wings, shining like a lighthouse beam from the old shrine. With a quick glance around to make sure no one could see me, I spread my own wings, following that distant, beckoning light.

"Go away," Faith said as I ducked into the ruined shrine. She was sitting in the center, hunched over a mobile phone. "I need privacy. I'm waiting for Billy-Bob to respond to my messages."

"Faith." She flinched as I knelt down next to her. "He's not real. Michaela said so. I think Ms. Wormwood was faking those texts and emails all along. That would explain why 'Billy-Bob' never sent you any pictures."

Faith shook her head stubbornly, staring down at the phone as if waiting for a divine revelation rather than a text message. "She's wrong. You're all wrong. I've known him for years. He's a real person. He'll call me, any minute now." Her knuckles were white where she gripped the handset. "I just have to talk to him."

"About what? If he *is* a real guy, he doesn't know about any of this stuff." I gently folded my hand over hers, forcing her to lower the phone. "Talk to me, Faith. I'm the only person who knows how you feel."

"No you don't."

"Hey, I found out I was half-demon too, remember?"

"So what?" Faith spat. "Your mum is *dead*. What do *you* care if she was a demon?"

I rocked back on my heels as if Faith had socked me in the gut. "That," I said when I could speak again, through the tightness in my throat, "was low, Faith."

Faith lifted her chin, her eyes as cold as the

Headmistress's. "It's the truth. You *don't* know what I'm going through, Raffi. Nothing's really changed for you. It might shake you up a bit to find out about your heritage, but at the end of the day you've still got your dad. I don't. All I've got is my mother and now Michaela wants to *kill* her." She collapsed like a folding deck chair, sinking into a huddle of misery. "I can't let her, Raffi, I can't!"

I had absolutely no idea what to say. Man, I wished Krystal was here. All I could do was curve a couple of wings over her, offering silent support as she cried.

"I was going to close the Hellgate for her," Faith choked out between sobs. "That's the real reason why I wanted to do it so badly. Not for the world. For her. I thought living on top of it for so long had influenced her mind, making her cold and remote. I thought that if I closed it, she'd get better. Because she *does* love me. I know she does. She can't be evil, she just can't—"

"Someone's coming," I interrupted, my angelsight alerting me to a couple of figures heading straight for us. I rose to my feet, shoulders tensing—and then relaxed as I recognized who was approaching. "It's okay. It's Michaela and Krystal. What are you two doing here?" I asked as they came in.

"Ask her," Krystal said sourly, jerking her thumb at

Michaela. "Tall-dark-and-overly-mysterious here just went charging off without explanation."

"My angel wanted me here," Michaela snapped. Her guardian was hovering above her in Heaven, two wings cupped over her head. "And now I see why." I moved back as she knelt next to Faith, putting a protective arm around her shoulders. "Faith, it will be all right. You don't need to stay here while we . . . finish things. You can go to Italy, to the Order. They'll look after you, just like they looked after me when I lost my home. I'll sponsor you."

Faith let out a brief, broken laugh. "My father was a heretic and my mother is a demon. I don't think a group of holy warriors is going to want me."

Michaela hesitated for a second. "Demons are just fallen angels. That means you're closer to Heaven than anything else. I'll tell the Order so. I can testify that you're pure. You're the most selfless, strongest person I've ever met."

Faith sniffed, swiping the back of her hand across her eyes. "Really?"

"Really." Michaela's hand tightened on her shoulder. "You never threw so much as a bad word at me, despite everything I did to you. And I've been told it would take a saint to put up with me at my worst."

That got a real laugh out of Faith. "Thank you," she said, putting her hand over Michaela's for a moment. She took a deep breath, straightening. "But I can't just run away." She looked around at us all. "She's my mother. If anyone can redeem her, it will be me."

Krystal groaned. "Oh God. Faith, it was bad enough when you wanted to redeem Michaela. This is a literal *demon from Hell*. You are not going to rehabilitate it!"

"'It' is my mother," Faith retorted hotly. "And I won't let any of you harm her. You said demons are fallen angels, Michaela. That means my mother is an angel, somewhere deep down. Why can't she become one again?"

"It's a . . . nice idea," Michaela said cautiously. She might as well have had glowing neon subtitles reading THAT IS AN UTTERLY INSANE IDEA scrolling across her forehead, but she still had her arm around Faith. "But I don't think—" She stopped midsentence. A funny look crossed her face, like a television presenter whose earpiece had just started malfunctioning.

"What is it?" Krystal and Faith said together.

"I think it's the angel," I said. The glow of the angel's wings had intensified, spotlighting Michaela in a beam of celestial light. "Is it talking to you, Michaela?"

"It doesn't work like that," Michaela replied absently,

her head still cocked to one side as if listening to something. "Believe me, my life would be a lot simpler if it did. I only get a feeling, like an intuition." She looked at Faith. "And when you were speaking, I had an overwhelming impression of . . . approval."

Faith caught her breath. "I'm right. You know I'm right. The angel wants me here. Even if I can't close the Hellgate, I can still save my mother." She bounced to her feet, determination wiping away all traces of her former tears. "And I know exactly how to do it."

We all looked at her.

"We," Faith stabbed a finger at me, "have to make out."

There was a silence.

"Uh," I said after a moment. "Not that I'm objecting, but . . . what?"

"We have to make out," Faith repeated, sounding more like someone ordering a pizza than someone proposing sexy times. "Think about it! All your wings and eyes and things, they all appeared after we touched, right? And I got *my* wings after we kissed. It's our soul mate connection, activating our powers. I need *my* full powers if I'm to confront my mother and bring her back to the light. So we have to make out. Right now."

"Aaaaand we'll just be going," Krystal said, heading for the door. "Michaela?"

Michaela folded her arms, looking as immovable as a tree. "I'm not leaving Faith alone with a half demon."

"*She's* half demon!" I said.

"Faith's Faith," Michaela said. "You're you. I'm not going anywhere."

"Well, I'm sure as hell not doing anything with you staring at me!"

"Please, Raffi!" Faith planted herself squarely in front of me, braced like someone about to undergo a root canal. "You have to kiss me."

What was I going to do, refuse? Scrunching my eyes tight shut, I leaned down to plant my mouth on hers.

Faith drew back after a moment. "Why isn't anything happening?" she demanded.

"I don't know!" I ran my hands through my hair, painfully aware of Michaela's eyes boring into us. At least Krystal had had the decency to turn her back. "Maybe it doesn't work unless we're, um, in the mood?"

"In that case it's never going to work," Michaela said acidly. "Rafael kisses like he's practicing artificial respiration."

285

"Hey, I'm feeling a little pressured, okay?" I snapped back. "I'd like to see you do better."

Michaela straightened up. "Is that a dare?" Before I knew what was happening, she'd shoved me aside, effortlessly snatching Faith out of my arms. Faith only had time to emit the briefest of startled squeaks before Michaela's mouth captured hers.

There was quite a long pause.

"There." Michaela straightened again, tossing her hair back. Faith sagged against Michaela's arm, looking somewhat shell-shocked as Michaela glared at me coldly. "*That's* how to kiss."

My mouth was hanging open. I shut it. "I . . . didn't quite get all the details there. Maybe you could show me again?"

"Someone *please* tell me when it's safe to turn around," Krystal said from the doorway.

Faith wriggled free of Michaela's hands. "Look, this isn't getting us anywhere," she said, breathless. "Michaela, you're the expert—on angels, I mean!" Her cheeks were flushed bright pink. "Do you know any faster way of awakening my powers?"

Michaela's eyebrows drew down. "I don't," she said slowly. "But my guardian angel might. It's dangerous . . ."

She trailed off, getting that faraway look in her eyes again. "And apparently she wants me to try it," she said after a second, not sounding at all happy at the prospect.

"Uh," I said as Michaela drew her daggers out from under her skirt. "What exactly are you going to try?"

"To act as a channel for my angel," Michaela replied. "And it requires a lot of concentration, so shut up." Drawing a deep breath, she crossed her daggers in front of her heart, closed her eyes, and started to murmur under her breath in Latin.

I felt Krystal move to my side. "Can *you* tell what's going on?" she whispered to me.

"Not really." The angel had stretched all six wings over Michaela. Its fires brightened, burning so fiercely that I had to squint my own angelic eyes against the light. "But the angel looks a bit like it did when it hit Ms. Wormwood. I think it's going to use Michaela as a bridge into our world again." Hopefully, not in order to smite me for lustful actions. Or, worse, offer me make-out tips. It was bad enough having Michaela criticizing my technique; I didn't need a giant ball of feathers doing it too.

Michaela's chant quickened. She flipped her daggers around, touching the points to her own throat and chest. Light shot down the metal as the angel brushed her with the barest tip of a single feather—

Michaela's eyes opened. They glowed pure white, without pupil or iris. Just for an instant, that infinitely old, infinitely calm gaze fell on me, and I felt as if my whole life had just been read like a book. Then the angel turned to Faith.

"You can save her." It was still Michaela's voice, but each word floated up from a deep, profound silence. "But you will lose her. Only by closing the Hellgate can she be freed."

"But how can I—" Faith stopped, going ashen. "My father's plan. To have me channel your power."

The angel said nothing, merely looked at her.

Faith's throat worked. "Will I die?" she asked in the barest whisper.

"Yes," the angel said with a terrible, bone-deep certainty. "All things die." It wore Michaela's face like a mask, unchanging and expressionless. Thin wisps of smoke curled from the ends of her hair. "But you need not sacrifice your body. There is another way." Its burning gaze swept over us all like a lighthouse's beam. "The greatest light is love. If two become one, the darkness will be lifted."

Krystal's breath caught. "Faith and Raf. You said it yourself, Michaela, demons are fallen angels, which makes nephilim half angels, in a way. Two halves make a whole. That's it, right? Together, they'd have as much light as a full angel, but it would be safer. That's why Gabriel wanted Raf as well as Faith."

"But we *tried* that." Faith cast me a faintly accusing glance. "It didn't work."

"Light cannot pass through lies or doubt. You must choose willingly." The angel took a step toward her, light fracturing around it as if its passage tore the very fabric of the world. It moved the dagger from its own neck so that the point rested gently in the hollow of Faith's throat. Faith held very still, her shadow standing out sharp and black behind her. "And with open eyes."

Light ran down the blade and into Faith. Wings burst from her back like a firework exploding. One pair, two, three—six wings, spreading as wide as the shine allowed. The angel's light faded, leaving only the starlight and silver glimmer of Faith's feathers.

Michaela coughed. Her skin was reddened as if with sunburn. She looked down at the dagger she still held at Faith's throat and jumped back as if it had burned her.

"Mother of God! If my guardian hurt you, I'll—" The words died on her lips as she caught sight of Faith's wings. "It worked?"

"And how," Krystal said, subdued for once. "Michaela, your angel just told us Raf and Faith can close the Hellgate."

Michaela stared at me. *What?*

Faith's eyes opened . . . all of them. In Heaven, I could see her angelic eyes emerge from under her wings. "Oh," she said weakly. "Oh, that's very strange." She flinched as she stared about her in Heaven. "Raffi, that's . . . you?"

"Yeah." I'd kind of just accepted my own extra parts, not really thinking about how they appeared. Now, with Faith also bristling with eyes and wings, I grasped just how freakishly alien we were. Judging from Faith's somewhat uncertain expression, she wasn't sure how she felt about being able to see the whole me either. I pointed with a wing at the angel, now hovering above us. "And that's what a full angel looks like, just to warn you. Personally, I think religion would be a lot less popular if they put *that* on stained-glass windows rather than winged dudes."

"Blasphemer." Michaela pushed back her dark hair, still sounding rather hoarse. "So now what?"

As if in response, the angel soared toward the main

school building. It hovered there like a star, its light shining at a particular spot, waiting.

"Now we get divine guidance," I said. "The angel wants to show us something."

Chapter 29

The angel led us to the gates of Hell itself.

"This is a *really* bad idea," I moaned, eyeing the grim portal. The matte-black surface of the door swallowed all light. There was no handle, no lock; only a single, red LED, glowing like a demonic eye over a fingerprint scanner. Gothic letters were chiseled deep into the stone above the door. Two simple words, warning all who read them that beyond the forbidding portal lay unimaginable horrors:

𝕿𝖊𝖆𝖈𝖍𝖊𝖗𝖘' 𝕷𝖔𝖚𝖓𝖌𝖊

"I think she wants us to go in," Faith said, glancing at the angel. The celestial being was bouncing up and down in Heaven over the door, like a dog desperate to be taken for a walk. She put her ear against the door. "I can't hear anyone inside. It's safe."

"Safe?" I yelped. "Are you nuts? Look at the place!"

"It's a door," Michaela said. She was still leaning on Faith's shoulder for support. "No wonder you are overcome with terror."

"You can't see it like we can," I snapped. I waved a couple of wings at the thick, ominous fog that curled through Heaven above the teachers' lounge. It was so dense that it blocked my angelsight, hiding the room beyond from view. "It's a place of darkness. Evil."

"I think it must be the heart of the Hellgate." Faith pushed at the door, but it didn't budge. "Don't worry, Raffi. Didn't you hear what the angel said? As long as love binds us together, we're as powerful as the angels themselves."

Yeah, but does it? said a tiny, traitorous thought in my head. I squashed it down, but a nagging doubt remained. Nothing had happened when we'd kissed in the old shrine. And if we weren't in love already, I really didn't see how a romantic date to the school staff room would help.

Krystal was fiddling with the fingerprint scanner. It let out a disapproving *bloop*, and she hissed in frustration.

"I hope the angel realizes we can't just walk through the wall."

"You can't," I said, staring up at the still-bouncing angel. I had the feeling it was trying to tell me something . . . "But maybe some of us can. Faith, remember when I jumped in front of you during the game?"

"Yes?" Faith's puzzled expression cleared into sudden enlightenment. "Oh! You teleported across the clearing!"

"Not exactly." I spread all six wings, their light shimmering in the gloomy corridor. "I flew. It was pure instinct, but I somehow leaped into Heaven for a second, and landed back on Earth somewhere else."

Krystal face-palmed. "Four-dimensional being. Of course! You can go *over* things by moving in the fourth dimension. Like we can just step over a line drawn on a piece of paper, moving in three-dimensional space to get around a two-dimensional object."

"Uh, if you say so. Anyway, I think I could do it again." Experimentally, I beat all six wings downward at once— and found myself hovering in Heaven, looking back down at Earth.

"Raf? *Raf!*" Krystal yelled, sounding panicked. Both she and Michaela were swiveling their heads, trying to work out where I'd gone.

"It's okay." Faith was staring directly at me with her angelic eyes. "He's up there. Raffi?"

I folded my wings again, dropping down to Earth. Krystal yelped as I appeared out of nowhere next to her. "Faith and I can get in." I glanced at the angel above our heads. "Michaela, I really need to ask your guardian something. Can you translate the response?" She nodded, and I hesitated for a second, wondering how I could tell if the angel was even listening to me. "Uh . . . hey, you up there. Can you do me a favor?"

Michaela squeezed her eyes shut in pain. "Did you really just start a prayer of supplication for divine intervention with 'Hey, you up there'?"

I decided to ignore that. "Can you watch over Michaela and Krystal for a bit?" I asked the angel. "Just in case the Headmistress goes after them while Faith and I are busy."

The angel's wings briefly enfolded Michaela. "Yes," she said simply. The angel retreated, and Michaela swayed on her feet. Faith hurried to support her. "I need to lie down now."

"Krys, can you get her back to her room? Actually, you'd both better wait there, it's too dangerous to hang around here. We'll meet up with you once we've investigated."

"Okay." Krystal took over the job of supporting Michaela, who leaned on her a lot less gratefully than she'd done on Faith. Krystal squeezed my hand briefly. "Good luck, Raf. Be careful."

"You bet." Faith had already flown over the door. I flapped my own wings to lift myself briefly out of the normal world, landing again next to Faith. "I really hate that." I rubbed my arms, half expecting to find them blistered and burned. "It's like jumping through an inferno."

"I guess our human halves aren't built for heaven." Faith was already poking through the coats hung up behind the door. "Come on, help me search."

"For what?" There was a small kitchen area in one corner of the room, with a humming fridge and a couple of cabinets. I opened one of them, discovering nothing more sinister than an enormous carton of bodybuilder's protein powder with a note stuck to it: *Oleander, if you so much as touch this, I'll practice discus with your spleen—Hellebore.* This was probably not what the angel wanted us to see.

"I don't know! The angel said we had to 'choose with open eyes.' There must still be some secret hidden away that we need to—Raffi, Ms. Henbane's got a pentagram on her key chain!"

"Yeah, she's a Satanist. Don't ask." Closing the

296

cupboard door, I tried to open the fridge. The handle resisted me. Something inside was jamming the mechanism. I tried to peer inside with angelsight, but was foiled by the dark clouds still masking the room. "I don't think she's dangerous, though."

"There has to be something in here." Faith rifled through the layered memos pinned to the notice board as if expecting to find one with the heading RE: HELL-GATE, CLOSING OF. "A hidden summoning circle with my mother's real name, or, or a diary, or—"

The fridge door finally sprang open. I stared at the contents. "Or a body."

"I think that's a little unlikely," Faith said, not looking up from the notices.

"No, I mean, literally, there's a body. In the fridge." She was curled into a tight ball of sticklike limbs and bony spine, completely filling the small space. One of her hands had flopped out when I'd opened the door. "It's Ms. Vervaine."

Faith's horrified eyes met mine. In the same moment, I heard footsteps approaching the door. There wasn't even time to kick the fridge closed again. Spreading our wings, we both leaped into Heaven, disappearing from normal sight just as the fingerprint scanner outside beeped.

That weird fog still shrouded everything, but the combined light of our wings was bright enough to cut through it somewhat, letting us see what was going on down below. Hovering invisibly above the mortal world, I watched as Ms. Hellebore came into the teachers' lounge, whistling. Her tune broke off midnote as she saw Ms. Vervaine's lifeless, limp hand sticking out of the fridge. "Oh, not again," she said in tones of deep disgust. Shaking her head, she poked the hand back in, shut the fridge door, and started mixing herself a protein shake.

"Ms. Hellebore?" Whispers carried weirdly in Heaven, but I could still make out the shock and confusion in Faith's voice. "Ms. Hellebore killed Ms. Vervaine? Is she *another* demon?"

Before I could respond, the fingerprint scanner beeped once more. "Vervaine's in the fridge again, Oleander," Ms. Hellebore said without looking around.

"Lazy cow." Ms. Oleander didn't so much as glance at the fridge. "And at a time like this." Faith and I stared at each other as Ms. Oleander heaved a large bucket up onto the table with a grunt. There was a biohazard symbol printed on the side. She peeled back the lid. "Can I have some of your protein powder?"

"No. It's disgusting enough watching you as it is."

"Squeamish, Fury?" Ms. Oleander said, scooping diced offal out of the bucket and into a large cereal bowl. "I thought your type loved blood." The door beeped and slid open yet again. "Henbane, didn't you tell Vervaine to stay out of the fridge?"

"Oh, honestly." Ms. Henbane gave a sniff of disdain as she swept past on her way to the coffee machine. "One of these days I'm going to *bury* her body while she's taking one of these little rests. It would serve her right to come back and find it half decayed." She poured coffee into a mug. It had a picture of a little red devil surrounded by hearts on its side. "If the rest of us can expend the effort to stay in possession, why can't she?"

"What d'you expect of a Sloth?" Ms. Oleander said with her mouth full. "Well, the Headmistress will expect her at this war meeting. Henbane, go haul her up."

"Excuse me?" Ms. Henbane said, looking offended. "I don't take orders from you, Glutton. Go get her yourself."

"Hen, you know it takes Oleander forever to reconnect to her digestive system," Ms. Hellebore said wearily. "And I'm possessing far more muscle groups than you bother to control. It'll be fastest if you go."

Ms. Henbane swore under her breath in a foreign language, but put her coffee cup carefully down on the work top. She straightened, closing her eyes—and dropped dead.

"Prideful cow," Ms. Oleander muttered, eyeing Ms. Henbane's collapsed corpse with dislike. "Thinks she's better than the rest of us."

"Shut up, Oleander, or I'll break your jaw. I don't need you stirring up trouble." Ms. Hellebore cracked her huge knuckles.

A group of lower-year teachers that I didn't know personally came in as she spoke. They sat down at the far end of the table, grumbling amongst themselves about the interruption to their day. Not one of them so much as batted an eyelid at the bodies on the floor. "You heard the Headmistress. It's more important than ever to work together, or we'll all end up like the succubus."

"I heard she got burned so badly, she'll never be able to possess anyone again," one of the other teachers chimed in. "She was only five years away from finishing her service here too."

"And I've only got two to go until I'm released," Ms. Hellebore said, raising her voice to address the room at large. "So if any of you worms puts a *feather* out of line, I will personally rip your tentacles off and floss with them. I'm not having any of you ruin the Prince's big day." She grinned wolfishly. "He's sure to be *very* grateful to those who prepared the way for him. I think I'll ask for a nice war. I rather fancy visiting France."

"You say that like there's still a chance our little nephil will agree to bind with him." Ms. Oleander gnawed nervously at her thumbnail. "You saw the light over at the old shrine. That has to have been Dante's pet, ruining all our plans. I don't understand why the Headmistress wouldn't let me eat the spare nephil the instant he left the sanctified ground, just to be safe."

"Always thinking with your stomach. Our nephil *definitely* wouldn't trust us ever again if you ate her friend in front of her. Anyway, the boy's got a father, you know. He'd be bound to raise a fuss, and do you know how much money it would cost to hush that up? Asking an Avarice demon as powerful as the Headmistress to part with that much cash is like asking you to go on a diet." Ms. Hellebore leaned back in her chair, looking unconcerned. "The Headmistress said she'd take care of the nephilim and she will. When have you ever known her to fail?"

"There's a first time for everything. I still think there's even odds on all of us finding ourselves cut loose from our host bodies and thrown back in the Pit before the end of the week." Ms. Oleander stared glumly into her bowl.

"If this is going to be my last meal, I should have brought ketchup."

"There," interrupted Ms. Henbane, sitting up again. "She hadn't gone far down." As she spoke, Ms. Vervaine climbed stiffly out of the fridge. "Oh, for Beelzebub's sake, Vervaine, get yourself under control. You're not even *trying* to look human."

"Why bother?" croaked Ms. Vervaine. Frost cracked off her clothes. "No pupils here." She rubbed at her eyes with one stiff hand, her arm moving as jerkily as a puppet with half its strings cut. "Too bright. Why?"

"You've frozen your corneas again," Ms. Oleander began—and then she looked sharply up from her bowl. "Wait. It *is* brighter."

Faith clutched my arm. "Raffi, I think they can tell we're here!"

With horror, I realized that Faith was right. The darkness surrounding the teachers' lounge had thinned considerably, driven back by our combined angelic glow.

Every one of Ms. Hellebore's impressive muscles tensed. "Dante's pet," she growled. Shadows flickered around her outline—

As one, Faith and I beat our wings hard, hurling ourselves higher heavenward as tentacles erupted from the mortal plane like a giant squid breaching out of the ocean. The grasping limbs missed our dangling feet by inches before sinking back out of sight. The mortal world blurred by under us as we fled as fast as our wings could carry us.

"Jesus, Mary, and Joseph!" Michaela yelped as we dropped into normal space inside her room. She whirled, daggers flashing. *"Sancte Michael Archangele—"*

"No, it's us!" I said from the floor. Michaela's daggers had missed me by inches. At least I'd managed to land on something soft. "Sorry, Krys," I added, rolling off of her. "You okay?"

"Fine!" Krystal squeaked. "Never better!" Face red, she scrambled to her feet, ignoring my outstretched hand. She cleared her throat, occupying herself with brushing at her clothes. "Did you guys manage to find anything out?"

Faith and I exchanged glances. "The good news is that your angel is right," Faith said. "The demons are afraid Raffi and I will close the Hellgate together."

"They are?" Michaela's eyebrows shot up—and then drew down again. "Wait, demons? Plural?"

"That's the bad news," I said grimly. "*All* the other teachers are demons."

Michaela and Krystal stared at us.

In the silence, the knock at the door sounded as loud as a gunshot.

"Good evening," the Headmistress said, entering without waiting to be invited. She looked around at us all, her expression cool and calm as ever. "I believe we need to talk."

Chapter 30

N O!" Faith shouted, tackling Michaela around the waist as the other girl leaped for the Headmistress with daggers raised. The two crashed into a shelf, textbooks and papers tumbling over their heads. Faith pinned Michaela's wrists against the wall. "You can't hurt her! She's still my mother!"

"She's a demon!" Michaela struggled against Faith's grip. "She's evil!"

"You heard the others talking, Faith." The instant the door had opened, I'd thrust Krystal behind me and snatched my keys out of my pocket. It wasn't much of a weapon, but at least they were metal. Angelic fire crackled around my wings, eager to be released into the mortal world as I pointed them straight at the Headmistress. "She's knows we're onto them. She's probably here to kill us all."

"If I wanted to kill you, Mr. Angelos, you would already be dead." The Headmistress did not appear the slightest bit perturbed by the sudden outbreak of weaponry. "And as for evil, Miss Dante, may I remind you that it was not I who attempted to shoot an innocent girl." She seated herself on Michaela's swivel chair. "But you have one thing correct." For an instant, a black aura flickered around her. All our breaths steamed in the suddenly freezing air. "I *am* a demon."

Michaela made another desperate lunge, Faith barely managing to hang on to her. "Let me go, Faith! You have to let me protect you!"

"Yes," the Headmistress said unexpectedly. "Release her, Faith. It is the fastest way I can prove my intentions." When Faith hesitated, her mother barked, "Now! Do not be afraid. She will not harm me."

The instant Faith's hands opened, Michaela scooped up her daggers and lunged for the Headmistress. Before I could even blink, let alone move to back her up, she had buried one in the Headmistress's throat, the other in her heart. "That was the last mistake you'll ever make," Michaela snarled. *"Sancte Michael Archangele, defende nos in proelio!"*

Nothing happened.

"Are you quite finished?" the Headmistress asked calmly, around the dagger in her neck. A trickle of blood ran down the blade, dark and sluggish. "We do not have long. Even demonic teachers will only sit around drinking tea and complaining at each other for so long before growing bored."

"Contra nequitiam et insidias diaboli esto . . . esto . . ." Michaela trailed off, baffled. She looked around as if searching for something. "Rafael? Where's my guardian angel?"

"Right above you, as always." The creature was at its customary station, hovering heavenward over Michaela's head. All of its eyes were fixed on the Headmistress, but its flames were low and dull, like a banked fire.

"The demon isn't doing anything to stop her?"

"Not that I can see."

"Or me," Faith added, frowning as she stared at the angel herself. Only two of its wings beat, slowly, while the rest had drawn tight about its body, muffling its glow. "Though it looks . . . sad."

"Doubtless due to your appalling pronunciation," the Headmistress said to Michaela. She took hold of Michaela's daggers between finger and thumb, drawing them out

307

of her flesh. The wounds closed up the instant the blades left her skin. "Latin may be a dead language, Miss Dante, but there is no need to desecrate the corpse."

Michaela backed off, looking down at her daggers as if they'd misfired. "I don't understand. You're a demon. Why won't my guardian attack you?"

"Because she knows what else I am," the Headmistress said. She sat back in her chair, steepling her fingers. "A traitor."

We all, as one, stared at her.

The Headmistress raised her eyebrows at us. "You never wondered how I could fail to notice for *sixteen years* that my husband was a demon hunter? You did not pause to ponder why I would allow a known Dante to rampage unchecked within my territory? You never calculated the odds of the one male I allow into this school turning out to be an unknowing nephil?" She shook her head. "Remedial critical-thinking classes for you all, I believe."

"Okay, hold it right there," Krystal said from behind me. She shoved at my shoulder. "And Raf, sweet as this is, stop squishing me into the wall. I don't think she's going to suck my soul out." She ducked under my arm to face the Headmistress square on, hands on her hips. "I'll accept that there are a lot of things that make more sense if you've secretly been on our side all along. But if you really are working for good, then the thing that *doesn't* make sense is why you're letting a dozen demons run around this school!"

"Better this school than the world, Miss Moon. Would you rather Ms. Hellebore was giving weapons lessons to terrorists instead of teenagers? I am powerful enough that here, on my home ground, they must obey me. I drag them in from around the world, kicking and complaining. While they are working for me I am able to curtail their worst excesses." She gestured around at us all. "The success of that may be judged by the fact that none of *you*, with all your knowledge, suspected what they truly were before today. Miss Dante, have you ever heard of demons behaving this subtly before?"

"No," Michaela growled. "But that just proves you're exceptionally dangerous, if you can command lesser demons to act against their natures."

"Miss Dante, you are quite willfully obtuse." The Headmistress sighed. "Please ask yourself, if I was evil . . . *why* would I command demons to restrain themselves?"

"You're reformed," Faith breathed. Rising hope shone in her face. Taking two steps forward, she reached out to clasp her mother's unresisting hands. "You're redeemed!

309

My father's love redeemed you!"

A pained look flickered across the Headmistress's usually impassive expression. "Sometimes," she said with a sigh, "you are *very* much his daughter." She looked down at Faith's hands, still clutching her own. "Suffice it to say that I have my own reasons for wanting the Hellgate closed. Gabriel thought that he was double-crossing a demon. He never realized that I was on his side all along."

"The side of Heaven. You're good, I knew you had to be good!" Faith paused, a shadow flickering across her expression. She drew back fractionally from her mother. "But . . . why did you fight with him after he told me about the Hellgate? You threw him out, leaving him defenseless against the demons."

"I had no choice. You see, he did not know about the other demons at this school. I kept them concealed from him, even as I ensured they did not discover his true nature." She sighed, pulling her hands out of Faith's and folding them in her lap. "He was still a Dante at heart, and I knew he would not be able to restrain himself if he knew their true nature. But that meant that when he decided the time was right to tell you the truth, he did not realize that the other demons were eavesdropping." She looked around at us all, lingering on me. "Hell is always under your feet. Listening. Watching. You would do well to remember that."

"So you just sat back and let the demons kill your own husband?" Krystal said. "Nice."

"It was that or have them kill him, myself, *and* Faith," the Headmistress retorted. "If I had attempted to defend him, they would have discovered my treachery, and that would have been the end of us all. I had no choice."

"You lie, deceiver." Michaela's dagger points were rock steady. "You're still trying to trick Faith into sacrificing her soul to your dark Prince."

"I will not see my daughter sacrificed to anyone," the Headmistress said with surprising force. "Not to a Prince of Hell. Not to an angel—oh, yes, Miss Dante, I know what my husband planned for Faith, and I would have killed him myself before I allowed him to risk her in such a fashion. Even a demon may grow to care for her child." She gestured at me. "Ask Mr. Angelos."

I thought of my own mother, and the flames flickering over my wings guttered uncertainly. I knew that she would never have done anything to hurt me, and she had been a demon too. "But even if you want to save Faith, why do you want to close the Hellgate? Won't you be banished too?"

"Yes, Mr. Angelos. I shall be cast down into the deepest depths of Hell, never again to return to the mortal world," the Headmistress said with perfect equanimity. "I am prepared to face that fate."

"She's sacrificing herself. That *proves* she isn't evil," Faith said fiercely, pushing my still-outstretched keys down and clouting me with a wing to force me to fold my own. "Stop threatening her." She turned her trusting blue eyes back on her mother. "I don't care what they think. I believe you, Mother."

"Good." The Headmistress rose. "Because I expressly forbid you to have anything more to do with these people."

"What?" Krystal, Michaela, and I yelled together.

"But, Mother, closing the Hellgate takes two nephilim. Two half-breeds united to produce as much light as a full angel." Faith reached back to take my hand. "Michaela's guardian said so."

"Did she? In those precise words? Naming Mr. Angelos specifically?" The Headmistress raised an eyebrow at Faith's sudden, uncertain silence. "I thought not. Mr. Angelos did not feature in your father's plans, Faith. Channeling the light of Heaven requires a pure soul. Ask Miss Dante. You have been raised specifically to be such a channel, but do you think Mr. Angelos is as virtuous as yourself? Has he not demonstrated the vast depths of his laziness, his arrogance, his wrath?"

"Hey!" I protested.

"Oh, come on," Krystal said to the Headmistress. "I'm not saying he's a saint, but he's not evil incarnate."

"He is an adolescent male, Miss Moon, which is bad enough . . . but he is also quite literally half demon. And he is rogue, raised by a mundane unaware of his true heritage, unable to provide the discipline required to overcome his tainted nature. Have you not realized that nephilim are balanced between Heaven and Hell? They can channel the light, true, but they can just as easily unleash the forces of darkness. If a nephil reflected *that* power into the world, the Hellgate would become immeasurably larger, rather than closing."

"Your aura was black." Michaela's voice had gone hard and cold. Her dark eyes were fixed upon me, wary. "When you broke my circle, you channeled darkness to do it. That was the power of Hell."

"You were trying to stab me with a dagger at the time," I snapped. "You can't blame a guy for getting angry!"

Krystal bit her lip. "It's not the only time, Raf," she said in a very small voice.

"I'm not evil!" Glaring around at them, I put a hand on Faith's shoulder. "Anyway, you don't have a choice. You need two nephilim to do this thing, so——" I stopped. Faith had twisted out from under my hand, backing away. "Faith?"

Her eyes met mine, agonized. "What if they're right, Raffi? My father *died* to give me this chance. I can't risk wasting it."

"But if we can't use Raf, how can we close the Hellgate?" Krystal asked, frowning.

"Not Faith and my guardian angel!" Michaela had lowered her daggers, but now she pointed them at the Headmistress's heart again. "It would destroy her. I'll kill you if you try to persuade her."

"Miss Dante, I may be a demon, but I have no desire to see my daughter harmed," the Headmistress snapped. "No. The Hellgate can be closed as you thought, Faith. With the power of love. That is what the light *is*, after all. Love itself."

The greatest light is love. The angel's voice rang in my mind like a distant bell. From the expressions on everyone else's faces, I wasn't the only one remembering those words. Even Krystal looked like she wasn't completely discounting the idea. "You're saying that if Faith's in love, it would amplify her light? Enough to close the Hellgate?"

"As I said, Miss Moon, Faith can close the Hellgate. She needs only to be united with a suitable partner."

"Well then, that's *still* me," I said, ignoring that recurring twinge of doubt. "So there."

"Is it, Mr. Angelos?" The Headmistress turned to Faith. "Or is it the one you knew it was, before a vain nephil boy caught your eye with his shallow charms?"

Faith's eyes widened. "Billy-Bob."

"It's a trap, Faith!" Michaela shouted. "I see her plot now. Hell still needs you. The Prince is too powerful to possess anyone other than a nephil. If you refuse him, he can't enter the mortal world." She dropped into a combat crouch, crossing her daggers as she glared at the Headmistress. "But you've been caught by your own lies, demon. There's no Billy-Bob at Winchester."

"There are, however, plenty of Roberts," the Headmistress said acidly. "Honestly, you thought 'Billy-Bob' was his real name?"

"I'm with Michaela. I know Ms. Wormwood was faking those messages." I started to raise my keys again, but a black tentacle flicked out of nowhere, knocking them out of my grasp before I could channel fire down them. "Faith! She's lying to trick you into binding with the demon Prince!"

"Kindly do not call my daughter an idiot to her face." The Headmistress grasped Faith's wrist, pulling her to her side. "Miss Dante, you well know that bindings cannot be forced. And that a manifesting demon cannot fully disguise their true nature. Forewarned as she is, Faith cannot fail to recognize the Prince, and she would have to accept him willingly. Do you honestly think her such a fool?"

Michaela and I exchanged glances across the tentacles holding me at bay. Faith, catching the looks, tossed her hair. "I *can* recognize a pentagram, you know," she snapped, sounding very much like her mother. "I'm not about to promise anything to a guy standing inside one." She hesitated, looking uncertainly at the Headmistress. "But even if Raffi's not my true love, he's still my friend. They all are. I—"

"You will obey me!" We all shivered as the temperature in the room dropped at least ten degrees with the force of the Headmistress's anger. "The other demons are always watching, Faith. They have no reason to fear you and Billy-Bob, for they do not realize the true strength of your devotion to him, but the mere thought of you together with Mr. Angelos fills them with terror. The succubus was assigned to do all in her power to stop that from happening. She failed. Give them any excuse, and their next attack will not be nearly so subtle."

"She's right." Krystal's fingers dug into my arm. "Even if she's lying about everything else. Which . . . I'm not so sure about."

"I never lie, Miss Moon. Now come, Faith."

Faith hesitated, caught between us and her mother in an agony of indecision. "I don't—I can't—I don't know what to believe! How am I supposed to know what to do?"

"Simple, my daughter." The Headmistress held out her hand. "You must decide if you trust me."

Chapter 31

All hell had broken loose. Girls crowded in the narrow corridor, fighting to get through to the notice board. Screams of excitement mingled with heartbroken sobs.

The Ball list had gone up.

"For God's sake." Krystal flattened against the wall to avoid getting squashed as yet another tear-stricken girl fled the scene of her humiliation. Krystal wasn't even trying to get a look at the list herself. She knew full well her Peer Assessment results had her in last place. "You'd think it was the end of the world."

"It might very well be," I said grimly. Averaging about a foot taller than the rest of my year meant I had a clear view of the top of the notice board, even from back here. "Look."

MASKED BALL PARTNER LIST (GIRLS)

1. FAITH JONES—*Billy-Bob*

Faith had just finished writing his name next to her own. I tried to push through to her, but before I could get more than three steps she'd seen me. Her blonde hair flashed as she turned and fled in the opposite direction, the crowd parting before her like water.

Someone's elbow caught me hard in the ribs. "That's what you get for sucking up to that conceited cow," Suzanne spat as she shoved her way past. "How does it feel to be rejected, Rafael?"

"You tell me," I called after her. "Who's *your* date, Suzanne?" She made an obscene gesture at me as she stalked away.

"Wow, it's a good thing the demon Prince needs a nephilim to possess," Krystal murmured, eyeing Suzanne's retreating back. "If anything even vaguely male-shaped and unattached turns up at the Ball, Suzanne will jump on him without question. Along with half the year group, by the looks of things."

"Well, he *has* got a nephil." Both my stomach and my fists clenched as I read the list one last time, confirming

319

that this wasn't some horrible nightmare. "I can't believe Faith fell for her mother's blatant lies."

Krystal was silent for a moment, her mouth set in that particular stubborn line that I'd come to learn meant she was deep in thought. Then she tugged on my sleeve, pulling me away from the crowd. Finding an empty classroom, she pushed me inside and shut the door behind us. "Not that that's likely to do anything to stop eavesdropping demons," she muttered, glancing at it. She shook her head, turning back to me. "Raf, there's a hole in the Headmistress's story."

I snorted. "Just one?"

"Yes, just one. You may not like her explanations, but at least they're consistent. Except for one thing. Michaela didn't know you were a nephil, right?"

I blinked at the sudden swerve in topic. "Right. So?"

"So that means Gabriel didn't tell the Order. In fact, he didn't say *anything* to them about a second nephil. And the Headmistress told us that he intended to use Faith and an angel to close the Hellgate. Not two nephilim."

"I still don't see where this is going, Krystal."

Krystal tugged on her hair in agitation. "I don't know

how much I dare say out loud. Not after what the Head-mistress said about the other demons always listening. Raf, we have no hints that Gabriel even suspected you existed. *So why are you here?*"

"Because you—" I stopped dead.

I was here because Krystal had summoned me. Using a charm from the last entry in Gabriel Dante's notebooks. An entry that he couldn't have written.

And there was only one person who could have planted that information in the notebooks that she knew her daughter was studying.

From Krystal's expression of relief, she'd seen that I'd followed her train of thought. "Someone wanted you here," she whispered, barely moving her lips. "Someone wants you to do something." She pointed significantly at the floor. "And that someone couldn't just come out and tell us."

I stared downward myself, imagining unseen demonic forms lurking on the flip side of the world. If the Head-mistress really was a traitor to Hell, she'd have to be incredibly careful about what she said. She'd have to appear to be telling us to do what Hell wanted, while actually giving us clues to the real plan.

Faith needs only to be united with a suitable partner.

And I heard again the angel's silence-filled voice: *The greatest light is love. If two become one, the darkness will be lifted.*

"Krystal," I said, matching her hushed tones. "The Headmistress said I might corrupt the light, that I'm not as pure as Faith."

"But you know you wouldn't." Krystal squeezed my hand briefly. "*I* know you wouldn't. I trust you, Raf. And I don't think I'm the only one."

I paced a few steps, my mind reeling as everything fit into place. The Headmistress *did* mean for me and Faith to close the Hellgate with our united light. The only problem was . . . "Do you think Faith has worked any of this out?"

Krystal winced. "I don't know. She's not talking to me either." She blew out her breath. "I hope that the Headmistress is right, and Faith *will* be able to recognize that 'Billy-Bob' is actually the demon Prince when she meets him."

"You do realize that we're staking the fate of the world on Faith's observational skills and common sense, right?"

Krystal groaned. "Oh, God. Raf, we're in deep trouble."

"Hey, Raffi!" Debbie poked her head around the door. From her ear-to-ear grin, I guessed she at least had a date for the Ball. "Hiding out? Good plan. You are gonna get ripped to *shreds.*"

For a heart-stopping moment, I thought she meant that the demons were after us. Then I realized Debbie had no idea what was really going on. "Huh? What do you mean?"

"Haven't you seen the list?" She winked at me. "Open season just got declared."

Krystal and I exchanged puzzled glances as Debbie withdrew again. "It's a bit clearer," Krystal said, leaning out to check the corridor. "Let's go see what she was talking about."

I felt like I had even more of a target painted on my back than usual as we stepped out into the corridor. The girls still lingering nearby were pinning me with identical stares of desperate hope. And as I got close enough to read the *other* notice on the board, I realized why.

MASKED BALL PARTNER LIST (BOYS)

1. RAFAEL ANGELOS—

That was all that was printed on the notice. Krystal and I both stared at the empty space next to my name.

"Do you think I can pick whoever I want?" I said slowly.

Chapter 32

I t's not much of a costume," Lydie said dubiously. She eyed a nearby group of sixth-year girls, glorious in white party dresses and feathered wings. The courtyard outside the chapel had been hung with hundreds of fairy lights, so that the milling girls seemed to waft through a star-filled night. "Everyone else's is much better."

"Hey, it's the best I could do." The theme of the Masked Ball was "Heaven and Hell." The Headmistress had a *terrible* sense of humor. "It wasn't like demon costumes form a big part of my daily wardrobe." I could have done a really *excellent* angel, but of course boys had to be the bad guys. I was making do with my regular all-black school uniform, minus the jacket and tie, and accessorized with Krystal's old pentagram charm and some other bits of occult jewelry my girls had managed to scrounge up.

"Tell everyone thanks for finding this stuff."

Lydie nodded, dropping her gaze as if having suddenly found something fascinating about the flagstones. "We studied medieval tournaments last year in History," she said, apparently at utter random. "Did you know, if a lady really liked a knight, she'd give him a token, like a scarf or something, for him to wear. It was called a 'favor.' It was to bring him good luck in battle." She thrust something out at arm's length. "Um. Here. I made you this. For your costume."

The homemade devil's horns were just cardboard, glue-gunned onto a red plastic headband, but Lydie had really gone to town on the glitter and sequins. Very solemnly, I knelt on one knee so that Lydie could fit them on my head. She adjusted them carefully. "Thank you, Raffi," she whispered. "For trying." Then she blushed from throat to hairline, and fled.

"What in the name of God have you got on your head?" Krystal said from behind me. "You look like a cow trying to pass as a unicorn."

"If you mock my knightly favor," I said, rising and turning. "I shall challenge you to—"

My words died in my mouth.

Her gossamer-thin white tunic floated over her curves,

fluttering with every movement. Golden chains secured the fabric, highlighting her slender waist. Matching gold sandals laced high over her smooth, elegant legs. She was wearing her hair up, exposing the delicate, vulnerable sweep of her neck. Another golden chain wound through the intricate braids, catching the light like a halo. A small pair of white-feathered wings completed the angelic effect. She could have just stepped down from one of the stained-glass windows.

"Wow," I said weakly. "You look . . . nice."

"Nice?" Krystal said from Michaela's side. Krystal looked pretty good herself, though even I could tell that gym shoes didn't really go with her party dress. She prodded me in the chest with the point of Gabriel Dante's sword. "Three hours of preparation and all you can say is *nice*?"

"No, I mean, literally nice! As in, a nice girl." I waved my hands in Michaela's general direction. "Rather than a terrifying man-eating lesbian dominatrix."

"Is that how I normally look?" Michaela said, sounding pleased. She looked me up and down, squinting a bit when she got to my disco-tastic horns. "Hmm. If more demons looked like you, we'd have less trouble with people agreeing to bindings."

I was pretty sure I'd just been dissed, but before I could

defend Lydie's costume-making skills, a gong rang out. An expectant hush fell over the courtyard, all the girls going as tense as runners at the starting blocks as they stared at the chapel doors.

"Ladies and gentleman." The doors opened to reveal the Headmistress, golden light and music spilling out around her. She stepped to one side. "The Ball has begun."

I grabbed Krystal's arm to keep her from getting bowled over by the sudden surge of the crowd. Michaela just deployed her best glare, effortlessly maintaining a bubble of personal space even as girls fought to be first through the doors. By unspoken agreement, we waited for the rush to subside before making our own way forward.

I hadn't even seen Ms. Hellebore standing guard until she moved to block our path. "No edged weapons on the dance floor, Krystal," she said a touch mournfully. "Much as I approve of your accessory choice, you'll have to leave it here."

"But it's part of my costume!" Krystal waved the sword. She'd wrapped orange tissue paper around the blade. "I'm the angel at the gates of Eden. This is my flaming sword, see?"

With a glance that clearly said that she knew what Krystal was up to, Ms. Hellebore plucked the weapon out of her hands. Krystal cast me a "well, I tried" shrug, then slipped past Ms. Hellebore into the hall.

"Rafael," Ms. Hellebore greeted me. Her expression turned sour as she looked at Michaela. "I cannot believe the Headmistress allowed this."

"Can't argue with school tradition," I said. "I'm the most popular guy in my year, I get certain privileges." I put my arm around Michaela's waist, drawing her closer to my side despite the way she stiffened. "And Michaela is still technically enrolled here."

"She *shot* you!"

"Yeah, well, just her passionate nature showing." I gave Michaela a warning squeeze. "Right, babe?"

"Ours is a tempestuous love," Michaela said through gritted teeth.

Ms. Hellebore growled. A shiver ran down my back as I remembered her tentacles lashing up through the world, trying to pull me and Faith out of Heaven. "Go ahead then," she said, stepping aside. "But I'll be watching you."

"I bet," I muttered. A shimmering curtain of crystal beads veiled the doorway, catching the light beyond like a waterfall. They chimed sweetly as I ducked through them, trying not to catch my horns. "Let's find—augh!"

"What? What?" Michaela nearly drew her daggers as

I bent over, clutching at my head. "What can you see?"

"Nothing," I said, straightening again and rubbing at my normal eyes, even though *those* ones were working perfectly well. "That's the problem. The instant I stepped through those doors, I went blind."

"Me too," Krystal said, appearing at my elbow. She was gaping, openmouthed, at the transformed hall. Pale stone columns soared up to delicate arches high overhead, where an enormous crystal chandelier blazed with rainbow-edged light. All-white mosaic tiles glimmered underfoot like chips of ice and pearl. White silk banners draped the walls and pillars, rippling gently and giving the impression that the whole structure was built from clouds and mist. "This is incredible. I had no idea the chapel looked like this under all the carpet tiles and temporary partitions."

"I didn't mean the decorations blinded me," I said, lowering my voice as a group of giggling girls pushed past us, heading for the buffet table. "You know how I said there was a darkness over the staff room? Well, it's back. And about a thousand times worse. Seriously, I can't see a wing in front of my eyes." Even Michaela's angel was just a dim, guttering candle flame amidst the choking black cloud.

"The Prince," Michaela said grimly, tugging her skirt

down over her daggers again. "He must be here already. We have to find Faith."

"Already ahead of you," Krystal said. She motioned us to follow her. "But you're not going to like this."

A dance floor had been set up in the center of the hall, under the chandelier. Couples spun in that wide, clear space, each radiant angel shadowed by a taller, black-clad form. As I watched, the boys lifted their partners in perfect synchronization, as easily as if the girls weighed no more than the feathered wings fluttering at their backs. Guess the reason for the limited number of guys was due to the size of Winchester's dance club.

"I could do that," I said under my breath, as one guy performed some complicated move that ended up with his starry-eyed partner bent backward over his knee. "If I wanted to." Nonetheless, I was suddenly very glad that my own escort was likely to disembowel me if I suggested we take a spin around the floor. "Bloody show-offs."

Michaela's breath caught in her throat. She stared through the dancers as if she hadn't even noticed them. "Faith," she whispered.

At the very center of the floor, Faith spun, her unbound hair shimmering in her wake like the tail of a falling star. It wasn't just a trick of the light that made her seem to glow——her halo was showing, just the merest sliver of gold edging her head. The crystal beads covering her long, white dress caught her divine light, shimmering as if she were clothed in raindrops. She wasn't smiling, but there was an air of intent solemnity around her, like a bride preparing to walk up the aisle. She was so dazzling that for a moment I didn't even see her partner. Then he twirled her around, dipping her nearly to the floor in his strong, confident hands, and I got my first good look at my rival.

My first thought was relief. The guy had a bloody great long tail sticking out of his butt, bright red and barbed, whipping around his legs as he danced. Even Faith couldn't fail to notice *that*.

Then my gaze dropped to the guy's feet, and the enormous expanse of perfectly white, perfectly pentagram-less mosaic floor surrounding him.

We all stared at one another, then back at Billy-Bob, as if we could make the pentagram reveal itself through pure willpower. "Could it be on the ceiling?" I muttered to Michaela.

"Does he *look* like he's hanging from the ceiling like a bat?" Michaela hissed back. Her hands twitched helplessly over her hidden daggers. "I don't understand. That *has* to be the Prince."

"They make a lovely couple, do they not, Mr. Angelos?"
I jumped. I'd come to rely too much on angelsight—I
hadn't noticed the Headmistress coming up behind us.
Now she stood at my elbow, watching Faith and Billy-Bob
dance, her face as neutral as ever. Her voice was dry enough
to shrivel a slug. "Ah, young love. How heartwarming."

It wasn't my heart that was getting hot. I shifted my
wings, stuffing my hands in my pockets to keep them
away from anything metal. If Billy-Bob really was an ordinary human being, had we been wrong in thinking that
the Headmistress had meant *me* to be Faith's true partner?
"Is he everything you hoped for?" I said bitterly.

"I do not hope for anything, Mr. Angelos. It is a poor
substitute for planning. Mr. McFly has appeared precisely
as intended."

"Like a certain other individual?" Krystal said.

The Headmistress regarded her in silence for a moment.
"You are a very intelligent young woman, Miss Moon."
She tilted her head, her eyes drifting from Krystal to Ms.
Vervaine, who was standing against the wall a little way
off, watching the dancers with an unusual, small, pleased
smile on her bony face. "And as such, you will recognize
when it is not the time nor the place to speak."

"What is it time for, then?" I asked. If I *was* supposed

to separate Faith from Billy-Bob, by the looks of things I would need a crowbar.

"It is time to party, Mr. Angelos." The Headmistress gazed at the crowds with the air of a naturalist observing the mating rituals of some rare species. "I suggest you enjoy both the company and the surroundings. Perhaps find a vantage point from which to admire the bigger picture. I trust you will do so." With a last nod to us all, the Headmistress moved off, effortlessly parting the crowd.

Michaela was looking baffled. I was glad I wasn't the only one. "What was all that about?" I muttered into Krystal's ear. "Did she really just tell us to go mingle?"

"I think she really did," Krystal murmured back. "Think about it, Raf. All the boys here go to the same school. All of them except one." As she spoke, the music ended with a few bright, final chords. Faith broke free from Billy-Bob's hold and turned to applaud with everyone else. I made a move to head for her, but Krystal dragged me back. "Faith doesn't think anything's wrong at the moment." Sure enough, Faith was already in Billy-Bob's arms again as the string quartet struck up a slower tune. "If we want her to listen to us, we need evidence."

"Let's go get it then. Krystal, you see if any of the

girls have noticed anything odd. I'll talk to the guys. Michaela—"

"I'm staying to watch Faith," Michaela interrupted. She glared at Billy-Bob as his hand slipped farther down Faith's back. "And if he goes any lower, I'm cutting in. With a dagger."

"Did I ever mention how glad I am you're here?" I said with heartfelt sincerity. I clapped her on the shoulder as I went past. "Keep up the good work, Mike."

"Mike?" Michaela could pack a lot of outrage into one syllable. I made a mental note never to call her that within dagger range.

I scanned the room, searching for the flashes of black in the sea of white. Most of the guys were firmly embedded within circles of girls, but I finally spotted a lone Winchester lurking in the shadow of an enormous flower arrangement. I felt weirdly nervous as I headed for him. I'd grown too used to hanging out with girls, who tended to supply the vast majority of any required conversation. What the hell was I going to say?

Apparently, nothing. The guy caught my eye as I sidled up to him, and nodded in acknowledgment. I nodded back. Crossing my arms, I leaned back against the urn myself, as if I'd just been looking for a convenient place to loiter. We spent a peaceful moment just standing there, side by side, idly watching the girls go past.

Man, I'd forgotten how much easier it was to get along with other guys.

He tilted his head at me. He was wearing horns too, glossy black prongs that jutted straight out of his temples. His movie-quality prosthetics might be cooler than Lydie's headband, but I wouldn't have traded. "Which one's yours?"

Now I was doubly glad I'd brought Michaela. "Over there. Black hair, gold chains, looks like she's about to rip out someone's spleen?"

The Winchester guy whistled under his breath. "Better you than me, brother. Getting anywhere?"

"Doing well so far." Given that my internal organs were still unpunctured, it was absolutely true. "What about you? Who're you here with?"

"Her," Horny said morosely, pointing. "I'm having absolutely zero success, no matter what I try. There's no chance she's giving it up tonight."

"Good," I said coldly. Over at the refreshment table, Debbie tossed her hair, laughing with a couple of other girls as they filled up their wineglasses. "Because that's a friend of mine."

"What?" Horny did a double take, his eyes flicking over me. "Wait—you're him!"

"You know me? Hey, wait!"

He was already backing away, looking as nervous as if I was an abandoned parcel that had just started ticking. Without another word, he scuttled off.

"Great," I said under my breath. I couldn't actually blame him. If the only guy enrolled at a school full of girls had approached me, I would have been sidling away with my back to the wall too. I cast around for another victim and found a couple of guys loitering under the sign to the toilets, muttering to each other. They broke off as I wandered up. "Hey," I said, nodding up at the sign. "What *is* it that girls do in there that takes so long?"

Actually, thanks to my stint as school guardian angel, I knew the answer to this mystery of life—that it takes an unbelievable number of powders and creams to look as if you haven't done anything at all—but moaning about girls was always a good icebreaker. From the alarmed looks on their faces, though, I might as well have opened with a comment about quantum mechanics.

"You're him, aren't you?" one said, staring at me wide-eyed. Given that he was wearing bright yellow contact lenses with vertical slit pupils, the overall effect was of a

337

cat who'd just seen a dog. "The—"

"—boy who goes to school here," the other one interrupted, giving his friend a surreptitious kick with one cloven hoof. I had to admit, their subtle demonic costumes were pretty awesome. "Rafael Angelos. We've heard of you. From the girls, of course."

"Oh, right." I leaned against the wall next to them. "Hey, do you guys know the ginger guy with the tail?" I jerked my thumb in Billy-Bob's direction.

"Yes, of course we do," Hooves said, and my heart sank. So much for it being that easy. "But not personally."

"He doesn't exactly move in our social circles," Catboy muttered, crossing his arms over his chest. His friend booted him again.

"Hi, boys!" Kate came out of the bathroom, followed by another girl. "Oh, hi, Raffi. Having fun?" Without waiting for a reply, Kate turned to Catboy. Sliding an arm around his waist, she batted her eyelashes up at him. "Sorry to leave you so long. Miss me?"

"Like the tide misses the moon," he said. I blinked at the sudden confidence in his voice. He brushed a finger over her smiling lips, his cat-slit eyes practically smoldering as he gazed deep into hers. "I warn you, I'm not letting you out of my sight again. We only have this one precious night. If these memories have to last me the rest of my life, then I want to brand you into my soul."

Rather than vomiting—which was what I considered an appropriate reaction to such utter cheesiness—Kate giggled. "Who says we've only got one night?" She leaned her head on his shoulder. "Come on, let's dance. See ya, Raffi."

"Hey, Raffi!" I turned at the tap on my shoulder to find Debbie behind me, her over-full wineglass tilting precariously. "D'you know where my date went? I thought I saw you talking to him."

"Yeah, about that." I took her elbow, drawing her aside. "You got a moment?"

"Sure, but make it quick." Debbie held up her drink with an evil smirk. "I'm on a mission. By the way, I spiked the punch. And so did Claire. And Julie. And probably more." She giggled. "And I saw Ms. Oleander empty a whole bottle of vodka into it. God, I love that teacher. So watch—Raffi! What the hell are you doing?"

"You a favor," I said, handing back her wineglass, which I'd just emptied into a vase of lilies. "Trust me. Debbie, your date is bad news. You don't want to get hammered around him. Take my word for it."

Debbie gave me an exasperated look. "That wasn't for

me, it was for *him*. The guy is sex on a stick." She sighed. "Unfortunately, the stick is up his arse. I'm just trying to get him to loosen up a little."

Why did girls always seem to go for total dicks? "Well . . . just promise me you won't go off alone with him, okay?"

Debbie burst out laughing. "Raffi, are you kidding me? That's exactly what I'm trying to do! I keep suggesting to him that we could leave this party and find somewhere more private, but he's not getting the hint." She shook her head, grinning. "What, were you worried about my virtue or something? That's so sweet." She patted me on the shoulder. "Now, in the nicest possible way, butt out. I'm a big girl, I'm not your sister, and it's none of your business."

I caught her arm as she tried to slip past. "Wait— you're trying to seduce *him*?"

"Hello? Have you seen the guy?" Debbie fanned herself with one hand. "Hot as hell."

I froze.

No. Impossible. They couldn't manifest outside a pentagram.

But both Michaela and the Headmistress had said that manifested demons couldn't hide their true nature. That costume had been *really* good . . . and if the guy wasn't after Debbie's body, maybe he was after her soul.

Good thing the Prince needs a nephil to possess, Krystal said in my memory. Just a casual, throwaway comment. But ordinary demons didn't need nephilim. Ordinary demons could possess ordinary people. And no Prince would travel without a proper entourage.

"Bit of a nerd, though," Debbie continued blithely as all this flashed through my mind. "I don't think he's met many girls. Talks like a cheap romance novel. And kind of disturbingly intense. He's already pretty much proposed to me—crap, Raffi, that hurts!"

My knuckles were white on her wrist. "Debbie," I said urgently, not letting go, "listen, don't talk to him again. Not another word. In fact, get out of here. Go for a walk or something—"

I stopped dead. We hadn't been speaking loudly. There was no way anyone should have been able to overhear us over the music. But Catboy and Hooves—neither of them closer than ten feet—had, totally independently, just turned around to look at us.

Too late, I remembered the Headmistress's warnings about demons' ability to eavesdrop.

"Okay, now you're getting weird." Debbie tried to twist free of me. "Raffi, don't make me hit you! What's your problem?"

I thought faster than I'd ever thought in my life, as the two guys whispered something to their respective dates, then started to converge on us. "My problem"—I dropped to one knee, grabbing for Debbie's hand and pressing it earnestly to my cheek—"is that I'm in love with you."

Both guys paused midstep. Debbie gaped at me. "Not again," she said. "Two in one night? What the heck did Ms. Oleander put in that punch?" Her expression turned suspicious. "Wait . . . you're playing a joke on me. Oh, very funny, Raffi. Get up."

"I'm dead serious." I surreptitiously leaned to one side, trying to peer past Debbie. Catboy and Hooves were exchanging glances with each other, eyebrows raised. "Seeing you with another guy made me realize. You're the only one for me."

"Oh, so that's how it is, huh?" Debbie's expression of deep disgust was not exactly the reaction I'd been hoping for. "You weren't interested in me at all before. But now you think I'm easy, so you've decided to try your luck? And here I was thinking you were a nice guy." She jerked her hand away from me. "Well, you can go screw yourself,

342

Rafael Angelos. Because I'm certainly not going to."

"Wait—" I was talking to her back. She flipped me off as she stalked away into the crowd. A couple of her friends converged on her, obviously scenting fresh gossip. From Debbie's gestures, my reputation was about to be thoroughly trashed.

More important, the two "Winchester" guys had drifted off with amused expressions. I didn't dare try to track them too closely, in case they got suspicious again. Heart hammering against my rib cage, I hurried off in search of Michaela.

"Get your filthy—" Michaela cut off as she saw who had touched her elbow. "Oh, it's you. Get your filthy hands off of me," she added seemingly as an afterthought. Then she frowned, peering more intently at my face. "What's wrong?"

"Nothing, babe," I said loudly, draping my arm over her shoulders despite the fact that this was about as wise as embracing a porcupine. "Listen, have any of the guys here been bothering you?" I stared into her eyes, willing her to understand. "Because there are a few here that I don't like much. I don't understand how *their sort* got in."

From the way Michaela went rigid, she'd gotten my hint. She leaned against me, nuzzling my neck. "Are you sure?" she whispered in my ear, her lips barely moving. "Manifesting, not possessing?" I nodded slightly, and she hissed under her breath. She broke free of me, pacing a few steps like a caged tigress. "But that's impossible—" She stopped dead, staring at her feet. Then, "Come on," she said, seizing my hand. "I have to go look at something."

"What?" I said as she dragged me through the crowd.

"The bigger picture."

There was a little spiral staircase in an alcove at the front of the hall, leading to a small pulpit halfway up the wall. A couple of girls were already up there, leaning over the edge to watch the dancing, but Michaela managed to dislodge them at ten feet just with the force of her glare. She waited impatiently for them to file out of the opening, then dashed up the stairs two at a time. I was out of breath by the time I caught up with her. "Good view," I said, looking down at the party. From this vantage point, we could see the whole hall. I picked Horny out of the crowd, though Catboy and Hooves were impossible to spot. "There's one of the guys I met earlier."

Michaela shook her head. She wasn't looking at the dancers at all, but rather at the floor. From this height, it became apparent that what at first glance appeared to be a random jumble of tiles was in fact a deliberate mosaic, all done in the same shade of white, but with some tiles polished to mirror-brightness. They stood out against the duller tiles, reflecting the candlelight in looping, shining lines. . . .

"Rafael, we have to get everyone out of here. Right now." Her fingers practically crushed my arm. "It's a pentagram. *The whole hall is a pentagram!*"

Michaela had forgotten about demonic senses too. Horny's head jerked up as if he'd heard a gunshot. He turned to stare directly at us.

As did every other guy in the room.

Including Billy-Bob.

Chapter 33

His eyes still locked with mine, Billy-Bob bent his head over Faith's, resting his cheek on her shining hair. She was tucked up against his chest, her back to us, as they swayed in a slow dance. Over the top of her head, he smiled at me.

He knew. He knew that we knew. And he didn't care.

Never breaking our eye contact, Billy-Bob trailed his hands down Faith's spine to rest on her hips, drawing her even closer against him. He spun her on the spot, one of his hands floating outward in a flourish that encompassed the rest of the hall. All through the room, as if Billy-Bob's smile had been some sort of signal, demons were turning back to their partners. Demonic hands on innocent backs, demonic lips whispering temptation into unsuspecting ears, demonic kisses on laughing mouths . . .

Completing his spin, Billy-Bob lifted his eyebrows at me in mocking challenge. The message was clear. *Well? What do you think you can do to stop us?*

I spread my wings, taking care to make sure they stayed invisibly in Heaven. My feathers burned so fiercely that the darkness around them boiled and seethed, but Billy-Bob just looked amused. At my side, Michaela made a low, distressed sound, the points of her drawn daggers twitching from target to target in an agony of indecision. Even if we took out Billy-Bob, we'd still be outnumbered ten to one—and the demons had hostages.

"Michaela?" I said under my breath. My fingers hovered over Krystal's pentagram charm. "Scream."

I grabbed the charm, whirled, and set fire to the nearest draperies.

Michaela had a good set of lungs. Her scream pierced the air like an arrow. Dancers stumbled in sudden gracelessness, every head turning in our direction.

"Fire!" someone yelled. "FIRE!"

A mass shriek erupted from the crowd. The hall exploded in a mad stampede for the nearest exit. Not even Ms. Hellebore could hold back the tide. Some of the demon boys were swept along like twigs in a torrent, only to hit the edge of the mosaic as if it was a solid brick wall. I caught a glimpse of Debbie frantically tugging at Horny, trying to haul him over the invisible barrier. He fought free of her, retreating back into the room, and she fled without him.

"Come on!" Michaela was already scrambling over the edge of the balcony. I grabbed her around the waist, manifesting my wings just in the nick of time to stop us from splatting headfirst on the marble. We still hit the ground hard enough to knock all the breath out of me. For a second, all I could do was clutch at my bandage, white-hot pain stabbing through my chest.

"*Sancte Michael Archangele, defende nos in proelio!*" Michaela's angel hurtled like a flaming meteor down from Heaven as Michaela leaped for Billy-Bob. He jumped out of the way of her daggers, flinging Faith aside—

Straight into my waiting arms.

I folded my wings around her. Beyond our embrace, all was chaos—Michaela's knives whirling, her angel battering against Billy-Bob's darkness like a moth against a windowpane, inhuman shrieks of rage and shouted prayers—but here, just for a moment, we stood in the eye of the storm, encircled by white light.

"It's us," I said, so close to Faith that we breathed the same breath. Our bodies pressed against each other, our hearts beating as one. My wings burned like the sun itself. "It's always been us. Faith, we have to save everyone. We have to close the Hellgate."

My lips touched hers.

I don't know what I'd been expecting—a blast of heavenly fire, some sort of shock wave, demons shrieking "Noooo!" as they were sucked into a closing vortex—but it certainly wasn't a knee in the groin.

I collapsed into a ball of pain, the light winking out as my wings folded like the rest of me. "I'm sorry, Raffi, I'm sorry!" Faith babbled even as she shoved me away. "But I can't do it. I can't send my mother to Hell. I can't!"

"Faith, no!" I wheezed through the agony, trying to catch her sleeve as she turned back to Billy-Bob, who was effortlessly forcing Michaela's daggers away from his throat. "He's the Prince, Faith!"

Faith let out a strange sound, half sob, half laugh. "I know he is. I deliberately stepped on his tail. He said *ow.*"

Even Billy-Bob looked rather nonplussed at that. Tossing Michaela to one side like a beanbag—she flew ten feet and hit the ground rolling, coming up at my side with broken wings and daggers crossed—he raised one red eyebrow at Faith. "You know what I am, and yet you come willingly?"

"Yes." She looked around at Michaela and myself, tears streaking her face. "I'm sorry, I can't close the Hellgate, I can't choose light with a willing heart." She spread her wings. Storm-cloud patterns chased across her feathers, light and dark locked in conflict. "I love my mother. No matter what, I can't condemn her to eternal torment."

"She's a demon!" Michaela guarded my back, her daggers and my light holding the demon boys at bay. "She's betrayed you!"

"I know. But this is my decision, Michaela. I'll take the consequences." Faith took a deep breath, raising her chin to meet Billy-Bob's curious eyes. "I'll bind myself to you. And then Michaela and Raffi will kill me."

"What?" Michaela nearly dropped her daggers in shock. Above her in Heaven, her angel seethed with furious light. "No!"

"Promise me you'll do it, Michaela!" Faith pleaded, opening her hands in supplication. "If you destroy my body with holy fire, the Prince has to go back to Hell. I may not be able to close the Hellgate, but I can make sure I'm the only one to suffer for it."

"Damn it, Faith, for once in your life open your eyes!" I yelled at her, struggling to my feet. I spread my wings, indicating the watching demons. "The Prince isn't the only demon who came through the Hellgate! *This is not all about you!*"

Faith blinked, looking around at the ring of grinning demon boys as if noticing them for the first time. She went pale. "No," she stammered. "My mother—she isn't evil. She wouldn't let demons possess her students."

"Of course I would." My heart froze in my chest as the Headmistress emerged from the back of the hall, Krystal struggling in her iron grip. The rest of the chapel was deserted now, though shouts drifted in from the open doors as the teachers tried to get the panicking students back under control. Bits of burning silk whirled over our heads as the fire spread. "I would advertise it as a unique feature of this school, if it would not cause undue comment. Why do you think we have a Masked Ball at all? Every year, the best and most promising girls receive the great gift of a demon companion. Not only do the girls gain powerful allies to help them on the path to wealth and power, they are also liberated from foolish hindrances like 'compassion' and 'kindness'. I would be remiss in my duty of care if I *didn't* give my students the opportunity."

The Prince caught Faith's wrist as she tried to back away. "Not so fast, pretty little nephil. I haven't yet decided which of the bodies on offer I prefer. It could still be you." His tail flicked lazily from side to side as he cast the Headmistress a pleased glance. "So kind of you to have offered a selection."

The Headmistress's face was an impassive mask in the flickering firelight. "Thank you, Prince Beelzebub."

"Beelzebub," Michaela whispered in horror-struck tones. "Lord of the Flies. Prince of Pride. Second only to Satan Himself."

"My reputation precedes me!" Beelzebub brightened as if this had made his whole day.

"Fly, Raf!" Krystal yelled, through her coughs. The hall was rapidly filling with smoke. Her face was red from the heat. "Get out of here!"

"I'm not leaving you!" I could possibly grab Michaela and fly into Heaven, but there was no way I could get to Krystal before the Headmistress ripped her apart. My fear for my friends fueled my own fire, my halo brightening until the closest demons had to take a step back. If I could just get to Faith, if she would join her light to mine this time—

"You think you have even the slightest chance of getting anywhere near me?" Beelzebub said as if reading my mind. "Me? A Prince of Hell?" He laughed. "You were right," he said to the Headmistress. "His vanity is indeed delicious. Perhaps I *will* possess him rather than your daughter."

"No!" Faith twisted to grab Beelzebub's sleeve. "I'll join with you, I will, if you swear on your name you won't hurt my friends!"

"Faith!" Michaela's desperate eyes met mine. "Rafael, I beg you, save her."

"Yes, Mr. Angelos." The Headmistress's emotionless stare bored into me. "If you are willing to sacrifice yourself, you can save her. You can save them all."

I froze.

All those tearstained letters, from Lydie and the others who suffered under the demons' rule. All those photos in the corridor outside the Headmistress's office, all those powerful women with hungry eyes. Hundreds of Balls. Hundreds of girls unwittingly corrupted with evil. Going out into the world and making it a little darker, a little crueler, a little more like this school . . .

And I knew what I had to do.

"Michaela!" I whirled on her. "Stab me!"

Michaela, understandably, stared at me as if I'd gone insane.

"Self-sacrifice," I said as fast as I could, grabbing Michaela's shoulders. Above her, the angel stretched its wings wide, burning like a thousand suns going supernova at once. It knew what I wanted, it knew I was choosing with open eyes, it was ready to use me as its channel to the mortal world. . . . "Like Gabriel's original plan, but me rather than Faith. I'm willing, I choose this, so for the love of Heaven, *stab me!*"

"NO!" shouted Beelzebub. The demon boys lunged forward.

Too late.

I didn't even feel Michaela's daggers enter my chest. The instant the tips pierced my skin, the angel's power burst into me. No human flesh could have withstood that supernatural heat for so much as a heartbeat. It seared even my nephil body, setting every one of my feathers alight with agony, but I forced my wings open before the fire consumed them. All three girls were knocked flat by the blast of light. The demonic darkness evaporated like mist at sunrise. Beelzebub and the demon boys twisted for a second, agonized shadows caught in the eye-searing whiteness—then they too went out like blown candles. Only the Headmistress was left, a lone dark shape in a world of white. Her eyes locked with mine.

For the briefest instant, she smiled.

Then, like a puppet with cut strings, she collapsed.

"Mother!" Faith cried out as my light died away. She struggled up and ran to her. "No, *no*, please . . . Mother!"

"Raf?" Krystal crawled over to me. "Are you alive?"

"Yeah," I managed to say on the second attempt. I felt like a spent match. Flat on my back, I stared up at the flames flickering across banners overhead and just wanted to go to sleep. "I think I closed—"

Before I could finish the sentence, something curled around my ankle, and yanked me down into Hell.

Chapter 34

Darkness and laughter.

I was sinking, sinking into the Abyss. Blind. Wings burned to nothing with that last shock wave of power. Angelic eyes, all gone. Just human. Falling into nothing.

Well done, Mr. Angelos. Well done indeed. The Headmistress coiled around me. I felt rather than heard her voice, as if she spoke directly into my bones. Her myriad eyes swam through the darkness, filled with a pale, cold light. *Look up, Mr. Angelos.*

High above, light sparkled, like the surface of the sea seen from underwater. Just a firefly glimmer now, as she carried me into the depths.

The mortal world, Mr. Angelos. The Headmistress shifted me in her tentacles, turning me away from that glimpse of warmth and light. *Bright again, our darkness dispelled. The world is like a pane of glass between Heaven and Hell, you see. Humans can polish it clean with virtue or smudge it with sin. We can only approach when so much cruelty and selfishness has accumulated that it blocks out the light from above. Many, many years carefully cultivating a grime of petty sins, Mr. Angelos, and you wipe it all away with one act of sacrifice. We are banished, thoroughly banished, for centuries to come.* Her satisfaction vibrated through my flesh. *I would write a special note of commendation on your end-of-year report, if you were going to have one.*

"It really was all your plan. All along, you *were* trying to close the Hellgate." Cold was spreading through my chest. I couldn't feel my limbs anymore. "Why?"

You find merely attending school a torment? Try a thousand years of running one, Mr. Angelos. Centuries of squabbling, self-obsessed teenagers. Centuries of pretending interest in your numbingly banal existences, each and every one of you just like the next, all convinced of your own uniqueness. And that, Mr. Angelos, that is not even touching upon the horror of the paperwork. A shudder ran through her titanic form at the mere thought. *I have been working to escape that place and return home for a very,* very *long time.*

"You could . . . could have just left."

Hellgates do not spontaneously appear, Mr. Angelos. They are grown. Few of my kind have the patience and skill for it. I am the very best. A thousand years of quietly influencing uncounted souls, turning a place of light into a place of darkness . . . no. I would never have been allowed to simply resign. The only way I would be permitted to leave was if there was no longer any reason for me to be here. So I set in motion a plan to undo all my own work.

"Me and Faith," I whispered.

Yes, Mr. Angelos. I knew it would take heavenly light to cut through my dark barrier, but I could hardly enlist the help of the angels. Nephilim were the answer. Two nephil could between them produce enough light to dispel the Hellgate. And I had an excuse to create at least one. Beelzebub has long desired to walk the earth, and no mere human could ever contain a Prince of Hell's power. . . . When I offered to bear a nephil for him to possess, he jumped at the chance. We demons rarely procreate, Mr. Angelos. Gestation is a remarkably tedious process.

"But you needed two . . ." Even as I spoke, the answer came to me. "My mother. You knew my mother. You told me so, the very first day of school."

Yes, Mr. Angelos. She knew my plan. She went into the world to bear her own nephil child in secret. She was supposed to send you to me at the proper time. Her arctic voice turned even colder, each word like ice in my mind. But she betrayed me. After your birth, she decided my scheme was too risky, with too great a chance that the Princes of Hell would realize your true purpose here. She cut all contact with me, hiding you away. Fortunately, I always have a backup plan.

I knew your name. I planted the summoning circle in my husband's notebooks after his death, knowing that my daughter would find it and call you here. All I needed to do then was let nature take its course, even as I outwardly pretended to separate you two. It should have been a simple matter. An edge of irritation crept into those slow, smug tones. *Perhaps I shall take up breeding giant pandas next. It would be a relaxing hobby compared to trying to orchestrate your love life, Mr. Angelos.*

I was too tired to defend my masculinity. "My mother," I mumbled. Everything was going vague and soft. Even breathing was starting to seem like too much work. "Is . . . is she down here? Are you taking me to her? I'd . . . I'd like to see her again."

No, Mr. Angelos. She is not. She paused, her tentacle bringing me level with one shifting, pulsing eye. *And you have already seen her recently, you know. Very recently. Demons are fallen angels, Mr. Angelos. Did it never occur to you that perhaps the reverse might also be true?* The Headmistress was silent for a long moment, the only sound, the whisper of air over her black wings. *Even though we are on opposite sides for now, it seems she has not forgotten me. I thought she had abandoned me years ago, becoming my enemy . . . yet she helped me at the end. It served the purpose of her side, no doubt, but still, I find that I am pleased by that. We had a long history together. Perhaps we will yet be reunited.*

What falls may rise, and fall again. . . .

The rocking motion as the Headmistress flew steadily down was almost soothing. I could just fall asleep. . . . "What happens now?" I whispered, barely able to form the words.

Now, Mr. Angelos? Now you die. If it is any consolation, you will serve me one last time. Your limp corpse will make the perfect present with which to convince Beelzebub of my continued loyalty. It will prevent him from taking out his frustrations on me. Her tentacle tightened around my chest, cutting off all air. That was okay. I didn't feel like breathing anymore anyway. *Good-bye, Mr. Angelo—*

"Mother! Don't you dare!"

I must be dying. An angel had come to collect me.

"Let him go! Let him go right now!" Bright wings in the dark, beating at the Headmistress like a butterfly attacking a whale. The squeezing tentacle paused. "Or I'll—I'll *hate* you! Forever!"

Without a further word, the Headmistress released me. The last thing I saw of her was her titanic bulk, studded with eyes, suspended under six, wide, motionless wings as she spiraled silently down into the dark.

Just for an instant, the black feathers gleamed with a flash of silver light.

Hands, human hands, grabbed me under the arms. Wings filled my vision. We shot up like a cork released underwater. The shining surface of the world hurtled nearer, nearer, until it broke across my face—

"I got him! I got him! Raffi, can you hear me?"

"Oh my God, the blood—you idiot, Michaela!"

"He *told* me to stab him! He didn't say how hard! Jesus, Mary, and Joseph, he's not breathing."

"Well, hurry up and heal him! You two are the ones with angelic powers!"

Something jolted into my chest, seizing hold of my muscles like an electric shock. Distantly, I felt the convulsions, but they seemed to be happening to someone a long way away. Delicious warmth spread over my skin. I was sinking into a soft pile of feathers, a cloud of wings wrapping protectively around me as all the noise and confusion started to swirl away into nothing. . . .

"*Faith!* Setting him on fire is *not helping*!"

"I'm sorry, I don't know how to do anything else!"

"*Sancte Michael Archangele*—"

"Exorcising him won't help either! Oh, for the love of—both of you get out of my way! Raf, don't you dare die on me, don't you dare!"

Air searing my raw throat. Someone pounding on my

chest. Pain roared back as I opened my eyes. I was being alternately hit and kissed. I kind of preferred the latter. Despite the fact that my body felt like one big battered block of ice, I kissed back.

After a moment, Krystal pulled away. "I'm *resuscitating* you, you moron."

"Oh. Sorry." I had to stop for a fit of coughing. I lay back in Krystal's arms, limp as a gutted fish. Faith and Michaela were tearing up their ball gowns into makeshift bandages. The sky beyond their heads was an orange glow, thick with smoke. Girls swarmed all around, screaming about fire and ambulances and dead teachers, too panicked to even notice the four of us.

Everything seemed okay. So I passed out.

Chapter 35

FIRE TRAGEDY CLOSES SCHOOL
Questions mount as teachers' bodies are recovered from site.

St. Mary's Boarding School for Girls and Boys will close for an indefinite period as police investigate the cause of the mysterious fire that broke out during the school's traditional Masked Ball three nights ago, claiming the lives of the entire staff. It is not yet known how so many teachers could have perished in the blaze, which appears to have been contained to the school chapel. Eyewitness accounts state that many members of staff safely evacuated the building before the fire took hold, and appeared to be completely fine before abruptly collapsing.

"It was like Ms. Hellebore had a stroke,"

said Deborah Hall, 16, a student at St. Mary's who was attending the Ball on the fateful night. "One minute she was shouting at me, trying to get me to go back in, the next she was lying dead on the grass."

Mysteries also remain concerning the identities and whereabouts of an unknown number of young men who were present at the Ball as dance partners. Despite multiple accounts from students that the girls' "dates" remained inside the hall regardless of attempts to get them to leave, no bodies matching their descriptions have been found by police. The Headmaster of Winchester Boys' School has now confirmed that none of his pupils are missing, and further stated that his school has never been in contact with St. Mary's.

The majority of the girls attending the Ball escaped unharmed, although a few were taken to the hospital with . . .

I let the newspaper fall onto the starched sheets. "I should have stayed in Hell. My dad is going to kill me."

"Relax," Krystal said, scanning through another paper from her seat at the side of my bed. "There's nothing here that suggests the police have any clue as to how the fire started."

"Did I ever tell you why I got thrown out of my last school? Believe me, my dad is never going to believe that I didn't do it."

"Well, you did," Krystal pointed out, folding the paper up. She stretched, giving me an evil grin. "And I know you did. I should demand hush money."

"Whatever happened to being the big hero?" I said plaintively to the world in general.

"Hey, that was practically last week. What have you done for us recently?" Krystal ducked as I tossed a pillow at her. "You must be feeling better after all."

"Yeah. Though the doctors are still puzzled as to how someone could be dragged out of a fire suffering from hypothermia." I scratched absently at the fresh bandages wrapping my torso. "Still, at least it distracted them from the stab wounds. I told them part of the chandelier fell on me."

"That idiot Michaela," Krystal muttered darkly. She looked down at her hands, fidgeting with the newspaper. "Has she done that trance thing again for you yet?"

"Yeah, I persuaded her to do it this morning." I was never going to be Michaela's favorite person, but even she'd had to admit that the Order of Dante owed me. I'd traded in the favor. "The trance didn't last long, but I was able to talk through her to . . . to the angel. It was . . . kind of a weird conversation."

It was hard to make sense of the angel's cryptic messages, but from what Michaela and I had been able to piece together, what the Headmistress had told me was true. My mother had been one of the St. Mary's demons, possessing the body of a former student. She'd been in on the Headmistress's plan to close the Hellgate, and had left the school to secretly bear the other required nephil child . . . but after I'd been born, she'd changed. She cut her ties with the other demons, instead devoting herself to good. Her job as an "investigative journalist" had just been a cover story for her real work—finding and banishing demons from the mortal world.

Her final mission had been at Michaela's old orphanage. Finding more demons there than she could handle alone, she'd anonymously called the Order of Dante. She'd stayed to help in the battle, even though she'd known that the Order, not knowing her true nature, would destroy her physical form too. That act of self-sacrifice allowed her to reascend as an angel. She'd attached herself to Michaela at the orphanage, thus bringing the young girl to the attention of the Dantes . . . and the rest was history.

"So Michaela's angel really is your mum?" Krystal asked.

At my nod, she blew out her breath. "Wow." She gave me a strange, sidelong look. "Raf . . . that's got to be tough, finding out about your mother right when you've lost your powers and can't see her yourself anymore. Are you okay?"

I thought about it. "Yeah," I said slowly. "Actually, I am."

I'd asked her why she'd turned away from the other demons. She'd smiled at me, through Michaela's face, and whispered one word before the trance broke.

Love.

It was enough.

"I might kind of miss the wings," I added. I shifted my shoulders, still feeling that strange, scarred emptiness where my angelic body parts had once been. "Flying was pretty cool. But the eyes were a bloody nightmare." I leaned back against my remaining pillows. "Nah, I'm happy to be just an ordinary guy again."

"Well, okay," Krystal said, looking unconvinced. "But if you ever want to talk about it—why are you looking at me like that?"

"Just enjoying the view. Your skin is so . . . *opaque.*"

Krystal snorted. "Oh, you really know how to woo a girl, Raf. Take me now, you irresistible stud."

I flipped her off. "I'm just relieved at being able to

see things properly again. You know, without getting an eyeful of all the squidgy bits inside." I cocked my head, something occurring to me as I studied her. It wasn't just my newly regained ordinary vision that made Krystal look so much better than usual. Her usually bloodshot, watery eyes were clear and bright. "Nice glasses, by the way."

"Raf!" Krystal threw my pillow back at me, her face going red. "I'm still waiting for my replacement contact lenses to arrive. My old ones got damaged by the smoke. So you can keep your comments to yourself."

"It was a *compliment*, you idiot—" My retort was cut short by a soft knock on the door. "Come in!"

"Hello, Raffi." Faith entered, Michaela behind her. "Can we talk for a moment?"

"Sure." I shifted my legs to make room for Faith to perch on the bed. Michaela leaned in a corner, glowering at me, though I suspected it was mainly just force of habit. "What's up?"

Faith's face was pale and drawn, with dark circles under the eyes. She took a deep breath, as if having to steel herself to say what was on her mind. "I've got some bad news."

I sat upright in bed, wincing as I jarred my bandages. "Is it the Hellgate? Is it reopening?"

"No. I'm afraid it's worse than that." Faith put one hand on mine, gripping my fingers as if to provide preemptive support. "I've decided to go back to Rome with Michaela. I'm going to become a Dante."

I blinked at her. "But . . . that's great! Why is that bad news?"

"Because you can't come," Michaela supplied from her corner.

My brow furrowed. "Why in hell do you think I want to become a Dante? No offense, but you guys are kind of weird. And I've had enough fighting demons for one lifetime."

"You don't get it." Faith's woeful blue eyes fixed on mine, begging me to understand. "Raffi, this means we won't be able to see each other anymore. I'm really sorry. But it's over between us."

Oh. I waited for the inevitable painful twist in my heart . . . which didn't come. I stared at her, and she was as beautiful as always, but she didn't shine anymore. The world didn't shift to put her at the center of all things. She was just . . . there.

A relieved grin spread across my face. "It's okay, Faith." I really was an ordinary guy again. "You go and be happy. I'll be fine."

"Oh, Raffi. You don't have to be brave. You can cry if you want." Faith's own eyes brimmed with tears. Krystal and Michaela were both studying the ceiling with identical expressions of acute embarrassment. "I feel so terrible about this, especially after everything you did for me. But . . . you lost your divinity and I didn't. We can't possibly be soul mates. You have to accept that."

"I do! Seriously, I'm not upset."

"In time, your pain will heal," Faith assured me earnestly. "The right girl for you is out there somewhere. You'll find her one day."

I gave up. "Thanks, Faith." Maybe she was right. And maybe the right girl would actually *listen* to me. Maybe she'd always have my back, rather than only ever demanding that I protect her. Maybe she'd be smart enough not to need me to solve all her problems. Maybe . . . she'd . . .

"What?" Krystal said warily. "Why are you staring at me again?"

"No reason!" I licked my suddenly dry lips. "Uh, Krystal? Where are *you* going next?"

Acknowledgments

First, my profound and eternal gratitude to my agent, Nephele Tempest, my editors Erica Sussman and Tyler Infinger, and all the fantastic team at HarperTeen.

There are some other friends without whom this book wouldn't exist. First, my gratitude to Eljas Oksanen, for long, long ago telling me about a boy he'd seen on the Brussels subway, thus planting the idea of Raffi in my head (no, really). Second, to my foxy friends Yoon Ha Lee and Nancy Sauer, for a late-night online conversation wherein the bones of this book first took shape. Nancy, I hope you approve of the Headmistress . . . and I apologize, Yoon, for the deliberate math mistake in Chapter 29 (though I'll be *very* impressed if anyone else spots it).

Book bloggers are simultaneously the most wonderful and terrifying people a newbie author like myself can encounter, and I am deeply in the debt of all the talented, passionate people who've taken the time to review my books. My particular thanks must go to Giselle Cormier of Xpresso Reads, who not only put together a fantastic book blog tour for *Fang Girl*, but also now daily entertains me on Twitter. And I will forever be grateful for the time Giselle put the wrong book in the mail, resulting in Jenni Arndt of Alluring Reads accidentally receiving *Fang Girl* . . . thereby introducing me to another marvelous and delightful blogger. Huge thanks to you both for all your support! (And I hope you got to read *Stealing Parker* eventually, Jenni.)

Final thanks go, as always, to my husband Tim, who is *my* angel . . . though not (probably to his relief) with hundreds of eyes.

Also by HELEN KEEBLE

You know something's
seriously wrong
when you wake up in a coffin....

FANG GIRL

HELEN KEEBLE

Sure, the idea of vampires is sexy, but who
actually dreams of spending eternity as a
pasty, bloodthirsty fifteen-year-old?
Not Jane.